Praise for Sarah Addison Allen

"You will love going to *Lost Lake* with Sarah Addison Allen and meeting all the fascinating characters who live there. This book is filled with mystery, magic, and wonderful surprises!"   —Fannie Flagg on *Lost Lake*

"Sarah Addison Allen delivers a feel-good story with touches of magic."   —*Entertainment Weekly*

"Allen is the master of magical details and plots that combine a fairy-tale sensibility with character-driven pathos."   —*NPR*

"It is always a pleasure to read Allen's work. Her signature magical touches are something readers anticipate. There's nothing like a little 'Allen magic' sprinkled on a book to make it a fascinating reading experience to be savored."   —*Times Record News* (Wichita Falls)

"Her eccentric cast of characters and charming Southern setting will win readers over."   —*Publishers Weekly*

"Allen always manages to nimbly mask her potent messages of inspiration and romance beneath her trademark touches of mirth and magic."   —*Booklist*

"Allen's work is such a treat . . . Like a cook who seasons just so, she adds flavor but not too much, and serves a satisfying literary meal without making you overstuffed."   —*The Herald-Sun* (Durham)

ALSO BY SARAH ADDISON ALLEN

Lost Lake
Garden Spells
The Sugar Queen
The Girl Who Chased the Moon
The Peach Keeper

FIRST
FROST

SARAH
ADDISON
ALLEN

St. Martin's Paperbacks

This is a work of fiction. All of the characters, organizations, and events portrayed in this novel are either products of the author's imagination or are used fictitiously.

FIRST FROST

Copyright © 2014 by Sarah Addison Allen.

For information address St. Martin's Press, 175 Fifth Avenue, New York, NY 10010.

ISBN: 978-1-250-19097-0

Our books may be purchased in bulk for promotional, educational, or business use. Please contact your local bookseller or the Macmillan Corporate and Premium Sales Department at 1-800-221-7945, ext. 5442, or by e-mail at MacmillanSpecialMarkets@macmillan.com.

Printed in the United States of America

St. Martin's Press hardcover edition / January 2015
St. Martin's Griffin edition / January 2016
St. Martin's Paperbacks edition / November 2018

St. Martin's Paperbacks are published by St. Martin's Press, 175 Fifth Avenue, New York, NY 10010.

10 9 8 7 6 5 4 3 2 1

To the magical Andrea Cirillo
For your faith in a strange little garden book

1

Bay Waverley-Hopkins raced down Pendland Street, her backpack bouncing and her dark hair flying behind her like blackbirds. The neighborhood homeowners always knew when she ran by, because they suddenly felt the desire to organize their sock drawers and finally replace those burned-out lightbulbs they'd been meaning to. We need to set things in order, they all thought as Bay ran down the street every afternoon after school. But, as soon as she passed, their thoughts quickly drifted back to where they'd been before—what was for dinner, why was a husband so moody lately, could a load of laundry wait another day.

Bay sped up as she approached the Waverley house. It was a rambling old Queen Anne with a wraparound porch and, Bay's favorite thing about it, a single, lovely turret. It had been the first house built in the neighborhood in the late 1800s, before even Orion College was founded, back when Bascom, North Carolina, had been nothing more than a muddy rest stop for people traveling through to the western mountains. The surrounding houses on the street had later tried to imitate the Waverley house in architecture, but nothing could ever compare. At least, not to Bay.

Instead of taking the steps from the sidewalk to the house, Bay ran up the steep lawn, sliding on the wet grass. Last night it had rained in sheets and strong winds had finally blown autumn into Bascom as if by the sharp sweep of a broom. There was a discernible chill in the air now, and wet leaves were everywhere—in yards, on the sidewalks, in the street, stuck on cars. It looked like the world was covered in a cobbler crust of brown sugar and cinnamon.

Bay hung her backpack on one of the bare branches of the tulip tree in the front yard, and it was still swinging as she took the front porch steps two at a time and opened the door.

The outside world might have finally turned into autumn, but inside the Waverley house it still smelled of summer. It was lemon verbena day, so the house was filled with a sweet-tart scent that conjured images of picnic blankets and white clouds shaped like true-love hearts.

Maybe it was Bay's imagination, but the house always seemed to preen a little when she entered, the dim windows shining a little brighter, the quilts straightening themselves on the backs of couches. Bay's mother said that Bay loved this place too much, that she was a lot like her great-grandmother Mary that way. Bay had never met her great-grandmother Mary, but all the same, she knew that her mother wasn't giv-

ing her a compliment. Her mother had never truly felt
at home growing up here.

Trying to catch her breath from her autumn dash,
Bay walked through the foyer, past the sitting room
decorated with the same old furniture from when her
great-grandmother Mary ran a boardinghouse here,
and into the large renovated commercial kitchen. Her
sneakers, almost covered by the frayed hems of her
baggy jeans, squeaked against the polished floor.

The air in the kitchen was heavy with sugary steam.
Bay found her quiet aunt Claire at one of the stoves,
her short, dark hair pulled back with mismatched clips
belonging to Claire's nine-year-old daughter, Mariah.
Claire's shoulders were tense from stirring and pouring the sugar and water and corn syrup, in the same
position, in the same large, copper sugar pots, into the
same molds, every day for months now.

Her aunt Claire used to run a successful catering
business, Waverley's Catering. What Claire could do
with the edible flowers that grew around the cranky
apple tree in the backyard was the stuff of legend.
Everyone knew that if you got Claire to cater your
anniversary party, she would make aioli sauce with
nasturtiums and tulip cups filled with orange salad,
and everyone would leave the party feeling both jealous and aroused. And if you got her to cater your
child's birthday party, she would serve tiny strawberry
cupcakes and candied violets and the children would
all be well behaved and would take long afternoon

naps. Claire had a true magic to her cooking when she used her flowers. Each Waverley had something *different* about her, but Claire was the most unusual in a family of unusuals. And Bay loved that about her.

But everything changed when Claire started Waverley's Candies less than a year ago. Last winter, Claire had been desperately looking for something to soothe her daughter Mariah's sore throats, ones that made Mariah lose her voice and kept her home from school for days on end. Rooms became tight when Mariah was sick, like the house wringing its hands. One day, when Claire had been fretting over another bout of Mariah's laryngitis, she heard something fall in her kitchen office, and she walked in to see that one of her grandmother Mary's old kitchen journals had fallen to the floor. That's when Claire found the hard candy recipe, tucked between instructions on how to rid the garden of shiny green beetles, and ingredients for husband-catcher cake.

The candies soothed her daughter's throat, and then became the newest thing everyone in town had to try. If it came from a Waverley, after all, there had to be something curious about it. When mothers at school heard about the candy, they found themselves knocking on Claire's door at two in the morning, bleary-eyed and desperate for something to ease sore throats that were keeping their children (and therefore the mothers) up all night.

When winter passed, the candies—beautiful, jewel-colored confections the size of wren's eggs and covered with powered sugar—began to be asked for as add-on orders for birthday celebrations Claire catered, then as bulk orders for trendy candy bars at graduations and weddings. It was at Lux Lancaster's wedding at Harold Manor, where the gift bags all contained small jars of Claire's honey-filled lavender hard candies, that Lux's cousin's girlfriend, who worked for *Southern Living* magazine, first tasted them. She wrote an article about the magical light purple drops on her plane trip back to Alabama, the words pouring out like water. She barely remembered writing the piece, feeling euphoric and a little drunk. When the article appeared in the magazine, then was shared through social media, orders began to flood in. People outside of Bascom were now curious about this curious candy, curious about the curious Claire Waverley who made them.

With her catering business, Claire used to hire help for bigger parties, but did the rest by herself. Her catering business had been the only size it could have been, just big enough for her to handle. But her candy business was getting so much attention now that it was busting at the seams. Bay worked for her aunt Claire every day after school. And Claire had another employee, a culinary student from Orion College named Buster, who was putting in so many hours that he was almost full-time.

And yet it always felt like they were running behind.

Changing from catering to candy had changed Claire, too. She was always tired, always working, and sometimes she would get this look on her face that was almost homesick. But she never asked for help, and no one could approach her about it. One of many peculiar things about Claire was that if she didn't want to talk about something, she could spring shut as quickly as a mousetrap.

When Bay walked into the kitchen that afternoon after school, Buster was talking, as he usually was. He could go on for hours, filling the kitchen with constant chatter that bounced off the stainless steel walls.

"So I told him his bread was ugly, and he called me a dough diva. *A dough diva.* Of all the nerve! We're going out on Saturday." Buster was tall and full-lipped with cropped hair that was dyed blue at the tips. When he finally noticed Bay had arrived, he stopped sifting the fine powdered sugar over a large batch of hard candies, just popped from their molds. "Hello, beautiful. Took the late bus again? I was just telling Claire about a guy I met in bread class. I hate him, but he could be my soul mate."

"'Dough diva'?" Bay asked. "I like it."

"I'm *so tired* of bread. I can't wait for next semester, when we do things with meat. What does your T-shirt say today?" Buster asked Bay. Bay showed him and he read, "'I Have Not Yet Begun to Procrastinate.' Oh, please. You probably had all your homework done before the bus dropped you off. Do you have any big plans this weekend? I hear there's a Halloween dance at your school on Saturday. Are you going with anyone special?" He wagged his eyebrows, one of them pierced.

Bay felt her face get hot, so she turned away and crossed the kitchen. She washed her hands and put on an apron.

Claire watched her, but didn't say a word. Unlike with Bay's mother, Bay had a silent understanding with her aunt Claire. Claire understood things about Bay without Bay having to say a word. Two months ago, when Bay had walked into this kitchen after her first day of tenth grade, her first year in high school after the purgatory that was junior high, Claire had known something had happened. Bay's mother had, too, but in a vague way. Claire had honed in on the problem right away and had asked, "Who is he?"

"No. No one special," Bay said to Buster, still turned away from him. "I'm just helping with the dance decorations."

"A face like that and the boys aren't falling over you." Buster tsked. "I don't understand it."

"If you were from here, you would," Bay said.

"Oh, *please*. Everyone in this town always says that, like you have to be *born* here to understand things. I understand plenty. You're only as weird as you want to be. Okay," Buster said to Claire, taking off his apron, "now that reinforcements are here, I'm off to my shift at the market."

"How many jobs do you have now?" Bay asked him.

"Just three."

"And yet you still have time to date?"

He rolled his eyes. "Like it's that hard. Bye, girls!" he said as he walked out of the kitchen. Seconds later, they heard him yell, "The front door won't open again! I'm trapped! I'm going to die in this house, having never known true love! Oh, wait. Now it's open. Oil your hinges!"

After the door closed, Claire turned to Bay. "I've been thinking. I could make something for you. To give to the boy, the one you like," she said, careful not to mention his name. "I could make mint cookies, and tea with honeysuckle syrup. Mint to clear his thoughts and honeysuckle to help him see. He'll be sure to notice you then."

Bay shook her head, though she'd considered it dozens of times, sometimes just because she wanted her aunt to cook something that wasn't hard candy again. "I doubt he would eat anything I gave him. He would know it came from you."

Claire nodded in understanding, though she seemed a little disappointed.

Bay suddenly put her hand to her chest, as if she just couldn't take it anymore, as if there were a knot there, all sinewy and hard, pressing against her rib cage. Sometimes it was an actual, physical *ache*. "Is it always like this?"

"You should talk to your mother," Claire said simply, her dark eyes calm and sympathetic. As different as they were in looks, in temperament, in *everything*, Claire and Bay's mother talked every day. Sometimes, when Bay would walk into the living room at home, she'd find her mother, Sydney, leafing through hair magazines, the phone at her ear, saying nothing. No sound came from the phone either.

"Who are you talking to?" Bay would ask.

"Claire," her mother would answer.

"Why aren't you saying anything?"

"We're just spending some time together," her mother would say, shrugging.

The Waverley sisters hadn't been close as children, but they were as thick as thieves now, the way adult siblings often are, the moment they realize that family is actually a choice. Bay didn't know many particulars about their childhood. But from listening to conversations through open windows and behind couches as a child—the only way she'd been able to learn any of the good stuff—Bay had gleaned that they were basically orphans. Their mother, a wild, lost soul, had brought them here to the Waverley house when Claire had been six and Sydney a newborn. They had been raised by their reclusive grandmother Mary. Claire had embraced everything Waverley as easily as breathing, but Sydney had rejected the notion that she was anything but normal until much later in life.

And, as magical as her mother was, Bay *still* wasn't sure she totally accepted it. It was one of many reasons Bay felt closer to her aunt.

Regardless, it was just a matter of time before Claire told Bay's mother about the boy.

"I don't think Mom would understand," Bay said.

"She would understand. Trust me."

"You know me better than she does."

Claire shook her head. "That's not true."

Bay turned to look out the window over the sink. The back garden was surrounded by a tall iron fence covered in honeysuckle vine two feet thick in places, and topped by pointy finials, like that of an old cemetery. She couldn't see the tree, but she knew it was there. That always gave her a small measure of comfort.

"It's finally getting cold. When will the apple tree bloom?" she asked. It was autumn, and the only time the strange apple tree in the Waverley's backyard, the one that had been there long before the house was built, was dormant. For no reason anyone could explain, the tree bloomed all winter, then it produced small pink apples all spring and into the summer. Some of Bay's fondest memories were of lying under the apple tree in the summer while Claire gardened and the apple tree tossed apples at her like a dog trying to coax its owner into playing catch. But as fall approached, the tree would lose its leaves overnight, and then it could do nothing but shake its bare branches miserably until the first frost of the season startled it back awake. The entire family felt its frustration.

"The almanac is calling for first frost on Halloween this year," Claire said. "A week from Saturday."

"That's late. Later than I ever remember. Will you have a party?" Bay asked hopefully.

"Of course," Claire said, kissing the top of Bay's head as she passed. Copper pot in hand, she began to pour the tart, yellow, lemon verbena candy syrup into small round molds to harden. "We always celebrate first frost."

On the day the tree bloomed in the fall, when its white apple blossoms fell and covered the ground like snow, it was tradition for the Waverleys to gather in the garden like survivors of some great catastrophe, hugging one another, laughing as they touched faces and arms, making sure they were all okay, grateful to have gotten through it. It was a relief, putting their world back in order. They always got restless before first frost, giving their hearts away too easily, wanting things they couldn't have, getting distracted and clumsy and too easily influenced by the opinions of others. First frost meant letting go, so it was always reason to celebrate.

Everything was okay after that.

To Bay, the day couldn't get here soon enough.

Because the way things had been building up lately, there was a lot that could go wrong between now and then.

After working a few hours for her aunt, Bay left at dusk and cut through neighborhoods and backyards, heading toward downtown Bascom.

As she approached the green in the center of town, she immediately noticed an old man standing in the park alone, a beat-up, hard leather suitcase on the ground next to him.

There was something magnetic about him. He had

a self-contained, silent confidence, as if a simple glance or a smile from him would feel like a secret he knew that would change your life, would change everything. Maybe he was a preacher or a politician or a salesman.

Bay considered it for a moment. Yes, definitely a salesman.

From across the street, Bay stopped to stare, a tendency she tried to curb because she knew it bothered people. Once, when she had stared too long at a woman in the grocery store, the woman had become angry and said to Bay, "I belong with him. He's going to leave his wife. Don't try to tell me otherwise." This had startled Bay because, number one, she'd had no idea Ione Engle was having an affair and, number two, she'd simply been staring at the tiny twigs caught in Ione's hair as, just an hour before, Ione had been rolling around the riverbank with another woman's husband. But people were always suspicious, because that was Bay's gift. Or curse, as her mother would say. Bay knew where things belonged. Just as her aunt Claire's gift was with the food she made from the edible flowers from the Waverley garden. And her mother's gift was her uncanny way with hair, how a cut from her could inexplicably turn your day around. Bay could put away silverware in a house she'd never been to before, in exactly the correct drawer. She could watch strangers in parking lots, and know exactly which cars they were walking to.

Bay watched the old man, his hands in his pockets, as he took in everything around him with a steady gaze—downtown Bascom's touristy stores, the fountain on the green where college kids would sometimes hang out. His eyes lingered curiously on the outdoor sculpture by the fountain, which had been made by the winning art student from Orion. The sculpture changed every year. This year it was an eight-foot-high, ten-foot-wide cement bust of the founder of Orion College, Horace J. Orion. The huge gray cement head was half buried in the grass, so that only the top of the head—from the nose up—was visible. Horace J. Orion looked like he was returning from the dead, peering out from under the ground, taking stock, before deciding if it was really worth the effort. It was actually pretty funny, this giant head in the middle of downtown. Local fervor had died down in the months since its installation, but it was still a source of conversation when gossip became thin.

The wind had died down, but the stranger's silver hair and trouser cuffs were moving slightly, as if he had attracted what little breeze left to him, the way birds flock to seed.

His light, silvery eyes finally landed on Bay. There was a road between them but, strangely, all the cars seemed to have disappeared. He smiled, and it was just as Bay had suspected. It was as if he could tell her everything she wanted to hear.

"I was wondering," the man called to her in a pearly voice, "if you could tell me where Pendland Street is?"

Bay paused at the coincidence. She had just come from the Waverley house on Pendland Street. Pendland

Street was long and winding and contained the oldest homes in Bascom, rambling, shabby-chic houses that tourists like to see. He could belong at any number of them. She looked at his old suitcase. Maybe at the inn on the street.

She pointed back the way she had come.

"Thank you," the man said.

Cars suddenly appeared again, racing down the busy downtown street, obscuring her view. She jogged to the nearby newspaper box and climbed on top of it, steadying herself with the lamppost beside the box.

But the green was empty now. The man had disappeared.

As Bay stood there on the box, a blue Fiat drove by. Inside were the upper-crust girls from Bay's high school—Trinity Kale, Dakota Olsen, Riva Alexander and Louise Hammish-Holdem. Louise leaned out the window and yelled to Bay in a singsongy voice, "We're going to Josh's house! Do you want us to give him another *note* from you?"

Bay, used to this, just sighed as she watched the car drive on. Then she jumped down from the newspaper box and walked to her mother's hair salon across from the green.

When she entered the salon, she saw her mother deep in conversation with her last appointment. Sydney was thirty-eight, but looked younger. She was a confident dresser, her preferences leaning toward shorts paired with striped tights and midcentury vintage dresses. Her skin was smooth and her hair was a delicious caramel blond—usually. Today, Bay could swear there were new, electric shadows of red in it, ones that hadn't been there that morning.

Bay dropped her backpack behind the reception desk where Violet, her mother's new (totally ineffective) receptionist was fast asleep in her chair. She was even snoring slightly. Bay took a tattered paperback out of her backpack and held it up for her mother to see, then she hitched her thumb at the door, telling her mother that she'd be outside reading.

Sydney nodded and gave Bay a look that had *driver's ed* written all over it. She'd been nagging Bay about signing up for driving lessons for months now. But Bay didn't want to learn to drive. If she did, there was no telling what sort of embarrassment she'd cause herself before first frost. No, she was fine walking and taking the bus to her aunt Claire's house and waiting for her mother to get off work in the evenings.

Too much freedom was a dangerous thing for a girl in love.

"Take your phone. I'll call you if I get through early," Sydney said, and Bay grudgingly went back to her backpack and took out her phone and put it in her pocket.

Her mother said she was, quite possibly, the only teenager in the world who didn't like talking on the phone. That wasn't necessarily true. It was just that no one but her mother called her.

Bay walked across the green, wondering for a moment where that strange elderly man had gone, and considering going back to her aunt Claire's house to see if that's where he'd ended up. But doing that would mean she couldn't walk over to Josh Matteson's house and back in time to leave after her mother's last appointment.

So she trekked through more backyards, then through the woods by the cold rush of the river, where the best homes in Bascom were. The new chancellor of Orion College lived there, as did a few doctors. And the Mattesons, who owned the largest manufactured housing plant in the state. Live in a double-wide? It was probably made here in Bascom, by the people who lived in this seven-bedroom Tudor. In the shadow of the half-bare trees, Bay climbed the hill that overlooked the Matteson's back lawn. She could see straight past where their pool had been covered for the season, to the hot tub and the open patio doors.

There were a lot of kids there already, some in the hot tub, some watching television in the sitting room off the patio. They were taking advantage of the fact that Josh Matteson's parents were away for the month. They were all trying a little too hard to look relaxed, like something they'd seen in a movie, but the truth was, none of them really belonged there.

The girls from the Fiat, for instance. Trinity Kale, whose parents were divorcing, belonged in Florida with her grandparents. And Dakota Olsen wanted to be working on her college essay, because she clearly belonged at Princeton. Riva Alexander, just this shy of plump, always on the bottom of the cheerleader pyra-

mid and always on a diet, wanted to be home, cooking. And Louise Hammish-Holdem, well, Bay couldn't
tell exactly where Louise belonged, she just knew it
wasn't here. That was high school in a nutshell. No one
was where they belonged. They were all on their way
to someplace else. It drove Bay crazy, and also made
her something of an outcast, because Bay knew exactly
where she belonged. She belonged here in Bascom.

With Josh Matteson.

She'd known about belonging in this town the moment her mother moved back here from Seattle when
Bay was five years old. It was the fulfillment of a dream
Bay had had a long time ago, a dream of lying under
the apple tree in the Waverley garden, everyone happy,
everyone in the right place. It took a while longer to
realize that Josh was who she was supposed to be with.
Bay and Josh had never had a chance to socialize, not
until this year, when Bay finally entered high school,
where Josh was now a senior.

Josh was sitting at a patio table, engaged in some
animated conversation with another member of the
soccer team. He was blond and beautiful and funny
and good-hearted, but so clearly miserable that Bay
was surprised no one else could see it. It radiated
around him like smoke, like he was smoldering, slowly
burning away.

She belonged with him. That alone was hard enough
to bear. But the fact that she knew he also belonged
with her, that he was on a path he wasn't meant for,
was excruciating. Getting him to believe that was the

hardest thing she'd ever tried to do. She'd made a fool of herself two months ago, writing that note to him, giving herself a reputation she didn't really need, on top of being a Waverley. So she kept her distance now.

She finally understood that, no matter how hard you try, you can't make someone love you. You can't stop them from making the wrong decision.

There was no magic for that.

Late that evening, Claire Waverley woke up and shivered. The bedroom window in the second-floor turret was open, letting in cold air. The chill hovered above the bed, twinkling in tiny white stars she could almost reach up and touch.

She got up quietly and went to the window to remove the board her husband, Tyler, had used to prop it open. Last night's big rain had finally blown colder weather into town, following a particularly scorching Indian summer. Outside, the neighborhood streetlights glowed in a blue haze, the way a warm glass will haze over when put in the refrigerator.

Claire looked over her shoulder at Tyler, blankets kicked off of him, his bare chest emanating heat in waves. He never got cold. The man even wore his Birkenstocks, without socks, all year round.

"I'm going to finish up some work," she said softly. The words barely took form, because she didn't want to wake him up. If he woke up, he would draw her back into bed with him, telling her that it could wait until morning.

She turned, just missing Tyler opening his eyes as soon as she left.

But he didn't stop her.

They had been married for almost ten years now, and Claire would still wonder, when she was tired and particularly short of temper, why he was still here, why he still loved her so much. He wasn't from here—he'd moved to take a job here at Orion College a decade ago, a time in Claire's life she always referred to as the Year Everything Changed—so he'd never fully invested in all of Bascom's superstitions and eccentricities. He'd never put much stock in the fact that everyone in town believed there were things about the Waverleys that couldn't be explained. In fact, deep down, she knew he didn't believe in any of it. He loved what *wasn't* special about her. Her hair, her laugh, even the way she walked. And it was confounding. Who she was without her gift was someone she couldn't even imagine. Being a Waverley, she used to think, back in the old days, back when she was alone, was her one redeeming quality.

She loved him with a force that could bring tears to her eyes, and the thought of losing him felt like standing on the edge of an endless black pit, about to fall in.

She shook her head as she walked down the hall. She was catastrophizing again. Tyler wasn't going anywhere. She knew her husband was as patient and happy as a leaf in the wind, blowing in whatever direction Claire went. But Claire had long ago realized, even after those constant dreams of her mother leaving faded away, that when you are abandoned as a child, you are never able to forget that people are *capable* of leaving, even if they never do.

Claire stopped at the end of the hall. She opened their daughter Mariah's bedroom door and saw that Mariah's window was open, too. Mariah was sleeping in a position similar to Tyler's, arms and legs outstretched, like she was dreaming of floating in warm water. She was so much like her father, and so little like Claire, that sometimes Claire thought it felt like loving another piece of him, wholly unattached from herself.

She picked up Mariah's ballet clothes and backpack as she crossed the room, looking around and feeling her child's normalcy like a crossword puzzle clue that made no sense to her. Mariah had wanted a pink room, perfect pink, the shade of watermelon cake frosting. She had wanted white furniture and a tufted princess comforter. She hadn't wanted old wallpaper or antiques or handmade quilts. Her daughter took ballet and gymnastics and was always invited to sleepovers and birthday parties. She even made friends easily. Just this week, she'd said she made a new best friend named Em, and Em was now all she talked about. That kind of normalcy never came so easily to a Waverley. And yet, here Mariah was, as normal as her father, as happy as he was, as oblivious to the eccentricities of Claire and this house as he was.

She reached the open window in Mariah's room and pulled it down. She thought of all she needed to do downstairs. She would make sure all her Friday candy orders were boxed and labeled. Then she would answer business emails in her office and save them in a draft folder to send during business hours so no one would know she was awake at 2:00 A.M., worrying about things that didn't need to be worried about.

Everyone was excited about Waverley's Candies, how much it was growing, how it was bringing so much attention to Bascom. Tyler, his brows raised when he'd found out what the profit margin had been over the summer, happily remarked that the new business was definitely good for Mariah's college fund. And even Claire had to admit that it was thrilling— seeing the Waverley name on the candy labels for the first time; the unfamiliar, but not unpleasant, jangle of nerves the moment she truly realized there were untold numbers of people out there, buying something she'd made. Claire. A Waverley. It was so different from catering, no longer personal, opening her talent up to a wider pool. It felt like the precipice of something big, and she wasn't immune to the idea of success. In fact, she was overcome with it, putting all her effort into the candy, thinking how proud her grandmother would have been. Grandmother Mary had been an intensely withdrawn woman who had sold her wares—her mint jellies and secret-love custard pies and rose geranium wine—only to people who would come to her back door, like it was a secret to be kept by all.

But as first frost approached, bringing with it that

noticeable uncertainty, Claire could no longer deny that something about Waverley's Candies was distinctly off.

When orders from gourmet grocery chains and specialty stores around the South flooded in after the *Southern Living* article, Claire couldn't keep up with making the flower essences that flavored the candy herself. The demand became too great for what she could harvest from her garden, so she'd had to quickly make the decision to buy the essences, instead of making them.

And no one noticed.

As the labels on the backs of the jars attested, the lemon verbena candies still quieted children and eased sore throats. The lavender candies still gave people a sense of happiness. And everyone still swore the rose candies made them think of their first loves.

But the candies now contained nothing from the Waverley garden, that mystical source of everything Claire held true.

In weaker moments, she found herself thinking, What if it wasn't real? What if Tyler was right and Waverleys were odd just because everyone had been told that for generations, because they just happened to live next to an apple tree that bloomed in the wrong time of year? What if the little girl Claire used to be, the one left here as a child, clinging to her grandmother Mary's apron, had latched on to the myth of this family simply because she'd so desperately wanted roots? What if the flowers weren't special? What if *she* wasn't? Instead of keeping the Waverley name local and mysterious like her grandmother, she'd opened it up to wider speculation. She'd wanted the attention, she'd wanted more people to know her gift, as if the more people who knew, the more real it would be. But she'd begun to wonder if she had betrayed a secret her grandmother had entrusted her with.

It didn't help that, at this time of year, Claire felt the loss of her grandmother Mary the strongest. Claire had been twenty-four when she'd lost her. That had been twenty years ago, but Claire could still smell Mary's fig and pepper bread sometimes, and there were times she was sure Mary was still here, in the way a carton of soured milk would tip over into the sink, or the mixing bowls on the shelf would seem to coordinate themselves by color overnight. She missed how natural everything felt with her grandmother around, how substantial.

She stepped away from Mariah's window to go to the kitchen. She paused, then turned back. Across the street, on the sidewalk in front of Mrs. Kranowski's house, she thought she saw a shadow. She squinted, her nose almost pressed to the glass, and the shadow began to take form.

There was someone standing in the darkness between the streetlights. He was tall and wearing something light, like a gray suit. His hair was silver. Everything else was obscured, as if his skin were invisible.

But he was definitely staring in this direction.

She made sure Mariah's window was locked, then she quickly went downstairs and pulled a flashlight out of the drawer of the table by the door.

She unlocked the door and opened it, stepping onto the porch. The chilled floorboards made her toes curl.

There was no one across the street now.

"Hello?" she called.

She flicked on the flashlight and aimed the light on the front yard. A breeze flew through, picking up some leaves and swirling them around, the sound like fluttering pages in a quiet library. Mrs. Kranowski's dog barked a few times. Then everything was quiet.

There was a scent of something familiar in the air, though, something she couldn't quite place, a combination of cigarettes and stout beer and sweat and, strangely enough, cheap cherry lip gloss.

Everything meant something, in Claire's experience. And this vision of a man made the hair on her arms stand on end.

First frost was always an unpredictable time, but this year it felt more . . . desperate than others.

Something was about to happen.

2

Earlier that day, when the old man had stepped off the bus and onto the green in downtown Bascom, he had looked around with dismay, wondering how his life had gotten to this point.

He was usually one step ahead of the colder weather as he traveled, doing jobs as he made his way from the north to Florida every year. Hoards of carnival people wintered there. Mostly old-schoolers like him, who never referred to the past as the good old days.

But he needed a quick infusion of cash first, which was why he'd stopped here. It wouldn't be a lot, but it would get him through the next few months. Business had been slow this year. There were fewer and fewer people on his list and, truthfully, he didn't have the skill he used to have. He once was able to blackmail people so smoothly he could make them believe giving him their money was all *their* idea. But his heart just wasn't in it anymore.

Or so the expression went.

He was fairly certain he didn't have a heart anymore. The only thing that kept his blood flowing through his veins was the thrill of the heist, and even that felt like going through the motions these days. The last time he could remember feeling an actual beat to his long-ago heart was when he'd been eight years old and his mother, the Incredible Zelda Zahler, Snake Charmer from the Sands of the Sahara, had left him during the night, never to be seen again. Her name had actually been Ruthie Snoderly, and she'd been from the tiny town of Juke, West Virginia, about as far away from the sands of the Sahara as one could get. She'd been neither pretty nor nice, but he had loved her. Under her thick pancake makeup, her skin had been pockmarked, but he would stare at her adoringly from his cot at night and imagine her scars were constellations, a secret map to a far-off, happy place. Her accent had been thick and rural, and sometimes when he heard that deep Appalachian accent even today, he found himself longing for something he'd never really had in the first place: home.

He set his suitcase down. It was a strange place, this North Carolina town. There was a huge gray sculpture of a half-buried head in the park. One of the eyes on the sculpture had a monocle, and the hair had been so expertly molded even the comb marks looked real. He sighed, thinking this almost wasn't worth the effort. If he hadn't put so much research into this already, he would wait for the next bus and go to Florida right now. Maybe he would get a job at Taco Bell for the winter.

The Great Banditi working at Taco Bell.

No, that was something even he couldn't foresee.

So, first things first. He had to find Pendland Street.

He turned and noticed a teenager across the street. She had long, dark hair and a steady gaze. She had stopped to stare at him. Not everyone could hold a stare that long and not seem rude. He quickly summed her up: too observant. He smiled to put her at ease.

"I was wondering," he called to her, "if you could tell me where Pendland Street is?"

She pointed west and he thanked her, picking up his suitcase and hurrying away. Best to be a mystery to some. Confusion was always the best way out of an unfamiliar situation. Any magician worth his salt knew that.

He found the street easily and walked slowly past the rambling old houses. Decent enough, he supposed. But the neighborhood didn't give him hope that he could make more money here than he'd already figured.

He had no idea where he was going to stay. He never did. Oftentimes it was in a park or a patch of woods somewhere. But his bones weren't what they used to be. He longed for softer things these days. Softer bus seats, softer beds, softer marks. And there was a chill in the air here that he didn't like. He wasn't moving fast enough to avoid the cold touch of autumn as it marched steadily from the north, and it made his joints stiff.

Halfway down the winding street, he stopped. His feet were already aching because, even though his shoes were so highly polished that they made perfect star-point reflections in the sunlight, there were holes forming on the soles, and he could feel every pebble he stepped on.

He looked up and saw that he had stopped in front of a house with a large sign on the front lawn that read, HISTORIC PENDLAND STREET INN.

He looked at the address number. It was a mere nine houses away from where his latest mark lived. This was fortuitous, indeed. Perhaps things were looking up.

Instead of walking to his mark's house to scope it out, which was better done under the cover of night, anyway, he walked up the sidewalk to the inn. The house was painted pink with brick-red shutters. The gingerbread trim along its arches was white, as was the porch. No fewer than four pumpkins were on each step leading up to the porch, each of varying sizes and colors; some pumpkins were even white, one was purple. Dried pampas grass was in an urn beside the door. Someone had put a great deal of effort into the autumnal decorations.

He opened the door, which had a wreath made of bittersweet on it, and entered.

It looked as most old houses turned into inns did, lots of shiny dark wood, a sitting room to the left, a dining area to the right, and a staircase leading to the upper floor. A check-in desk was in the foyer. More pumpkins were in here, too, and displays of dried silver dollar plants and Japanese paper lanterns. Someone had also taken their floral arranging class very seriously.

He set his suitcase down and looked around. There was no one here this evening. They must not offer dinner to guests. But the dining area hinted at breakfast or lunch, which meant there was a kitchen he could quietly raid. It had been hours since he'd last eaten. He tapped the bell on the desk and waited, studying the photos on the wall. Most were of a prissy, prudish-looking man in his sixties, shaking hands with people who appeared to be local bigwigs.

But the man in the photos wasn't the person who appeared from a room behind the staircase.

It was an excruciatingly thin woman, someone who reminded him of a contortionist he once knew named Gretel. This woman was in her late fifties or early sixties. Her hair was dyed dark brown and her skin was the sallow hue of someone with a two-pack-a-day habit. Her eyes, probably her one beauty as a youth, were quite green. He sized her up right away. This was a woman who had long ago figured out she wasn't getting her own happily-ever-after. But, like all disappointed women, she still believed in it, just that it was meant for someone else.

"May I help you?" she said, without much enthusiasm. She reeked of cigarette smoke.

He smiled at her, holding her eyes with his own. He was older than she was by twenty years, but he knew he was still attractive, in a genteel kind of way. His hair was thick and silver, and his eyes were an unusual bright gray. They were eyes that could hypnotize, which was the only reason he'd been allowed to stay on with Sir Walter Trott's Traveling Carnival when his mother left. Well, one of the reasons. "I'd like a room, please."

She turned to the computer on the desk and woke it up with a shake of the mouse. "Do you have a reservation?"

"Sadly, no."

She looked at him with exasperation. "This is leaf-looker season. We're booked. Sorry."

He leaned in slightly, showing his appreciation for the small effort she'd made with lipstick by looking at her mouth. "Surely you could make an exception for this weary traveler? I've come a long way."

She looked startled, as if this kind of attention was unexpected. Unexpected, but not unwanted. No, he had not read her wrong. He rarely did. "My brother would have a fit," she said, her hand going to the collar of her white polo shirt with the Pendland Street Inn logo embroidered on the chest.

"But something tells me you know how to work around that," he said with a smile. He let her know that he noticed she wasn't wearing a wedding ring by looking at the hand that was playing with her collar. "I've always found that the smartest people aren't the ones in charge, it's the ones who let them think they're in charge. Older brother?" He could see from the photos on the wall that he was.

"Yes. How did you know?"

"I had an older brother, too." He didn't, of course.

"Was he a prick, too?" the woman asked. Her use

of the familiar, the colloquial, let him know he was already in.

He shook his head in solidarity. "The stories I could tell."

"I do love a good story. What the hell," she said, turning back to the computer. "It's your lucky day. My brother doesn't usually let me man the front desk. He says I don't have front-desk qualities. I can cancel a reservation." She typed something into the computer. "Credit card and ID?" she said, looking up at him.

"In my suitcase," he said, gesturing to the banged-up leather case he'd set by the door. "If you don't mind, could I be shown to my room first? I'll rustle through my things and find them for you. Perhaps after a nap."

If that tripped her up, she didn't show it. He was fairly certain that she was past the point of caring if her brother got paid or not. "Room six, then. Breakfast starts at eight and there's tea at four." She handed him a key. "Don't mention this conversation to my brother."

"My lips are sealed," he assured her. "Thank you, Mrs . . . ?"

"Ainsley. Anne Ainsley. *Miz*.," she said pointedly. "And you are?"

The Great Banditi smiled and gave her a half-bow. "Russell Zahler, at your service."

The next morning, Sydney Waverley-Hopkins sat at the kitchen table while Bay ate Cocoa Puffs and reread her worn copy of *Romeo and Juliet*. She was already dressed for school, wearing a T-shirt that said, COME TO THE DARK SIDE. WE HAVE COOKIES.

Sydney looked at Bay pointedly, but Bay didn't look back.

"Ahem." Sydney cleared her throat and lowered her head, trying to meet Bay's eyes over the book.

Nope.

Sydney sighed and got up to refill her coffee cup. She didn't have to be at work until ten, but she didn't want to miss this opportunity to be with Bay. She was determined to be around when her daughter finally decided to confide in her about what was bothering her, about what was making her so distant and miserable lately.

Whatever it was, it was making Bay want to spend more and more time with her aunt Claire. But Sydney wasn't going to give up these mornings. She would just sit and wait. One day, Bay was going to need her advice. Sydney could remember her teenage years here in Bascom with a clarity she wished she didn't have. Sometimes it made her lose her breath, remembering how those years had felt like drowning. She knew what her daughter was going through, even if Bay didn't believe it.

It was just before daybreak and the window over the kitchen sink was dark. Sydney could see Bay's reflection behind her in it. She tied her red kimono robe tightly around her, feeling a hollow in her stomach every time she realized that her only child would be an adult in just a few short years. She had an unnerving suspicion that there was a void Bay was standing in front of, and as soon as Bay moved, Sydney would get sucked into the blackness. Sydney had always assumed she would have more children by now. She tried not to think of it every month. She thought if she acted like she wasn't watching the calendar, that maybe fate would laugh and surprise her. But it didn't. Sydney had been almost frantic about it these past few weeks, taking her lunch hour and surprising her husband, Henry, in his office, and jumping on him the minute she got in bed at night.

She'd had no experience in mothering before she had Bay, and she'd not always made the right decisions. She wanted another chance. She'd stayed with Bay's father, David, far longer than she should have. It was one of those things women simply *assume* about themselves—that they weren't the kind to stay after the first hit, that they would never let their child live in that kind of environment. But a woman's ability to surprise herself is far stronger than her ability to surprise others. Sydney had stayed, not knowing where else to go. She'd left her hometown of Bascom when she was eighteen, burning bridges with the fire of her resentment, never intending to return. She'd hated her Waverley reputation, hated all of her teenage peers who had rejected her, hated that she was never who she really wanted to be here. But the person she'd been with David hadn't been who she'd wanted to be, either. She'd fled Seattle and David when Bay was five. She'd finally realized, if she'd been so wrong about life outside of Bascom, maybe she'd been wrong about leaving Bascom in the first place.

There were times when she would still wake up in the middle of the night and feel a remembered fear, aches like bruises along her sides and cheekbones, thinking that David was still alive, that he was going to find her and Bay here. But he was long gone, she would remind herself. Ten years now. The Year Everything Changed, Claire called it. He'd died suddenly in prison after Sydney had finally pressed charges.

Yes, she'd made a lot of mistakes. And she so desperately wanted to get it right this time.

Maybe then she would feel like she was finally forgiven.

She was startled out of her thoughts when she heard Bay's spoon clatter against the bowl. She saw Bay's reflection stand up from the table.

"The last Halloween dance decorating committee meeting is this afternoon, isn't it?" Sydney asked as Bay came up beside her and put her cereal bowl in the sink.

"Yes. But I'll be done in time to baby-sit Mariah while you and Claire go on your double date."

That made Sydney laugh. "You make it sound so distasteful. *Dating.* Bleh. What a horrible thing to do. You should try it sometime. You'd like it."

"No one has asked me," Bay said, zipping up her hoodie. "Can I spend the night at the Waverley house tonight, since I'll be there anyway, baby-sitting Mariah?"

"If Claire says it's okay. You know, you could do the asking. I mean, you could ask a boy out."

Bay rolled her eyes. "Right."

"No, really," Sydney said, pulling Bay's long hair out from under the hoodie and smoothing it down around her shoulders. "Ask Phin. I see you two talking at the bus stop all the time."

"We're fellow outcasts. That's all."

"You are not an outcast. The more you say it, the more it becomes true in people's minds." Sydney looked her daughter in the eye. "I wish I could make you see yourself the way I see you."

"Five years old with an apple tree for a best friend?" Bay asked, putting her copy of *Romeo and Juliet* in her back pocket.

"No." Although it was true. Sydney would always see Bay as a black-haired, blue-eyed little girl, the summer they'd moved back and lived with Claire. Bay would lie under the tree in the Waverleys' backyard for hours, daydreaming.

"*Fifteen years old* with an apple tree for a best friend?" Bay asked.

"Bay, stop it," Sydney said, following her through the farmhouse to the living room. "That apple tree is not your friend. Phin is your friend. Riva Alexander is your friend. She asked you to be on the decorating committee, didn't she?"

"Riva is . . . decent, I guess. But she's not my friend. She only put me on the committee because she saw how teachers kept asking me to rearrange the desks in

their classrooms to where they made the most sense,"
Bay said. "You know what some kids call me? Feng
Shui Bay. Riva *put* me on the committee. She didn't
ask me."

"Because you're so good at that kind of thing. Interior design is in your future. I'm sure of it. That's what
you should study when you go to college," Sydney said
encouragingly, letting her know that this misery didn't
last forever.

Bay shrugged as she picked up her backpack from
where it was sitting on the large beige couch facing the
fireplace. When Sydney had married Henry, putting
down roots here in a way she'd never imagined when
she'd left town at eighteen, the farmhouse had been
decorated in Early Man. Henry and his late grandfather had lived here alone for years and had never
minded the dark walls and the rugs with worn paths
in them: front door to living room; living room to
bedroom; bedroom to bathroom; bathroom to kitchen,
kitchen to back door. Henry had followed his grandfather every day of his life. When Bay and Sydney
had moved in, they had infused the place with light-
colored furniture and curtains, new rugs and yellow
paint that sparkled in the sunlight. A few years ago,
they'd even renovated the kitchen with glass-front cabinets and an apron sink and golden floorboards. The
decor might have changed, but Henry's route never
did. He still made the same trail through the house
every day. But, unlike his grandfather, he didn't have
a son or grandson to follow him.

That made Sydney put her hand to her stomach.

Bay walked to the front door. "I don't want to argue with you, Mom. I'm doing my best. I really am. No matter how hard you try, you can't make it easier for me. I know you want to. But you can't. I love you."

That was where she was wrong. Bay was drowning. She just didn't know it yet. And Sydney's job was to keep her head above water.

Sydney followed her to the front door and watched Bay walk down the front steps. The sun was beginning to rise. "I love you, too, baby girl," she said.

Bay walked down the long driveway from the farmhouse, passing cold, wet fields. It was getting lighter now, and ghostly mist floated over the ground, not quite touching. She could hear the cows in the distance as they were being herded to the milking parlor in the barn. It was a slow, steady job. It was like a dance, every morning. Her father Henry dancing with his cows.

When she reached the road, Phineus Young was already there. He was tall and reedy, with white-blond hair and light green eyes. His rough-around-the-edges family lived across the road, on property strewn with old cars and tractor tires used as flower planters. The Youngs were known for their strength. They were the town's manual laborers and strong backs. Many had worked at the dairy over the years.

Legend had it that, once in every generation, a Young child would be born with even more strength than the average Young, and that child would always be named Phineus. He would be the strongest man in town, the one everyone would call for the truly hard work—lifting old well caps by himself, moving large rocks out of tight spaces, or chopping down looming trees when babies were sleeping and a noisy chain saw couldn't be used.

But Phin was not what you would call a tower of strength. Despite his name and everyone's expectations, he wasn't the strongest man in town. No one asked him to move anything. He was, in his own words, a dud. They'd been meeting here at the bus stop every morning since first grade. Bay's mother had stood with them for years, worrying about them alone on the road. Phin's parents were never worried. No one would ever mess with a Young, especially one named Phineus. Sometime around sixth grade, Bay finally convinced her mother that she and Phin were fine.

"Hi, Phin," Bay said, coming to a stop beside him. Her breath made a visible cloud in front of her. She tucked her chin into her hoodie. They never talked in school, only here. They had a bus stop understanding.

"Hey, Bay."

He knew about the letter she'd given Josh. Everyone in school knew. But he was kind enough never to mention it. They stood in cold, comfortable silence. There was very little traffic at this time of morning.

"So, are there going to be good decorations for the Halloween dance tomorrow?" Phin suddenly asked.

"Yes." Bay looked at him curiously. "Are you going?"

He made a snorting sound and scrubbed the gravel

shoulder of the road with the toe of his old military boots, ones that had belonged to his dad, who had died in Afghanistan. "Me? No way." He paused, then said, "Riva Alexander is on the decorating committee, too, isn't she?"

"Yes."

"I heard her talking about the food she was going to bring. It sounded nice," Phin said wistfully. "She's nice."

"Riva? Seriously?" She shook her head as if disappointed in him. "Phin."

"Oh, come on. You can pine away for Josh Matteson, but I can't like Riva?" He saw the look on Bay's face and said, "Sorry."

"It's okay." When you take your heart out of your chest and hold it out for all to see, it's not like you can expect everyone not to notice.

Phin gave a short laugh. "We can always dream of a normal life, can't we?"

"No, Phin, we can't. And we shouldn't. We're fine like we are! We're great," she said, up on her high horse again. She was up there a lot lately.

She didn't used to be like this. She'd always been confident about where she belonged and who she was but, lately, she'd been so *insistent* about it. She would hear herself sometimes, and even she found herself annoying. She was overcompensating. She knew that. But her emotions were so hard to control these days. She would cry at the drop of a hat. She would get angry at her mother for absolutely no reason. She was fifteen. That was part of it. But it was also the time of year. As soon as first frost was here, she was sure everything would get better. She'd be nicer to her mom. She'd sign up for driver's ed. And maybe Josh Matteson would even fall in love with her and everything would be perfect.

"I want to live in your world," Phin said.

"What are you talking about, weirdo?" She gave him a playful nudge. He was so thin it was like pushing at something pliable, like a bendy straw. "You already do."

After school that Friday, Bay headed to the last meeting of the decorating committee in the school gymnasium—a state-of-the-art, embarrassingly large facility that dwarfed the three other academic buildings of Bascom High. A few years ago, the high school booster club had raised the funds for the gym in less than six months. Apparently, there were a lot of parents with deep pockets and memories of their glory years in sports here. The place smelled like fresh paint and new rubber and missed opportunities.

At the first after-school decorating committee meeting a month ago, Riva Alexander had let Bay sketch out how she'd wanted the gym to be decorated, then she had Bay make a list of things to buy, while the other girls on the committee talked about the costumes they were going to wear. At the second meeting, Bay did her chemistry homework while Riva regaled the committee with what food and drinks she and her mother were bringing: flaky pastries that looked like knobby, weathered fingers, with slivered almonds for fingernails; big plastic drink dispensers with plastic eyeballs floating inside the punch. They'd spent the entire two hours huddled around Riva's laptop, looking up where Riva had gotten her ideas on Pinterest.

When Riva had asked Bay to help decorate, she'd hinted that she'd hoped Bay would get her aunt Claire to cater the dance, too. Riva loved food, and she would have loved to have spent hours talking to Claire about menus, going off on tangents about flan and crème fraîche and pink Himalayan salt. But Riva was out of luck. If it wasn't about candy, Claire didn't have time for it.

Claire normally would have a lot of catering work this time of year. She used to have a party to cater almost every night in October. Bay remembered the Waverley house full of pumpkin pie scents in the fall. There had been *mountains* of maple cakes with violets hidden inside, *lakes* of butternut soups with chrysanthemum petals floating on top. But not this year. When Claire wasn't making candy, she was on the phone, talking about the candy, or filling out orders for the candy, or boxing up the candy. There were even companies calling, asking about buying Waverley's Candies. The way Bay saw it, Claire making candy was like the perfect chair in the perfect color in the perfect place in a room—only it was made of the wrong fabric. And when something that small was wrong, most people didn't bother fixing it.

The dance decorations had arrived that week, so this final committee meeting was to be spent putting them up. Bay tried to do her homework on the bleachers, but the other girls kept interrupting her, asking where everything belonged. She finally put her books away and joined them. Some boys from the soccer team—boyfriends and want-to-be boyfriends—showed up with duct tape and butcher's twine and ladders pilfered from the janitor's closet, acting very manly about it.

Bay stood in the middle of the gymnasium, directing them all, feeling like an ice skater in a snow globe, spinning and spinning. It was nice. She always had this image in her head, the end product when everything was where it was supposed to be, and it was thrilling when she could actually make it happen in real life.

She didn't realize at first when everyone had gone quiet. The music from Riva's laptop was still blasting. Bay was admiring the lighted ball that was hanging from the steel rafters. It was shrouded in paper cut-outs that cast shadows on the walls, which looked like a dark forest. Surrounding it were glittery paper bats chasing full moons made from wrapped, store-bought popcorn balls, which students could reach up and pluck from their strings from the ceiling. She finally looked around with a smile, only to see the whole group staring at the gymnasium doors.

There was Josh Matteson, bits of stray smoke curling off his shoulders, smoke only she could see. Her hand almost went to her heart, but she stopped herself halfway and pretended to scratch her neck instead.

He, too, seemed confused as to why everyone had gone silent. That's when he saw Bay.

Bay cursed that stupid note. It had taken her weeks to write. When school had started in August, she'd seen Josh in the hallway on that first day, and suddenly she'd had honey in her veins. The note had laid it all out as passionately and sincerely as she could make it. She'd described her feelings as best she could, though she wasn't sure she'd gotten it just right. She'd told him she'd be outside on the front steps after school every day, waiting for him if he ever wanted to talk—which she was *still* doing, almost making her late to her job at her aunt Claire's house every afternoon, but she couldn't help herself.

Funny, when she'd given him the note—in front of his friends, which had been her first mistake—it had never occurred to her that he wouldn't believe her.

To Josh's credit, he smiled from the gymnasium doors. "I was wondering where everyone went," he said in that deep, bright voice of his, like fresh water in a dark cavern.

"We'll be out at your house later," Riva said, quickly stepping forward. Riva looked like she was already wearing a costume. She favored billowy skirts with colorful scarves tied around her waist. Her eyes were slightly tilted in a way that gave her an exotic, gypsy-ish air, despite her fair, WASP-y coloring. There was something about her that was just slightly west of center, making her the odd one out in her group, the one gotten mad at the most and excommunicated for days on end for mysterious mean-girl reasons.

"Want to stay and help decorate?" Riva added, but it was said insincerely, because if she had wanted him there, she would have asked him before now. But she hadn't. Because of Bay. Josh was avoiding seeing her, and his friends knew that. And what Josh thought mattered to them. Josh was a star soccer player, class vice president, and he had been voted most likely to succeed in the senior superlatives—based entirely on his last name, some conjectured. But they only saw how perfect and beautiful and easygoing he was. They couldn't see him burning with unhappiness.

"No," Josh said. "I'm not very good at that kind of stuff. I'll just watch."

Everyone tried to act normal, giving Josh deference while still trying not to slight Bay, presumably so Bay wouldn't run out and leave them in a lurch. They needed her. All the county high schools had been invited to this soiree, so it had to be special, it had to be the *best*, to show off to their rivals.

But Bay would never do that—would never run from herself.

It was so excruciatingly awkward that everyone, Bay most of all, was relieved when it was over and they all went their separate ways, Josh leaving a trail of soot behind him that blew away in the breeze.

3

Bay walked from the school to her aunt's house in the growing darkness, having just missed the late buses because of the meeting. She didn't feel like running today like she usually did, always so anxious to get to the Waverley house. So she crunched slowly through the red leaves on the sidewalk, her face to the sinking sun, thinking about Josh. When she saw herself with him, she saw snow, so maybe this winter something would happen. Maybe she just had to be patient. She'd discovered long ago that getting things to where they belonged was sometimes a timely process, so she'd become good at waiting. If only there wasn't this longing that felt like actual *pain* sometimes. No one ever told her it was going to be like this. It was a wonder that anyone fell in love at all.

"Hello again."

She had just reached the Waverley house. She stopped on the sidewalk and turned. Across the street, she saw the same man she'd seen yesterday on the green downtown, the elderly man in the gray suit. He didn't have his suitcase with him today.

Bay smiled in surprise. "I see you found Pendland Street."

"Indeed, I did. Thank you."

"Are you visiting someone?"

"As a matter of fact, I am," he said.

Bay was momentarily distracted by the Halloween lights flipping on in Mrs. Kranowski's yard behind him—orange twinkle lights strung in her boxwood bushes, tattered glow-in-the-dark ghosts hanging in her spindly maple tree. The decorations had obviously been in storage, because Bay could smell mothballs from across the street. Mrs. Kranowki's elderly terrier, Edward, was at the front window, barking wildly at the man.

When Bay's eyes flicked back to the man—it had only been seconds—he was gone.

Edward stopped barking, as confused as she was.

Bay's dark brows knit and she slowly backed away, then ran to the house. She slid up the wet hill, then hurried to the front door, looking over her shoulder as she entered, half expecting the man to have followed her.

First frost falling on Halloween this year seemed to be making everything just that much weirder.

It had been rose candy day in the Waverley house, the scent still permeating the air, even though the kitchen was closed for the evening. It smelled as if there were a garden hidden in the walls some-where.

The back labels on all the rose candy jars read:

> *Rose essence is for memory*
> *of long ago first loves,*
> *have a taste and you will see*
> *the one you once dreamed of.*

Bay took a deep breath and felt her shoulders relax. But then she gave a start when her aunt appeared at the top of the staircase. She was in a bathrobe, obviously getting ready for her night out. "Bay?" Claire asked. "What's wrong?"

Bay pushed herself away from the front door. "Oh, nothing. Just this elderly man I've seen outside two days in a row. He wanted to know where Pendland Street was."

"It's a popular street."

"He just seemed strange. He was wearing this shiny gray suit, like a salesman, maybe."

"Hey, Bay!" Mariah said, running down the stairs past Claire. She had brown eyes and curly brown hair like her father, hair that always looked somehow in motion, even when Mariah was still, as if someone were running their fingers through it, lovingly.

"Hey, squirt," Bay said, giving her a hug. "I've got homework. How about you?"

"Yes."

"Let's do it together in the sitting room."

As Bay walked into the sitting room with her backpack, she almost missed the look on Claire's face, the look that maybe this man in the silver suit was not someone Claire was unfamiliar with.

Sydney arrived not long after Bay and Mariah had settled on the floor in the sitting room with their homework. She had just come from work and looked beautiful, as always, that perpetual scent of sweet hair spray floating around her like she was encased in fine mist. Again, her hair seemed a little more red than it had that morning. The change was subtle, but getting more noticeable. Her mother was slowly but surely turning into a redhead. Something like this happened to Sydney every year around first frost—an unexplained cut, or an odd change in color. But it was worse this year than most. Her restlessness was worse. It was for all of them, as if they all wanted something they suddenly feared they couldn't have.

Sydney asked how school was, and Bay gave her vague answers. Sydney finally gave up and headed upstairs to help Claire with her hair. Honestly, if it weren't for her mom's skill with hair, they would all have birds' nests on their heads.

Henry showed up next. He sat with the girls in the sitting room and waited, his blond hair still wet and the scent of Irish Spring soap clinging to his skin from his recent shower. Henry was a good man, a steady man who worked hard and loved unconditionally. He was a grounding force as strong as gravity in Bay and her mother's lives. Henry was Bay's adopted father, the only father she'd ever really known. She lost her biological father years ago. Bay could barely remember him now, the edges of his existence corroding like faxed paper. Her mother, always trying to make things right, never talked about him, for the same reason she kept trying to make Bay go out more and be more social, less Waverley. She was trying to make up for things that weren't her fault. Sometimes Bay just wanted to hug her and tell her that it was all right. But that would put a serious crimp in her effort to avoid talking to her mother, an effort so concerted that it baffled even her sometimes.

After the adults left, Bay put some frozen dinners (a dreadful staple in the Waverley house lately) in the microwave and she and Mariah ate and talked. Mariah mainly liked talking about her new best friend, Em. Apparently, they'd only met this week, but Em was already Mariah's entire world. Mariah was such a normal kid—a braces-wearing, dirty-fingernailed, bright-eyed *normal* kid. In this family, that was curious. Sometimes Bay thought her own mother should have had Mariah, and Claire should have been Bay's mother. That would have made more sense. Everyone would have been happier that way. Her mother would then have a normal daughter she didn't have to worry about being made fun of, and Claire would get someone just like her, someone who accepted being strange, whose entire identity counted on it.

When Mariah fell asleep in the sitting room later that night, Bay set aside the book she'd been reading. The furnace fired up on its own. Like an old woman, the house hated a chill. Bay lifted Mariah's feet off her lap and grabbed her hoodie off the back of the old couch. She walked through the kitchen and out the back door, crossing the driveway to the garden gate. She found the key hidden in the honeysuckle vines and entered, closing the gate behind her. The place was completely enclosed. The nine-foot fence covered in honeysuckle was as thick as a wall. Because the tree was dormant, nothing else would bloom in the garden, either, not even the rosebushes, which were still in bloom around town in clusters of pink and magenta from Indian summer.

The solar-powered ground lamps glowed with steady yellow light, marking the footpaths all the way to the back of the lot, where the apple tree was.

It was a short tree, barely reaching the top of the fence, but its limbs were long and wide, almost like vines. This tree was a presence, a personality, an influence on every Waverley who had ever lived here. Legend around Bascom was that if you ate an apple from the Waverley tree, you'd see what the biggest event in your life would be. Claire had once told Bay that the mere fact that someone wanted to see the biggest event in their life meant they weren't concentrating on what was good about every day, so Claire kept the gate locked and the finials sharp so no one could get in. As for the Waverleys themselves, they were all conveniently born with a severe dislike of apples, so they were never tempted to eat one. There was a long-ago saying that was still heard from time to time in town: *Waverleys know where to find the truth, they just can't stomach it.*

Bay reached the tree and touched its weathered trunk, the swirls and ridges of the bark like a mysterious chart to untold places. She lowered herself to the brown grass and looked up through the bare branches at the half moon like a black-and-white cookie in the sky.

This was Bay's thinking place. It had been since she was five, since she'd first arrived in this town and knew, *knew* she was home. Just a girl and her tree. Being here in the garden always made her feel better.

She thought about how she wished Josh Matteson would love her the way her dad loved her mom, and her uncle loved her aunt. The Waverley sisters had married men as steadfast and normal as the women were mercurial and strange. The men in their lives loved them the way astronomers loved stars, loved the promise of what they were, knowing there was something about them they would never truly understand.

"I wish you could tell me what to do, tree."

She thought she saw the barest movement along its limbs, just a slight tremble, the way eyes flicker under lids while dreaming.

Maybe it wished so, too.

Russell Zahler was too late for afternoon tea at the Pendland Street Inn, but purposely so. It was best not to be noticed by too many people, and the inn guests were all from out of town, anyway. They had nothing useful to share with him about what he needed to know.

The proprietor of the inn, Anne Ainsley's brother, Andrew, was at the front desk when Russell came back from his walk. Anne was clearing away the dishes in the dining room from tea. She smiled at him when she saw him. Her teeth were crooked and yellow, but she always showed them when she smiled, as if she didn't care.

"Hello, Mr. Zahler. You missed tea," Andrew said from the front desk. He was a fat man, but his movements were small and birdlike, his elbows always held closely to his sides, his footsteps clicky and dainty. From the way he was sitting back in the desk chair, his hands resting on his rotund belly, Russell guessed Andrew had eaten what had been left over from afternoon tea.

Russell had yet to offer any payment or ID, but Anne had obviously worked around that. Her brother had no idea. Andrew Ainsley was curious about Russell, though. He was probably wondering if Russell was a man of substance or means. He had peppered Russell with questions during breakfast, probably wondering if he deserved a photo on the wall. Russell had given him the story he gave most: he was a retired businessman on vacation from Butte, Montana. If ever asked what business, Russell would say he'd once owned a plant that manufactured clips for pegboards. Most people would lose interest after that.

"I lost track of time, exploring your lovely neighborhood," Russell said. "There's one house that's quite extraordinary. The yellow one with the turret, on the small hill."

"The Waverley house," Andrew said, waving his hands dismissively. "It was the first house built in the neighborhood. The Pendland Street Inn here, our Ainsley family home, was built by my great-grandfather, a mere seven years later. Our house still has all its original—"

"Waverley," Russell interrupted, before Andrew could hit his stride. "The name sounds familiar."

Andrew frowned. "Yes, well, they're an odd bunch. They keep to themselves." The phone rang and Andrew leaned forward with a small, involuntary grunt to pick it up.

Russell saw Anne catch his attention as she pointed toward the kitchen. She picked up the last of the plates and teacups and he followed her through the dark, doilyed dining room to the small kitchen. There was a nice oak butcher block island in the center, littered with crusts and flour, where Anne had obviously prepared the tea sweets and savories that afternoon.

His stomach grumbled. Though Anne had made sure he'd had extra large portions of scrambled eggs, bacon, and berries that morning, it was the last time he'd eaten today.

The large breakfast was a direct result of last night. When he thought everyone had gone to sleep in the inn, he'd crept downstairs, having automatically memorized where the creaks were on the staircase and along the old floorboards. He'd entered the kitchen for food, only to find Anne there, puffing on a cigarette in the dark, standing next to a window she'd cracked open to let the smoke out.

She'd reached over and turned on the light when he'd entered.

Because things like that could happen—and he always considered every possibility—he'd taken care to cover his old, torn pajamas with his heavy silk paisley robe, which had a gold rope sash with tassels on the ends. It made him look elegant and old-fashioned. He'd used the robe in his act as the Great Banditi, after the original Banditi had met his demise under mysterious circumstances. Perhaps he'd had too much to drink and hit his head on a rock in that field in northwest Arkansas. Or perhaps the rock had been wielded by an unknown assailant. The original Banditi had had many enemies on the carnival circuit. Russell had been one of many young boys he'd taken to his trailer on moonless nights, to do things no one would speak of.

After Russell had walked into the kitchen last night, Anne had fed him a snack of salad, cheese, and beer. In exchange, he had regaled her with the story of the time he'd watched the sausage and pepper stand explode at the carnival when he was a boy. The smell of fried sausage had brought every feral cat and stray dog in the city to the midway. There had been hundreds of them, so many it had been like wading through sand. The city hadn't known what to do. Russell told Anne that he'd had the genius idea to fence in the midway and turn it into a pet sanctuary. To this very day, he said, children of all ages still visited the sanctuary to throw sticks for the dogs and let the cats sit on their laps.

The story wasn't true, of course. Well, part of it was true. He had watched the sausage and pepper stand explode, but it had been his fault for spilling the grease when he'd tried to steal a sausage.

Anne hadn't seemed to care if it was true or not.

He got the feeling she'd given up on expecting the truth a long time ago.

That afternoon, when Russell followed her to the kitchen, Anne smiled as she set the pink, hand-painted teacups and plates into the sink. "I saved you some sandwiches and tea cakes," she said, wiping her hands on her jeans and reaching under the butcher block to produce a plate covered with a white cloth napkin. "Otherwise, Andrew eats all the leftovers." She removed the napkin with the flourish of a skilled magician's assistant. There were several triangles of crustless sandwiches and a few small scones and petit fours on the plate. Anne was, if nothing else, fairly competent in the kitchen.

"Thank you, Anne," he said as he took the plate, giving her a slight bow, like it was a gift of some great importance.

She liked that. "Come with me," she said, opening the kitchen door, which had lace curtains on it. She led him outside and around the house, away from the windows, to a small corner alcove formed by the heat pump and a nearby rose trellis. There were two cheap plastic picnic chairs there. "Until the sun goes down, it's still warm enough to find some peace outside. Andrew never finds me here."

Russell sat down. Anne took the other chair, obviously a new addition to her hidey-hole. She apparently didn't invite many people back here. Russell supposed he should feel honored. But one would need a heart for that.

"I heard you asking about the Waverleys," Anne said as she took a pack of cigarettes and a lighter from under an overturned flowerpot.

"Yes," Russell said simply.

"Andrew doesn't like to talk about them. He thinks their house gets too much attention. And Claire Waverley is sort of a local celebrity, especially since she got featured in a magazine. Andrew has been trying to do that for years. He's always saying about them, 'You can't compete with strange. Strange always wins,'" Anne said, lighting a cigarette. "But I'll tell you anything you want to know about them." She paused to exhale a plume of smoke. "But first, tell me another one of your stories."

Russell sat back and popped a petit four into his mouth.

It was a small price to pay.

"I once saved an entire town from bankruptcy when I was twelve. It was in Nero, Nebraska, and I was walking along the carnival midway, minding my own business, when I saw the cops chasing a man carrying a huge bag of money. He'd just stolen it from the town bank, and it was all the money they had. Bills were flying out as he ran. Most people at the carnival darted around, trying to catch the money. But not me. I was eating cotton candy, but I dropped it in the dirt and ran to the shoot-the-bottle booth. I grabbed the rifle. I knew the sight had been tampered with to keep people from winning the game, so I aimed high and shot the robber in the knee, sending him down. The town threw a parade in my honor, and the carnival owner made sure I had cotton candy every day for an entire year."

"That's good," Anne said with a smile, taking another puff of her cigarette. "I almost think you believe it."

"You wound me. Would I lie?"

Anne snorted, and he smiled back at her.

The real story was that one day Sir Walter Trott had chased one of his employees out of his trailer with a riding crop, after discovering he'd been stealing from him. The employee ran wild, pushing people out of the way and knocking things over as he fled. Russell had taken advantage of the distraction to steal dozens of funnels of cotton candy from one of the vendors. He'd sat behind the shoot-the bottle-booth and ate them all.

It had made him sick, but, to this day, he still considered it one of the best days of his childhood.

He didn't know why he didn't just tell Anne the truth. There would have been no real harm to it.

But, somehow, it's the real stories that are hardest to tell.

Claire, Tyler, Sydney and Henry were the last to leave the campus gallery. The showing that night had been for the same art student who had won the honor of designing that year's sculpture on the downtown green in Bascom, the one of the founder of Orion College's half-buried head. All the student's sculptures on display that night had the same theme: Horace J. Orion's face hidden in a bouquet of flowers; Horace J. Orion's hand emerging from a book; Horace J. Orion seemingly tangled in a long sweep of a lady's hair—that one presumably referencing the fact that Orion had been a school for women when it had been founded.

Horace J. Orion had been a man ahead of his time. He'd been an effeminate creature with a high voice and a close shave, and he'd moved to Bascom at the turn of the twentieth century with a mysterious man-friend he called, simply, "My love." A champion of women's rights, he'd used most of his family money to start a college for women in this small North Carolina town in the middle of nowhere, a sanctuary for women around the world who wanted to learn. Years later, upon his death, it was discovered by an understandably startled undertaker that Horace J. Orion had actually been a woman, a one Ethel Cora Humphreys. Her family had been cruel, died-in-the-wool misogynists. She'd been determined that her family line would end with her, but first she would do all the good she could for her fellow women. And, as many student term papers would posit over the years, living as a man was the only way she could do it.

After the lights in the campus gallery were turned out and poor Horace could finally get some rest, Claire, Tyler, Sydney and Henry walked across the old college campus with its brick towers and wall murals. It wasn't a sports college, so students spent Friday nights at Orion on the quad with picnic baskets full of culinary students' latest efforts, or mapping the stars with their college-issued telescopes.

As the sisters walked ahead, Tyler and Henry lagged behind. The tall, lanky art professor and the shorter, muscular dairy farmer didn't have much in common except their wives, but that was enough. Sometimes one big common bond is stronger than a dozen tiny ones. They frequently got together on their own, Henry meeting Tyler at the college for lunch, or Tyler stopping by the dairy after work. When Claire asked what they talked about, Tyler always said, "Man stuff." She wanted to believe that meant electric shavers, athlete's foot and maybe golf. But she was pretty sure "man stuff" meant "you and Sydney."

"Thanks for letting Bay stay over at your house tonight," Sydney said, looping her arm through Claire's as they walked.

Sydney was sparkling tonight in a beaded navy dress that looked like something a tiny, pampered housewife would wear to a cocktail party in the 1960s. Her hair was in a French twist, and her blue wrap fell off one elbow and fluttered behind her. Claire's hair was in a sleek bob, and she was wearing a red floral dress, one of Sydney's, but it was a little too short and tight on her tall frame. Claire had long ago accepted that she would never have the fine bones and blue eyes most Waverley women had. She was tall and dark-eyed and curvy, genes probably donated by the father she would never know.

"You know it's no problem. I appreciate her baby-sitting Mariah tonight," Claire said. It had been a much-needed night out, with wine and laughter, and yet Claire's mind kept going back to the business she needed to take care of at home, the extraneous things that had nothing to do with making the hard candy it-self: email to check, labels to print, boxes to unfold, orders to track.

"I'm looking forward to spending some time alone with Henry," Sydney said with a wink.

Claire looked over her shoulder at their husbands following them. She wondered if Henry knew what Sydney had in store for him. Probably not. Sydney had been secretive lately.

"Maybe tonight we'll finally . . ." Sydney let the words trail off. Claire knew what she was going to say. It came and went in cycles, but never fully went away, Sydney's desire to have more children. It had taken a while, probably five years of living back in Bascom, married to Henry, life going well, for Sydney finally to trust it, to realize she was back for good. And with that realization came the desire to make it *more,* more stable, more settled, more to keep her here, as if she were really afraid she might leave again and never come back this time, just like their mother had done.

"Maybe tonight," Claire agreed. "Love your red hair, by the way."

"Thank you. I can't seem to help myself. I just look at it lately and it gets more red."

"You're going to have to tell Henry what you're doing," Claire said in a low voice. "He's going to figure out what the red hair and all these nights you're spending alone together mean. And he's going to be hurt that you didn't come to him." Secrets were in the nature of the Waverleys. The men they chose never expected to be totally enlightened. Claire's husband Tyler's way of dealing with this was to be unfailingly patient, in addition to his good-natured disbelief of anything odd. Henry was different, though. He'd been born in Bascom. And he was a Hopkins. All Hopkins men were born with old souls. It was his nature to be depended on.

"I know. I will," Sydney whispered back. Once they reached the parking lot, she changed the subject and said, "You're not going to let Bay work for you tomorrow, are you? Saturdays should be spent doing something fun at her age."

"Don't worry. I'll shoo her out of the kitchen,"

Claire assured her, though she'd never understood why Sydney never wanted Bay to spend too much time at the Waverley house. But she didn't question her. Motherhood is hard enough without judgment from others who don't know the whole story. And the way the sisters mothered was as different as they were. Their own mother had abandoned them here, the names of their fathers long forgotten, to be taken care of by their agoraphobic grandmother, Mary. Claire and Sydney were, the both of them, forging new ground with their own children, having no firsthand knowledge of how to do it right. Just the fact that Sydney wanted to do it again made her seem so *brave* to Claire.

"And the backyard," Sydney added.

"And the backyard."

Sydney shook her head. "I'll bet you a million dollars she's out there right now, with that tree."

"You'd win that bet."

"She's doing okay, isn't she?" Sydney asked.

"I think she's doing fine. Bay knows herself. She likes herself. She doesn't care what other people think."

"But I want her to have a good time in high school."

"You want her to be popular," Claire said. "She doesn't want to be popular. She just wants to be herself."

"She doesn't date, or go out with friends, or anything. Has she talked to you about anyone she likes?"

Claire hesitated. She didn't want to keep this from her sister, but it was Bay's secret to tell, not hers. "She's mentioned a boy once or twice. You'll have to ask her about that."

"You're never going to have this problem with Mariah when she turns fifteen," Sydney said. "She's so social. That child is your husband made over."

"I know."

"Ever get the feeling our daughters were switched at birth, six years apart?" Sydney joked. Meaning to Claire: *Ever get the feeling your child isn't anything like you?*

"All the time." Mariah had no interest in cooking. Like Tyler, she didn't seem to notice when doors opened on their own, or mysteriously stuck in their frames in the house. When she went out to play, it was always in the front yard, not the garden, though the tree loved her and seemed hurt by her inattention. It morosely threw apples at her bedroom window at night in the summer. And then there was this new best friend, Em. In a period of five days, Em had become everything to Mariah. Em told her what books to read and what games to play and to brush her teeth before going to bed and always to wear pink. It drove Claire crazy. In her mind, Em was a deranged ballerina-child who smelled like bubble gum and only ate McDonald's Happy Meals.

But it was all misdirected frustration, Claire knew. Because Claire didn't have time to meet Em. She didn't know anything about Em's parents. But Tyler probably did. Over the past few months, Claire had been so busy with Waverley's Candies that Tyler had taken over most of the parenting duties. Tyler knew all the particulars that Claire used to. Homework. PTA meetings. Ballet and gymnastics moms by name.

Grandmother Mary had always had time for the day-to-day minutia of raising her granddaughters. She had memorized school schedules. She'd ordered notebooks and pencils and new shoes and sweaters when the sisters had outgrown their old ones, and the supplies had been delivered (back when downtown stores still delivered). She'd cooked and gardened and ran her back-door business and still made sure the girls were tended to.

Claire had always assumed the reason Grandmother Mary hadn't branched out, hadn't made more money with her special food, was her painful introversion. Now, Claire wondered if Grandmother Mary hadn't wanted the public to know about her curious recipes because it wasn't really about the recipes at all, it was about selling the mystique of the person who created them. She also wondered if maybe, just maybe, Grandmother Mary had taken into consideration the effect a growing business would have on her ability to care for her granddaughters, too.

Which made Claire feel worse.

And yet, how could she stop? She'd put so much effort into getting her name out there in the world, success making her like a crow collecting shiny things. There was so much to prove. Was it ever going to be enough? Giving up, especially now with all these doubts, would feel like conceding that her gift really was fiction, a belief contingent upon how well she sold it.

"Hey, are you okay?" Sydney asked when they reached Henry's truck in the parking lot and Claire had fallen silent.

"Sorry. I'm fine." Claire smiled. "You know what I thought of last night for the first time in ages? Fig and pepper bread. When I woke up this morning, I could have sworn I even smelled it."

Sydney took a deep breath, almost like she could smell it, too. "I loved fig and pepper bread. Grandmother Mary only made it on our birthdays. I remember she always said to us, 'Figs are sweet and pepper is sharp. Just like the two of you.' But she would never tell us which one of us was fig and which was pepper."

"I was obviously fig," Claire said.

"No way! I was fig. You were pepper."

Claire sighed. "I miss fig and pepper bread."

"You're burned out on candy. You need a vacation." Sydney hugged Claire then got in the truck with Henry. "See you later."

Tyler put his arm around Claire as they walked to his car, a few spaces away. When Tyler hesitated getting in the car, Claire looked up at him, his curly hair in need of a cut, his beloved Hawaiian shirt almost glowing in neon under his blazer.

"What's wrong?" she asked, because sometimes he did that, just stopped and daydreamed. She loved that about him. Her own sense of focus never ceased to amaze him. She wasn't magic to him. She never would be. What she cooked had never had an effect on him, either. Years ago, when they would argue, she would serve Tyler chive blossom stir-fry, because Grandmother Mary always said chive blossoms would assure that you would win any argument, but it never seemed to work on him.

Tyler gestured behind her. "I'm just waiting for Henry to start his truck. Do you think anything's wrong? He was talking about winterizing his truck. I had no idea what he was talking about. Maybe he did it wrong."

Claire looked over to Henry's king cab. The windows were beginning to steam and a faint purple glow was emanating from inside. "Nothing's wrong."

"Wait," Tyler said. "Are they doing what I think they're doing?"

"Voyeur," Claire teased, getting in the car. "Stop looking."

Tyler got behind the wheel and grinned at her. "We could give them a run for their money."

"And risk getting caught by one of your students? I don't think so. Stop it," she said, when he reached for her. "Let's go home."

He thought about it for a moment, then nodded. "Home. Okay." He started the car. "But I have plans for home now."

"Oh no," Claire said with a smile. "Plans."

The road leading off campus was lined with hickory trees, their leaves so bright yellow they shone like fire, as if the road were lined with giant torches. Claire rested her head back as Tyler drove, his hand on her knee. Houses in town were decorated in full Halloween regalia, some more elaborate than others. Jack-o'-lanterns flickered on porches, and red and yellow leaves swirled. This wasn't her favorite time of year, but it certainly was gorgeous. Autumn felt like the whole world was browned and roasted until it was so tender it was about to fall away from the bone.

Stop feeling so anxious, she told herself. It was just this time of year making her feel this way, making her have these doubts. First frost was almost here. If she could make it until then without a big drama, she felt sure everything would be okay, everything would fall into place and feel right again.

Tyler turned down Pendland Street with its winding curves, uneven sidewalks and sloped yards, which suddenly made Claire remember her grandmother Mary walking her and Sydney to school on this street on autumn mornings. Mary had become anxious in her old age, and she hated being away from the house for long. She'd hold the girls' hands tightly and calm herself by telling them what she would make for first frost that year—pork tenderloins with nasturtiums, dill potatoes, pumpkin bread, chicory coffee. And the cupcakes, of course, with all different frostings, because what was first frost without frosting? Claire had loved it all, but Sydney had only listened when their grandmother talked of frosting. Caramel, rosewater-pistachio, chocolate almond.

Claire settled back in her seat, starting to relax a little from the wine that evening. She began to wonder, if she had the time, what she would make for first frost this year. Fig and pepper bread, because she'd been thinking about it. (Of course *she* was fig. Sydney was *definitely* pepper.) And pumpkin lasagna, maybe with flowers pressed into the fresh pasta before she cooked it. And—

She sat up straight when she saw him again, out of nowhere. The old man on the sidewalk. And not just his gray suit this time. She saw his skin and his eyes and the tiny smile on his lips. He was standing near the corner, his hands in his pockets, like he was on a summertime stroll.

Tyler drove right by him.

"Wait. Did you see that?" she asked.

"See what?" Tyler asked.

Claire looked behind her and he was gone, as if he hadn't been there at all.

But if that was the case, how could he leave behind that scent, like a smoky bar, now coming through the car vents?

When Tyler parked in front of their house, his wife got out quickly. She stood on the sidewalk and looked down the street from where they'd come.

Tyler got out and locked the car with the remote, then he walked over to Claire, who was silhouetted by the light from the street lamp, her curves like a map that took him to a different place every time he

consulted it. He put his arms around her from behind
and bent to rest his chin on her shoulder. Her arms
were cold, so he rubbed them.

"What do you see?" he asked.

She stepped away and turned to him. "Nothing," she
said, shaking her head. "Why don't you go inside and
check on Mariah and Bay? I think I'll take a quick
walk around the neighborhood."

One side of his mouth lifted into a half smile, confused. "At this time of night? In those heels?"

"I'll just be a minute."

He took off his blazer and put it around her shoulders. "I'll go with you, for protection. That Edward is
a slippery one. He might have escaped and is now on
the prowl."

Claire laughed at his reference to Mrs. Kranowski's
elderly terrier, who only prowled a few feet into his
yard every day, long enough to do his business. Then
he skittered back inside, where he stood at the window
and barked at birds and bugs and the occasional threat-
ening leaf.

Claire held the lapels of his blazer together, then
looked back down the sidewalk. "No, you're right. It's
too late. Too cold," she said, turning to walk up the
steps to the house.

Tyler watched her navigate the concrete steps slowly
in her heels, her hips swaying. All the lights in the
house were out except the porch light, which appeared
to flutter in happiness as Claire approached. If lights
could actually feel happiness, that is.

Tyler had grown up in a manner similar to Claire's. His parents were potters and potheads who still ran an artists' colony in Connecticut. Their version of reality wasn't based on anything anyone else considered normal, either. His parents fed him kale sandwiches, let him draw on their Volkswagen, often walked around nude but dressed *him* in ridiculous things like T-shirts that read POTTERS DO IT ON WHEELS for school pictures.

A lot of it was embarrassing to remember, but Claire often reminded him of the better parts of his childhood, back when everything seemed possible. He wouldn't exactly say he'd lost his ability to believe now, but his role with Claire was to be the rational one. He laughed out loud, there on the sidewalk, when he thought of that. He was spacey and forgetful and, before he'd met Claire, he'd traveled restlessly, chasing happiness like it was something he secretly believed couldn't be caught. He'd taken a teaching position here in Bascom, North Carolina, because, like every decision he'd made up until meeting quiet Claire that night she'd catered an Orion art department party, he thought this was only the next step. He thought he would soon be on his way to someplace different, as distracted and easily led as a cat following a fly. He loved that, within their relationship, he was the grounded one. He loved that she made him something he never thought he'd been capable of being. Someone who stayed.

Tyler snapped out of it, realizing he'd been staring

into space. He saw that Claire had reached the front porch. He loped up the steps to catch her. But she crossed the threshold and the door closed just as he reached it. He turned the knob, but it was locked. He took out his key and tried it, but the door still wouldn't open. He wasn't surprised. It had done this for years.

He knocked on the door and called, "Claire, I can't get in!"

He heard the tick of her heels on the hardwood floor as she walked back to the door and opened it. She smiled at him. "If you ask it nicely, it will open for you. All you have to do is talk to it."

"Mmm–hmm," he said, putting his arms around her and backing her up. He closed the door with his foot as he kissed her. "So you say."

He could no more talk to the door than accept the apple-throwing tree. He'd once even developed an elaborate system of strings and bells in the garden as an experiment. As long as the warning system was up, no apples were thrown in the garden, which he took as proof that the tree wasn't really doing anything. He knew Claire wanted him to believe her explanation instead of trying to make sense of it. But, whether she knew it or not, she needed someone who believed in *her,* not everything else in this crazy house.

Claire stepped away from him after a few kisses. "Go on upstairs. Check on the girls. I'll be there shortly."

"Where are you going?" he asked.

"To the kitchen," she said. "I have some catching up to do."

Her dark eyes were tired. When he held her, he could feel the tension she was holding in her back muscles. The air around her was cool lately, as if she were creating a vacuum with her unhappiness. His wife would tell him what was wrong in time. He'd learned that long ago. He shook his head and took her hand.

"Not tonight," he said, leading her up the staircase. "Plans. I have plans."

4

At that moment, across town, old Evanelle Franklin suddenly woke up. She stared into the darkness of her room, trying to grasp at what she'd been dreaming about. The steady whir of her oxygen machine was like white noise now. It used to bother her, that machine. Just its existence used to make her angry, angry that her body, which had been steady and reliable and treated well for over eight decades, had suddenly decided to fail two years ago. She'd been diagnosed with congestive heart failure and, without the oxygen, her lungs felt like they'd been zapped by one of those shrinking machines in the sci-fi movies she liked to watch with her companion Fred. With the oxygen, she felt okay, though the tube that sat at her nose and looped around her ears was damn uncomfortable and chapped the skin at her nostrils. She had to have oxygen all the time now, even when she went out. Fred carried the portable oxygen container for her when she had to leave the house. It looked like a big, unwieldy purse. Fred would put the strap over his shoulder and say, "It's medical chic." Gay men were a lot of fun.

Evanelle sat up and moved her legs off the bed. She had to give something to someone. Every once in a while she would get this overwhelming itch that could only be scratched by giving someone a plum or a coffee grinder or a book on animal husbandry. She had no idea why she had to give these things, and she had no idea why the recipients needed them, but they always did, whether they liked it or not.

That was her Waverley gift.

There'd been times when she wished it had been different, that her special gift could have been more pretty, or at the very least she could have made a living by it. But she'd long ago accepted that this was what she was supposed to do—she was supposed to give people she knew, and sometimes people she didn't know, people she met on the street, a strange gift. She couldn't change who she was, and she no longer wanted to, even if she could. She knew that who you are is a stone set deep inside you. You can spend all your life trying to dig that stone out, or you can build around it. Your choice.

Sitting there in bed, she thought about what it was she was supposed to give. A spatula. Good. She had one of those. No need to go out and buy one. Now, who did she have to give it to? She thought about it, then shook her head. No, that was silly. But the name kept coming back.

Her cousin Mary Waverley.

Who had died twenty years ago.

Huh. That was a new one.

Evanelle hoisted herself out of bed and put on her slippers. The home oxygen machine was located in her bedroom. It was squat and square, like a dopey monster just sitting there, humming to itself. There was an extremely long oxygen tube attached to it so that Evanelle could walk around the house. She had to roll up the tubing like a rope and loosen it as she walked, leaving a trail. Fred told her that her hide-and-seek days were over.

She gathered up the long, clear tubing and shuffled out of her room to the kitchen.

Once there, she rooted around in her green-painted cabinets until she finally found an old spatula, the sturdy kind with an old wooden handle. It had been years since she'd used it. Come to think of it, her cousin Mary was the one who had given it to her.

She heard Fred's footsteps on the attic steps. He had a nice apartment up there. He could afford his own place, but he liked it here. He didn't like being alone. He'd moved in with her after he'd broken up with his boyfriend years ago, spending months renovating her attic—in a way, renovating his life, too. It was an odd little relationship they had but, Evanelle had to admit, she liked having him around. But as much as she needed him, she thought he needed her more.

She didn't know how much time she had left on this earth, a thought that didn't bother her as much as it did fifty years ago. She knew a lot more people on the other side now. Even though it sure took a long time to get Mary's granddaughters on the right path,

Claire and Sydney had each other now, had their husbands. It was Fred that she worried about the most. What was he going to do when she left him?

He turned on the kitchen light. He was in a pair of old plaid pajamas, the kind you wore for comfort, not style. She'd given him a pair of silk pajamas, monogrammed on the pocket and everything, for Christmas last year, but he never wore them. He was too set in his ways, Evanelle thought, and told him so often. He was only in his sixties, with a nice square face and sharp eyes, too young to be hanging out with an old lady all the time. He hadn't dated anyone in years. Maybe he just forgot how. She was going to have to help him along a little.

"Sleepwalking or midnight baking?" he asked with a smile, leaning against the doorjamb and crossing his arms over his chest.

"Neither. I woke up and needed to give my dead cousin Mary a spatula." She held up the spatula and Fred's brows rose. It sounded crazy, even for her. She laughed. "Oh, don't look at me that way. I know it's crazy. I probably have to give it to Claire. I was having a dream about Mary when I woke up. Wires probably just got crossed."

"Do you have to give it to her tonight?" Fred asked, because sometimes her Waverley gift worked that way; she had to give something to someone *immediately*. Which was pretty inconvenient for someone with a plastic hose connected to her nose. Going out took planning these days.

Evanelle reached under the sink for one of the hundreds of paper bags she'd collected from the grocery store, because you never know when you'll need a good paper bag. She put the spatula inside, then set it on the counter. "No. I'll give it to her when I see her next," she said, already out of breath.

Fred pushed himself away from the doorjamb. "How about I make us some nice pumpkin spice coffee?"

"You know, that's exactly what I need," she said as he helped her take a seat at the table in her small arts-and-crafts home. She and her husband had bought this house over sixty years ago. She missed him. He'd been a lot like Fred, only he'd liked women. And he'd *loved* her. Loved everything about her. "Every crooked pot has a lid," he used to say. He didn't care that she was weird. This had been a good house. Good memories. She was going to miss this place. She was going to miss her stuff. Then again, it would be a relief that in heaven she'd never have to give anyone anything. Everyone already had what they needed up there.

Fred started tinkering with the coffeemaker, as comfortable in this place as she was. "You're getting more and more like me every day, Fred."

Fred turned and looked at her like she had given him the best compliment anyone had ever given anyone in the history of all the world.

He was a hoot.

The next morning, as Sydney unlocked the door to her salon, she saw Fred Walker, a square, tidy man in his sixties, doing the same at Fred's Fine Foods, his small, touristy market down the street.

"Hi, Fred!" she called, waving to him. "How's Evanelle?"

Fred turned, startled, and waved back. "Fine," he said, looking distracted and lost in thought. "She's fine."

Fred wasn't much of a conversationalist.

Sydney walked into the White Door Salon. The door was clear glass, but the previous owner thought "the White Door" sounded mysterious, like a door Alice might walk through to Wonderland. It's what everyone knew the salon as, so Sydney didn't change the name when she bought the place a few years ago.

She turned on the lights. It still made her smile, this big open space with its comfortable couches and the stylish chandelier that looked like icicles hanging over the reception desk. Her first job after moving back to Bascom ten years ago was here. This place was a part of the thread that wove her new life together. She had seven stylists, all but two younger than she was. She liked that. She liked how they dressed and how fearless they were in their style.

Bay wasn't interested in any of that kind of stuff. She liked her slouchy jeans and snarky T-shirts.

After turning on the computer at the reception desk, Sydney made coffee and set out cookies that she persuaded Bay to make every week. Claire used to make them, but then she became a candyhead and didn't have time anymore.

Sydney had told Violet, her new receptionist, that part of her job was to get here before anyone else and do this, but Violet always had an excuse. No one knew why Sydney hired her. Sometimes even Sydney wondered.

She went to her station and turned on her curling iron to style her hair, which was easier to do here than it was in the tiny bathroom in the farmhouse. She looked at herself in the mirror, then did a double take.

There were more red highlights in her hair. She was sure of it. It was like they had crept in during the night. Henry had even commented on them this morning before he'd left. He'd called her fiery.

Claire had told Sydney to tell Henry what she was doing. And she was probably right. Claire always gave good advice. She handled things in such a contained way. She made everyone around her calm, just by being near her. If it were a perfume and she could bottle it, she'd make millions. Forget candy.

But Sydney knew what Henry would say if she told him why she was all over him lately. He would say that he didn't care that they couldn't have any more children. But Sydney knew better. His grandfather passed away not long after Sydney and Henry married, and Henry missed him intensely, a longing that was so strong it sometimes made the cows go quiet and gave their milk a strange strawberry sweetness. Henry's grandfather had raised him, taught him everything he knew about being a good Hopkins man and the dairy business. Henry had spent his whole life wanting to grow up and be old like his grandfather. He needed a son, someone to teach. Henry had adopted Bay. There'd been no hesitation about it when they'd married. After that, Bay had followed him around wherever he went. Henry had loved it, Bay getting up early with him and helping at the dairy. But what Bay had been doing, what she was always doing, was making sure things were as they were supposed to be, that he was where he belonged. After a few months, she'd stopped getting up at oh-my-God-thirty with him.

Suddenly, the door to the salon burst open. Sydney checked the clock on the wall.

"I know, I know," Violet said as she hurried in, an adorable moon-faced one-year-old boy on her hip. She had a plastic thrift-store bag over her shoulder that Sydney knew didn't have enough diapers in it to get through the day. "I'm late. Sorry."

Sydney did a few quick twists with her hair and secured the twists with clips so that she could go take the baby from Violet.

"No one would baby-sit him," Violet said when Sydney took him in her arms and snuffled his dark hair, which made him laugh. "My neighbor across the street, who usually takes him, went to Dollywood this weekend. I had to bring him."

"It's okay," Sydney said, even though it wasn't. But Violet knew how much Sydney loved baby Charlie. She knew she had something Sydney wanted. Young girls always know. They know older women look at them and see what they've left behind and can't get back. It's a truth everyone knows but no one acknowledges: There's nothing more powerful than an eighteen-year-old girl.

Violet had dropped out of school when her mother, a Turnbull—a family known for their wild ways and unparalleled ability to have children at the drop of a hat—left town with her latest boyfriend. Violet partied all the time, did some drugs, and soon got pregnant. If she knew who the father was, she never said. Charlie looked every bit like his mother with his dark hair, widow's peak, and coffee bean–colored eyes.

Sydney had met Violet a few months ago when Sydney had taken her lunch break and grabbed some orange juice and yogurt at Fred's market, intending to sit on the green and eat. It had been prom season and her arms had ached from creating all those updos.

Sitting cross-legged on the green in her tie-dye harem pants and black racer-back tee, she'd put the OJ and yogurt on the ground between her legs, then closed her eyes and lifted her face to the sun, soaking it in.

A few moments later, she'd felt something tug at her leg, and looked down to see a dark-haired baby in an unsnapped onesie trying to crawl into her lap. She'd remained perfectly still, the way you do when you realize you have a bee on you, waiting to see where it was going before you overreacted. She'd finally had to reach for him when he'd crawled over her knee and was about to go face-first into the ground.

She'd stood and put him on her hip as she looked around the green. There hadn't been a lot of people around that day, but she did see a teenager with long, stringy hair on a bench near Horace J. Orion's half-buried bust, the one college students would pass and joke, "Horace may be dead, but he's not buried."

"Excuse me," Sydney had called to the skinny girl in oversized sunglasses. "Is he yours?"

The girl hadn't moved.

"Excuse me?" Sydney had called, louder this time.

The girl had startled awake and turned her head to Sydney.

"Is he yours?"

She'd nodded and yawned, but made no move to get up, so Sydney bent to get her OJ and yogurt, then walked over to the bench. As she'd gotten closer, she realized she recognized the girl, who was just a few years older than Bay.

"You're a Turnbull, aren't you? Your family lives near the mobile home manufacturing plant?"

"We used to," Violet had said, not taking the baby from Sydney when she sat down beside her. "My mom left. I had to move out."

Sydney had discovered that Violet now shared a trailer with a woman and her old common-law husband, who were on disability and had plenty of prescription pills to give to those in need, for a price. Violet had been looking for a job, but said no one would hire her. "My mom was right," Violet had said when Sydney had given her the OJ and fed the yogurt to the baby. "When she left, she said there's nothing good here."

Sydney's old receptionist, Amber, had just gotten married and had immediately gotten pregnant (of course) and was moving to Fayetteville, where her husband was stationed at Fort Bragg. So Sydney had offered Violet the job. She'd recognized something in Violet, something Sydney had felt at the same age. Violet wanted to leave. She almost vibrated with it. She looked at life outside of Bascom as the promised land. She thought everything wrong with her life was the fault of this *place,* therefore happiness would surely be hers if only she could escape.

Sydney had left at eighteen, feeling the same way. She'd wanted so badly to escape the burden of her family's name and reputation. Out there in that big wide open was where she'd met Bay's biological father, and escape had taken on an entirely new meaning. It had taken her a long time to realize that a prison sometimes isn't a prison at all. Sometimes it's simply a door you assume is locked because you've never tried to open it.

The job was like throwing Violet a lifeline. Violet needed something to tether herself here. Without this job, it would only be a matter of time before Violet left and took Charlie with her.

Violet dropped the plastic diaper bag as soon as Sydney had taken Charlie, and made a beeline for the coffeemaker and cookies. "Can you watch him while I do my hair?" Violet asked, spitting crumbs. "I didn't have time before I left."

"Use my station. The curling iron is already hot."

"Thanks."

People wondered why Sydney put up with Violet.

Sydney held the baby in the air above her and looked up into his sweet round face while he smiled and curled his toes and stuck his fist in his mouth.

It was because of this.

5

Bay slept late into Saturday morning at her aunt Claire's house. When she woke up, she immediately knew Claire had been making her lavender candies that day. The scent spread through the house like a long, soft blanket, settling over everything, calming all worries.

The labels on all the honey-lavender candy jars read:

Lavender essence is for happiness,
with a touch of honey to raise your spirits.
A joyful attitude is ravenous
consuming everyone who is near it.

She got dressed and went downstairs to help. A day spent here, away from the world, would get her mind off the Halloween dance at school that night, wondering who Josh was going to bring. His group of friends included a lot of girls, but Bay couldn't discern an attachment he had to any particular one.

Bay walked into the kitchen, shoving her long hair under a ball cap, prepared to put on an apron and get to work. Instead, she found the honey-filled lavender candies already on the counters, ready to be funneled into jars. It surprised her because the honey-lavender hard candies were the hardest to make and took the longest. Claire must have gotten up very early. The lavender candy had to be worked constantly, rolled into long strips after it was poured from the sugar pot, then threaded with local honey from the farmer's market, rolled again, cooled, and cut by hand, instead of just using the molds like with the other two flavors, rose and lemon verbena. Claire used just the right amount of organic food coloring to make the candies the color of springtime. Today's candies looked like purple flower buds.

There was a single plate on the stainless steel kitchen island and Claire turned from the stove and slid pancakes onto it from a skillet. "Breakfast is served," Claire said. Once she'd put the oatmeal pancakes on the plate, she drizzled some syrup on them, then sprinkled the last of the yellow and orange calendula flowers she'd picked from the garden before it went dormant. It was from a stash she'd been saving in the refrigerator.

"You cooked!" Bay said.

"This was what my grandmother used to make for me and your mom on Saturday mornings."

"I didn't mean to sleep so late. Are you all done for the day?" Bay asked, pulling a stool up to the island. "I was going to help."

"I got up early. Your mom wants me to drop you off at her shop as soon as you're finished eating."

Ah, now Bay understood. "She doesn't want me working here today." Thus the reason for the calendula flowers. They were supposed to remove negative energy. Claire didn't want Bay mad at her mother.

"It's a beautiful day," Claire said, looking out the kitchen window. "You shouldn't be cooped up here." Bay studied her aunt's profile while she ate. With her dark eyes, elegant nose and olive complexion, Claire looked timeless, old-worldly.

"What are you going to do today?" Bay asked.

Claire shrugged. "Tyler took Mariah to gymnastics, then she's going to spend a few hours with him at his office. I have paperwork to catch up on, but I thought I'd pick up some things at the market while I'm out. I'm feeling cooped up, too."

Now that was unusual. Claire never felt cooped up here. "Can I ask you a question?"

"Sure," Claire said.

"Do you actually *like* making candy?"

Claire hesitated, then said carefully, like it was rehearsed, like she'd been expecting someone to ask, "It's a little monotonous, and it's not what I imagined I would be doing when I started my catering business, but I'm good at it, and there's a big demand for it right now. And it's padding Mariah's college fund."

"I miss your cooking," Bay said, looking at her plate, not wanting to finish, not wanting it to be gone.

"Especially this time of year. Are you going to cook for first frost?"

"If I have time."

Bay nodded, knowing that meant no.

Still, the tree was going to bloom, and that alone was always reason to celebrate, food or no food.

Bay looked at the kitchen wall calendar.

Still one week to go.

Bay hoped they all could make it until then without doing anything crazy.

After breakfast, Claire drove Bay downtown. When they got out of Claire's van, Bay happened to look across the street to the green and saw Phineus Young there with some of his friends, sitting in a group in the grass, playing a complicated flip game of cards and dice.

It looked like she wasn't the only teenager in town whose parents wanted her out of the house for some fresh air.

Claire started walking to the White Door, but Bay said she'd join her in a minute, and ran across the street to the green.

"Hey, Phin," Bay said as she approached them, playing in the shade of Horace's half-buried head. "What are you doing?"

Phin didn't look up as he tossed another card onto the pile. "Losing."

"Big-time," Dickus Hartman said, throwing down his winning card and laughing. Dickus was fat and oily and crude but, truthfully, he belonged right here with these other boys. They were the only ones who would put up with him.

"Are you sure you're not going to the dance tonight?" Bay asked, aware that she'd asked him before, but she had to make sure, even if it meant Phin's friends would make fun of her. At this point, it wasn't like she could make it any worse. She wanted an inside informant who would tell her on Monday who Josh took to the dance, what he wore, how he acted.

"No," Phin said as Dickus snickered and dealt the cards again. "Are you?" Phin looked up at her, squinting his pale green eyes at the sunlight like a mole.

Bay shook her head.

"Then some people are going to win a lot of money tonight," Dickus said.

"What are you talking about?" Bay demanded. Dickus just looked smug. Bay nudged Phin with her foot. "Phin?"

Phin looked embarrassed. "There's a bet going around about whether or not you're going to the dance to try to *bewitch* Josh," Phin made twirling motions with his fingers, "and create some big drama."

"A bet," Bay repeated evenly.

"Don't worry about it," Phin said, playing a card. "They're just being stupid."

"Is Josh in on this bet?" Bay asked.

"He thinks you won't come," Dickus said.

"That's just what he said," Phin said, trying to soften the blow. "He's not in on the bet."

Why was Josh even talking about her? If he wanted her to go away, if he wanted all this teasing about her letter to go away, he should just let it go. He should tell her *to her face* that she was wrong and he didn't want anything to do with her. He should stop acting so awkward around her, avoiding her like a bad smell. He certainly shouldn't be chiming in on whether or not Bay would show up at a stupid dance to . . . do what, exactly? Cast a spell? Is that what he really thought of her? "Phin, be ready at six tonight," she suddenly said.

"Why?" he asked.

She walked away, her hands fisted at her sides. So much for not doing anything crazy. "Because you're taking me to the dance."

Claire was standing at Sydney's station, thinking about things that needed to be done at home, while Sydney gave Madison Elliott's hair a blowout.

"Charlie said my name this morning, didn't he?" Sydney said, yelling over the blast of the blow dryer. Baby Charlie was by Sydney's station in a bouncy swing that Sydney had bought for him. He had a smile on his fat little face as he babbled to everyone who passed by. Charmer. He was already learning that the lone guy in a beauty salon is always the center of attention.

Violet Turnbull, skinny in a way that made her look like all points and knobs, looked up from where she was surfing the Internet at the reception desk. "I think it sounded more like 'kidney' than 'Sydney,'" she said.

"Why would he say 'kidney?'" Sydney asked, giving Charlie an affectionate look that made Claire feel scared for Sydney, scared she was going to get hurt, that she was too enamored of this baby. "Either way, he's such a smart boy."

"I need to go," Claire said. "Do you want me to pick you up some lunch?"

"That would be great," Sydney said, palming the brush and blow dryer in one hand, the dryer still going, and handing Claire some cash out of her hip apron. "Would you get me an olive sandwich and a caramel apple latte at the Brown Bag Café?"

"Anyone else?" Claire asked the other stylists.

One of them, pink-haired Janey, said, "A café americano."

"I don't have any money," Violet said woefully from the reception desk.

"You got paid yesterday," Janey said, clearly not Violet's biggest fan.

"I'm saving," Violet said.

"I'll get it," Sydney offered. "What do you want, Vi?"

Violet perked up and said, "A club sandwich, chips, extra pickles, and two cans of Coke."

Janey gave Violet the stink eye from across the salon.

"What?" Violet said. "I didn't have breakfast."

Sydney nodded to the cash she'd just given Claire. "Would you get some bananas and Cheerios at Fred's market, too? I usually keep some for Charlie in the break room, but I think Violet ate the last of them yesterday." Claire must have given Sydney a look she'd seen before. "Don't say it."

"I didn't say anything," Claire said.

Sydney turned off the blow dryer. Madison Elliott hadn't heard a thing. She looked up from the magazine she'd been reading and smiled. Her hair looked stunning. Sydney was always booked. She could do magical things with hair. When someone got a cut by Sydney, it was always a perfect day—DMV lines were always short, bosses gave raises, and kids made their own dinner and went to bed early. Claire felt a pinch of envy. Sydney never had to work very hard for her gift. She'd worked harder at denying it when they were younger. It seemed to come so easily to Sydney and Bay and their old cousin Evanelle. But Claire worked tirelessly. She always had. And it felt even more difficult lately.

Claire had just collected the money for the rest of the lunches when Bay walked into the salon. Her pale skin was shining, her cheeks pink, as if she'd swallowed something bright and it was now glowing from within. Everyone stopped what they were doing, knowing something was up.

"I'm going to the Halloween dance," Bay announced.

Claire almost laughed at her sister's reaction. Sydney's arms fell to her sides, as if in defeat. "You've got to be kidding me."

"No," Bay said. "I'm not kidding."

"You've known about this thing for weeks, and *now* you're deciding to go? You don't even have a costume!"

"I don't need a costume."

"Of course you need a costume!" Sydney said. "Girls, do any of you have a Halloween costume Bay could use tonight?"

"I have a slutty vampire costume," Janey said.

"No."

"Slutty nurse?" Janey said.

"No."

"Slutty—"

"Nothing slutty," Sydney interrupted. "Oh, God, this is a disaster. Come here. Maybe I can do something with your hair." Sydney patted her chair as Madison Elliott left, and Bay walked over to her, head down, beyond embarrassed. She didn't meet Claire's eyes as she passed, and Claire suppressed a smile. Once Bay sat, Sydney whipped off her baseball cap and Bay's long, dark hair cascaded down. Sydney ran her fingers through it, watching her daughter in the mirror.

Lined around the mirror in front of Sydney's chair were photos of Bay. One when she was six, lying under the apple tree. One from her ninth birthday party when Claire had made her a blackberry cake. Another from when she was twelve, standing beside Phineus Young at the bus stop, the first time Sydney had let them wait alone. And now here Bay was in the middle of the mirror, fifteen and getting ready for her first dance.

Sydney seemed to sense the moment Bay was going

to say something about her mother's banjo eyes, so Sydney cleared her throat and called to her receptionist, "Violet, when Mrs. Chin comes in, have her wait a few minutes, then shampoo her for me."

"But what about lunch?" Violet said.

"Claire hasn't even gone for it yet. You'll have time."

Bay squirmed in the chair. "Mom, costumes are optional. This is not a big deal."

"This is your first dance. It *is* a big deal. I will not let you go without a costume. Does anyone have any clothes from the eighties?" she asked her stylists. "I do excellent mall hair."

Claire finally decided to throw Bay a rope. "Grandmother Mary had a few old dresses I kept. Long, filmy things, like party dresses from the 1920s. I think they might have belonged to her mother."

Sydney smiled, as if remembering something she'd almost forgotten. "I used to think you were the only person in the family to ever throw parties in the garden, like your first frost parties, but now I remember that Grandmother Mary once told me about picnics she had in the garden. She would invite people in and dress like a garden nymph."

"That's what I'll be, then," Bay said quickly, definitively, wanting to put an end to this. "I'll wear a Grandmother Mary dress and be a garden nymph."

Claire and Sydney exchanged glances. This was a big step for Sydney, accepting this about her daughter. Bay was a Waverley who wanted to dress up like a Waverley, and not in jest, like the time when they were kids and Sydney dressed up as Claire one Halloween, wearing a long, black wig that covered her face and an apron that said KISS THE COOK, which she'd thought was funny, because no one had wanted to kiss weird Claire. Of all the things Bay could be, a Waverley is what she'd chosen. That's who she was. It wasn't really a costume at all. Sydney gave in, ultimately lured in by the possibilities of styling Bay's hair. Bay had only let Sydney trim it for years.

"Fine," Sydney said, pumping up the chair. "Claire, will you pick up some flowers at Fred's so I can put them in her hair?"

"I'll be back as soon as I can."

"Wait, get me some pie, too, will you?" Violet called as Claire passed the reception desk and walked out.

When Claire stepped outside, the autumn light was slanted and orange, like the noontime sun had fallen to the ground somewhere far away in the flat distance. The light at this time of year had a different feel to it, like a beacon slowly fading.

She was about to turn right, toward the café and Fred's market, but to her left she caught the glint of something silver, and she turned to see two ladies standing outside of Maxine's clothing store, speaking to an elderly man in a gray suit.

It was *him*. The old man she'd seen outside her house, twice. She hurried up the sidewalk toward them, bypassing a group of college students who had stopped in the middle of the sidewalk to take a group selfie, as if the act of walking on the sidewalk itself needed to be documented. Claire edged around them, losing sight of the old man for a moment.

When she looked again, he was gone.

Puzzled, Claire approached the ladies. She knew them well. Claire used to cater all of Patrice's anniversary and birthday parties. Patrice was with her sister, Tara, who often visited from Raleigh. Claire had gone to school with Patrice. Sydney put a lot of emphasis on her own high school years, how pivotal they were to her. And Sydney wanted so much for these years to be good for Bay. But Claire could honestly say she didn't remember much of her own high school experience. She went, kept to herself and waited to go home in the afternoons so she could join her grandmother in the kitchen. It was, like most things in Claire's experience, something she glossed over in favor of better memories. Sydney called it her revisionist history.

"Claire, we were just talking about you," Patrice said. She was in her early forties and fighting it. Her hair was long, super-blond and shiny. Facial fillers kept her mouth from moving too wide, so she spoke with a slight fish-face expression. Her blue eyes were deeply rimmed in black eyeliner, a look she wasn't young enough to pull off, and her pupils were always a little dilated from taking one too many anti-anxieties, though she thought no one noticed.

"That man, who was he?" Claire asked, trying not to sound like it was urgent, because it wasn't really urgent. At least, she didn't think so.

"What man?" Patrice said.

"There was an elderly man standing here a moment ago," Claire said. "He had silver hair. He was wearing a silver suit."

"There was no one here," Tara said. Tara was older than Patrice and not fighting it as well, in large part because Tara didn't have the kind of money Patrice married into. Her hair was darker, and she wore tunics covering a perfectly acceptable middle-aged belly, hiding it from her go-to-the-gym-every-day sister.

"He was right here," Claire said, getting frustrated. "Right where I'm standing."

"I'm sorry, Claire," Patrice said. "We haven't seen anyone like that."

"You were *talking* to him," Claire said, frowning.

"We were talking, but just to each other," Tara said. "What was it we were saying?"

"I don't remember," Patrice said.

Tara laughed. "That's funny, I don't remember, either."

"We came out of the store, and you walked up to us. I thought we'd been talking about you, but I suppose we hadn't." Patrice shrugged.

Claire said good-bye and walked away, leaving Patrice and Tara staring off into space, as if someone had put them in a trance.

Someone who smelled like smoke.

6

Back at the Pendland Street Inn, Anne Ainsley stood outside room number six with a set of fresh sheets in her arms.

"Mr. Zahler?" she called as she knocked.

He didn't answer. She knew he wouldn't. She'd seen him leave for downtown after breakfast.

She unlocked his bedroom door and entered.

In every one of Anne's three marriages, she'd found herself surprised by her husbands' lies. Genuinely, knocked-off-her-feet surprised. After her third husband cheated on her and emptied her bank account of the last of the money she'd inherited from her parents, she swore she would never allow herself to be surprised like that ever again. Men lied. She accepted that now. They couldn't help it. It was their default position. They denied it, but that just proved her point.

Russell Zahler was lying about something. And she truly didn't care. It actually gave her some satisfaction that Andrew was being conned. But she was curious and bored. Andrew didn't let her have a television in her room. There wasn't a television in the whole damn inn. *It isn't authentic to the house,* Andrew would say. Sometimes she wanted to say, *What about electricity, Andrew? That's not authentic to the house, either.* God, he was so much like their father sometimes. So, Anne had to find her own entertainment.

Her entertainment mostly consisted of the Internet on the front-desk computer, and spying on guests and rifling through their things when she cleaned their rooms. She never stole anything. Andrew would toss her out in a millisecond if she did that. She just liked to see what people brought from their homes, what their perfumes smelled like and what sizes they wore. She liked the stories she would make up about them.

Anne had always been a bit of a sneak. She knew that about herself. Anne and Andrew's father had been an optometrist and their mother had run his office, but their mother had also secretly sold naughty lingerie in her spare time, mostly to the Clark women in town, who were known for their sexual prowess and always married well because of it. Their father had never known about their mother's side business. And Andrew had been aghast when he'd found their mother's catalogs and wares after she died.

But Anne had known all about it. She'd found the stuff when she was ten, after discovering the locked trunk in the back of her mother's closet. She'd searched all over the house until she'd found the key to it hidden in the toilet tank.

Their parents had died on their first road trip after they retired. They'd saved a fortune and had intended to live very well into their old age. The several hundred thousand they'd left had made Anne soft in the head. That's the only explanation she had for letting Andrew have the house. She'd been married to her first husband back then, and Andrew had still been living at home. He'd always been a prissy man. Women made him uncomfortable and he never dated, so Anne had thought she was being magnanimous by letting him have a place to live out his lonely years.

Two husbands later—two husbands and their two failed businesses, both of which Anne had funded— and Anne was broke. For the past five years, she'd been living here in her childhood home, which Andrew had turned into an inn. She'd always secretly felt it was a little creepy, like creating a shrine so people could visit their dead parents. Andrew gave her room and board (their two tiny bedrooms were now in the basement) and minimum wage, which she spent on beer, cigarettes and magazines. This was her life now. She accepted that. She was fifty-nine, so close to sixty she could taste it, and she had no expectations for her own happiness anymore.

She closed the door to Russell Zahler's room behind her. This was officially called the Andrew Ainsely Room. It was even written on a small plaque on the door. This was Andrew's old bedroom from when they were children. It was decorated in dark purples and aubergines, which Andrew called royal colors.

He'd named Anne's old bedroom the Hopes and Dreams Room.

She wasn't sure, but she thought that was a dig.

She set the sheets on the queen-sized bed and looked around. Russell Zahler had left the heat turned up and the clear glass lamp by the bed on. But he hadn't hung anything in the closet, and there were no toiletries in the small attached bathroom. There was only his large leather suitcase on the luggage rack at the bottom of the bed. She walked over to it and clicked it open. There wasn't much inside. Another gray suit and a white shirt, folded; a threadbare pair of pajamas; that outlandish lord-of-the-manor robe he'd worn that night he'd walked into the kitchen and scared Anne to death because she'd thought it was Andrew, catching her smoking again; socks and underwear; and a black toiletry bag containing a comb, toothpaste, a tooth-brush, deodorant, a bar of soap, a razor and a bottle of aspirin.

That was it.

That wasn't much of a story. She was a little disap-pointed.

She frowned as her fingers touched the bottom of the suitcase. It didn't feel like she had reached all the way down. She tapped at it with her fingernails. It sounded hollow. She found the corners and pulled the divider up, revealing a secret space.

Ha! she almost said out loud, satisfied as she always was when she discovered something someone didn't want found.

Inside was an old deck of tarot cards, a small white crystal on a cheap chain necklace and a thick pile of tattered office folders held together by a large rubber band.

Anne took the file folders out and slid off the rubber band. The tabs on the folders had names of people on them, each folder containing newspaper clippings and photographs and copies of public documents like land deeds and marriage certificates. She didn't recognize any of the names until she came to the tab on the folder that read: *Lorelei Waverley*.

That was Claire and Sydney Waverley's mother. Anne had been a few years younger than Lorelei. Lorelei had been odd, like all the rest of that family. But wild and sad, also. Lorelei had left town years ago and died somewhere in Tennessee, from what Anne had heard. Was that why Russell Zahler was so interested in the Waverleys? Because of Lorelei? Had he once known her? Anne looked inside the folder. There were several copies of a single old photograph. It was taken in the 1970s, judging by the pointed collars and the mustard and brown colors of the clothing. In the photo, there was Lorelei Waverley when she looked to be in her twenties, sitting next to a middle-aged Russell and another dark-haired couple with a baby. They were in one of those curved corner booths found in older bars and Pizza Huts. She glanced at the rest of the contents of the folder, which, interestingly enough, seemed to be all about Claire Waverley, not Lorelei; articles about Claire's business, and tax documents, which she wanted to take a closer look at, but she nearly jumped out of her skin at a knock on the door.

"Anne?" her brother called. "Are you in there?"

"Yes," she said calmly. She was about to put the file folders back when she suddenly noticed a few antique flyers, yellowed with age, that had been under the folders in the suitcase. She picked one up. It was an old advert for a traveling carnival, featuring a magician and psychic called the Great Banditi.

On the bottom right-hand side of the flyer was a circular photo of a man wearing a large turban with a jewel in the center. He had his hands out in front of him like he was going to shoot lightning out of his fingertips.

It was Russell Zahler.

Now *here* was a story.

"Anne!" her brother called again.

"Coming," she said as she folded one of the flyers and put it into her pocket, then put the rest of the things back into the suitcase, exactly in the places they'd been. She snapped the case closed, then went to the door.

"What are you doing?" Andrew asked.

"I'm changing the sheets," she said with a shrug, "like I do every day."

He pointed to the sign hung on the doorknob. "There's a DO NOT DISTURB sign here. We take these things very seriously."

She hated when he referred to himself as *we*.

"Oh. I must have missed it." She went back into the

room and grabbed the folded sheets she'd left on the bed. "Sorry," she said as she walked out.

"Don't let it happen again." Andrew glanced around the room, then firmly closed the door behind him.

Several hours later, Claire, Sydney and Bay were searching through the Waverley house for one of Grandmother Mary's dresses for Bay to wear to the Halloween dance, which felt to Bay like trying to find a specific drop of water in a well. The Waverley house was large and stuffed to the rafters. The only place that had any order was the commercial kitchen, which made sense, because that's where Claire spent all her time. As for the rest of the house, Claire had apparently kept everything that had once belonged to her grandmother. And when Tyler had moved in, he'd brought all his things, including his painting stuff, which took up most of the guest room.

Bay was secretly hoping they wouldn't find a dress in time, then she could take these ridiculous daisies and green leaves out of her wildly curled hair and go as herself. All she wanted to do was make sure Josh saw her, saw her ignoring him, not making a scene, then she'd leave. He said she wouldn't come. She'd show him. He had no idea who she was or what she would or wouldn't do. He'd never even *talked* to her.

They'd just come from the attic when they met Tyler and Mariah in the hallway, home for the day.

"What are you doing?" Mariah asked brightly, instantly intrigued. She was still in her gymnastics uniform. Her hair was in a messy bun that her father had obviously tried to execute. "Is this a game? Why do you have flowers in your hair, Bay? You look so pretty, like my new best friend."

Bay put her arm around her cousin, who smelled like peanuts. "Thanks, squirt."

"Hi, baby," Claire said, almost guiltily, like she was caught doing something that wasn't work. "How was gymnastics?"

"It was fine. What are you doing?" Mariah asked again.

"We're looking for old dresses for Bay to wear to a Halloween dance, dresses that once belonged to my grandmother," Claire explained.

Mariah screwed up her face for a moment, thinking, then said, "Have you tried the guest room closet?"

"Not yet. That's a good idea."

Mariah turned and ran into the guest room, where the springs of the bed were soon heard squeaking as she jumped on it.

Claire turned to Tyler. "When you get time, would you caulk around the vents in the attic? I felt some cold air coming in when we were up there."

"You'd feel cold air if you were standing on the sun," Tyler teased.

Claire smiled. "Did you and Mariah have fun today?"

"Gymnastics, and then office hours. It's been the longest day anyone has ever had, ever. Seriously, I win." Tyler scrubbed the stubble on his cheeks tiredly.

"Sorry. Don't forget to eat. I bought some rotisserie chicken at Fred's today." Claire leaned in and said in a low voice, "Was Em at gymnastics practice?"

Tyler shook his head, as seemingly perplexed by this new best friend as Claire was. "Apparently Em doesn't do gymnastics. Or ballet."

"Wait," Claire said, drawing back. "You mean you haven't met her yet?"

"You two can play old married couple some other time," Sydney said. "The dance is in two hours!"

Bay snorted. "Like you and Dad don't act that way all the time."

"I feel like I'm in competition with good old Henry. Come here," Tyler said, grabbing Claire and bending her back over his arm and kissing her.

"Please," Bay said. "Not in front of the kids." She turned and walked to the guest room, rolling her eyes for effect. Tonight, of all nights, she really didn't want to see how well love worked when two people felt the same way about each other.

Claire and Sydney soon followed her. The guest room closet was so small only one person could get inside it, so Claire went in and started bringing out boxes. Sydney and Bay opened them while Mariah jumped on the bed, happy to be with them. They found old linens, a box of antique cracked leather purses, candles that had gone soft and melted into each other, and a cat bed. But no dresses.

"There's one last box in here," Claire said from the

back of the closet. "They have to be in this one. Otherwise, I don't know where they might be."

"That's okay," Bay said, reaching up to scratch her head, which felt tight and itchy. "I really don't want to wear a costume."

"Don't you dare touch that hair," her mother warned, and Bay dropped her hand.

"It's stuck in a corner. Wait, I've almost got it!" Claire pulled the box free, hitting her head on the low shelf in the closet as she stood, upsetting the contents on the shelf. A shoe box fell, scattering old photos all over the bedroom floor.

Bay started to duck inside the closet to help Claire. "Are you all right?"

"Stop!" Sydney said. "You'll mess up your hair!"

Bay threw her hands in the air with exasperation. "I think you used thirteen cans of hair spray on me. My hair is not going to move for a decade!"

Claire emerged from the closet with the cardboard box in one hand, rubbing the top of her head with the other. When she noticed the photos on the floor, she immediately set the box down and went to her knees, her mouth forming the word *Oh*. "These are photos of Grandmother Mary! I'd forgotten about them."

Sydney went to her knees beside Claire, helping pick up the photos. She stopped to examine one. "Hey, Claire, look at this. This must be the fairy picnic Grandmother Mary told me about."

Claire leaned over to look. "Must be. Grandmother

Mary told you a lot more about that time in her life than she told me."

Claire and Sydney were shoulder to shoulder now, an image Bay would always think of when she thought of them together, how close they were, like they knew what was inside each other's pockets.

"Why did Grandmother Mary tell you more than she told Claire?" Bay asked, curious.

Claire looked up at her and answered, "Because your mom was pretty and popular, like Grandmother Mary was when she was young."

Bay felt her world shift slightly, like when you think you're on the last step of a staircase, only to discover there was still another step left. "*You* were popular?" Bay said to her mother.

That made Sydney laugh. "You sound so surprised."

"But you're a Waverley."

"One has nothing to do with the other," Sydney said, staring at the photo. "Grandmother Mary had a lot of suitors when she was young, before she married, before she got old and . . . strange."

"Agoraphobic," Claire corrected, putting the rest of the photos in the shoe box and crawling back to the last box she'd taken from the closet. As soon as she lifted the lid, she laughed in surprise. "We're finding everything of Grandmother Mary's but her dresses. Look, here's another one of her kitchen journals. She hid these things all over the house. I once found one inside a mattress." Claire brought out a small, thin black notebook with *Waverley Kitchen Journal* on the cover, as all her journals had. But written beneath this one was also the word *Karl*.

"How many journals have you found now?" Sydney asked.

"Over a hundred." Claire opened the journal and her brows fell in confusion.

"What is it?"

"Look at this," Claire said. "She blacked out every single page." On each page, every line Grandmother Mary had written had been crossed out with thick black horizontal ink stripes, obscuring the original script.

Sydney shook her head. "She was a funny old lady. She was always scribbling in those journals. She was almost manic about it."

"She did the best she could," Claire said, leafing through the journal. "I've been thinking about her a lot lately. Raising us couldn't have been easy for her."

"You always gloss over the fact that when Mom brought us here, she stayed for almost *six years* before she left again," Sydney pointed out.

"But it was still Grandmother Mary who took care of us."

"Mom took care of us while she was here. Evanelle said it took Grandmother Mary almost a year to get used to people being in her house again. She barely talked to any of us." Sydney waved her hand dismissively at Claire, as if this was a familiar argument. "But you never remember those parts."

Claire seemed to think about it, then said, "Well, after Mom left, Grandmother Mary took care of us."

"After she left, Claire, *you* took care of us."

"No, it was Grandmother Mary," Claire argued. "She ordered food and clothes and shoes for us. Washed our sheets."

"*You* did all of that. You were twelve when Mom left us. I remember getting so frustrated with the things you would pick out for me to wear. You dressed me in gray dresses and black sweaters, like an old lady, for most of elementary school."

"I did not." Claire paused. "Wait, I did, didn't I?"

Sydney shook her head with a snort. "You and your revisionist history."

As Bay watched them bicker and coo, she began to realize how much she didn't know about the Waverley sisters, their histories, their lives before Bay knew them as the unit they were now. She knew, she'd always known, how protective they both were of her, so they'd never offered up much information. Then again, Bay had never asked before, and questions now over-whelmed her. Who was Mary, really? Why was she one person when she was young, and another when she was old? Why was she raising her own daughter's daughters? Why did Lorelei leave?

Claire reluctantly set the journal aside and looked in the box again. She took out several sheets of yel-lowed tissue paper, then said, "Jackpot! Here's a dress." She brought out something so thin and delicate it looked like it was made of vellum. Claire put it to her nose. "It even smells like her soap."

Sydney set aside the photo of the fairy party and took the dress. "Her gray smoke soap. I loved that stuff." Sydney stood and held the dress against Bay. "Yes, perfect for a garden nymph."

Bay looked down at the wispy dress, her fingers trailing over it. It really was perfect. It was a faded teal green with layers of beige netting forming a sheer cowl neck. Old sequins were sewn down the side, forming the shapes of flowers, and a silk sash sat below the hips.

"It's the same dress she's wearing here," Sydney said, bending to pick up the fairy picnic photo. The picnic table in the photo was an old door set up on sawhorses, and the seats were old tree stumps, or maybe thick pieces of firewood, topped with square cushions. Six men were sitting there, not looking at the camera, but at the beautiful woman with long, dark hair, almost to her waist, standing at the head of the table. She was smiling, her arms outstretched, as if welcoming everyone to her world. The apple tree in the background, just barely visible, was stretching a single limb out to her, as if wanting to be in the photo with her.

Even it looked a little in love with her.

"Okay, enough reminiscing," Sydney said, pushing Bay into the hallway, toward the bathroom. "Hurry and get dressed!"

*   *   *

When Bay and Phin walked into the gymnasium together, Bay very nearly grabbed Phin's hand, she was so nervous. But his hand was impossible to get at. He was covered from head to toe in a white sheet dotted with tiny rosebuds. Two crude eye holes had been torn into it.

"I can't believe you wore a sheet," she said.

"When you came to my door in a costume, I had to think fast," Phin said, his voice muffled. "My mom is going to kill me for poking holes in her best sheets."

"Why didn't you use your own sheets?"

He hesitated before he mumbled, "They weren't clean."

Boys.

"So, what do we do here?" Phin asked.

"I don't know. I've never been to a dance before."

"You helped decorate it."

"That didn't give me any insight into the social dynamics of the thing."

"It looks great." He moved his head around, as if trying to see through the eye holes. "What I can see of it."

"Take that thing off."

"No way." He sidestepped her when she reached to grab the sheet. "No one knows it's me. I'm in disguise."

Bay looked around. The place did look great. The lighted, covered ball on the ceiling cast shadows on the gym walls that looked like dead trees. And there was a corner where stills from classic horror movies flashed onto a white screen. Riva had gotten Maisy Mosey's dad, who was a professional photographer, to take photos of kids posing in front of the movie stills as they acted like they were being chased by the Blob or Hitchcock's birds.

Unfortunately, without telling the decorating committee, it appeared that some parents had the brilliant idea of bringing bales of hay for everyone to sit on, and also cute little scarecrows left over from the kindergartners' party. The gym ended up looking like a square dance gone horribly, horribly wrong.

All the county high schools had been invited, and Bay could see the soccer players from Hamilton High making fun of the scarecrows, pretending to be afraid of them.

It was trouble having Hamilton High here. Everyone knew that except maybe the principals, who had set this whole thing up. The Bascom High soccer team didn't make the state playoffs, but Hamilton High did. They were old rivals, Hamilton High, the rural school with great sports teams, and Bascom High, the city school with a disproportionately large number of students from wealthy families. The two teams were sizing each other up from across the gym. All the soccer players on both sides were dressed as zombie players with white face paint, fake blood on their jerseys, and fake skin peeling off their arms. The only way to tell them apart was by the color of their uniforms and the numbers on their backs.

Josh was number eight. She found him right away. He'd spiked his blond hair and had poured some fake blood on his head so that it streaked down his face and onto his jersey. His mouth was painted to look like it was monstrously large, with extra teeth. Some of his friends had red eye contacts. One of them had hidden one arm inside his jersey so that it looked like his arm had been ripped off.

"Let's get something to drink," Bay said to Phin, the moment she saw Josh. Bay felt strange, like something in her had changed, which she thought was silly, because only the outside had changed. It was this magic dress, but also the cleverness of her mother's gift with hair. Her hair made her feel pretty, but tender, vulnerable to thoughts of Josh taking one look at her and seeing her in a whole new light, of him walking up to her in front of everyone and telling her he hadn't realized how beautiful she was, that everything she'd written in the note made sense now.

She and Phin walked to the refreshment table while "Thriller" blared over the DJ's speakers.

"Nice spread," Phin said, trying to pick up a cookie through the sheet.

"Take your hand out, for heaven's sake."

"No way. I don't want anyone to know it's me."

"They'd know you by your hands?"

"They might," he said, picking up a cookie with his hand covered by the sheet, like a puppet. He brought it up to his mouth, forgetting he had no mouth hole.

Bay shook her head and looked away. A few seconds later, Phin said, "The cookies are really good." But she could barely make out the words. She turned back to see his mouth making chewing motions behind the sheet. He'd obviously risked someone seeing his distinctive hands and grabbed at least half the cookies off a plate.

"Riva came up with the idea for all of this," Bay said. And it *was* a nice setup. The drink dispensers looked appropriately ghoulish, with plastic eyeballs floating in one, and a giant plastic brain floating in another. The finger pastries did actually look like real fingers, and the ghost cookies were clever—Nutter Butters dipped in white chocolate with chocolate chip eyes. There was also a platter of black licorice rats, hot dogs wrapped in dough to look like mummies, and a bowl of square white mints simply labeled, *Teeth*.

But, there again was some parent's brilliant idea to use red gingham tablecloths and napkins that read, *Ya'll have a safe Halloween!* This had to be the weirdest hoedown ever. Hamilton High was yukking it up.

"Where is Riva?" Phin asked.

Bay looked around and found Riva near the DJ's setup. She was dressed in a big bee costume, like the bee girl in that Blind Melon video from the early nineties. All her friends' costumes looked inspired by iconic, retro videos. Dakota was in a Madonna cone bra. Trinity was in a suit like Annie Lennox, and Louise had on her Jamiroquai hat. Bay had to give them props for the clever costumes. Much better than all the zombie soccer players. "She's with her group. Over there."

"What's your plan?" Phin asked, still eating his

cookies under the sheet, like a little boy sneaking sweets into his bed at night.

"I don't have a plan," Bay said.

"If this is about the bet, you have to let them see you. Shh, be quiet," Phin suddenly said.

"Be quiet? Why? Are you always this crazy, or are you just too sleepy at the bus stop in the mornings and I haven't seen it?"

"Riva is coming over here," Phin whispered. "Don't tell her it's me."

"Why would I tell her it's you?"

"Bay, is that you?" Riva said as she walked over. "Great costume. The dress is so Gatsby! And your *hair*! Oh my God. Your mother must have done it. You might get the award."

"Super," Bay said, having no idea what the award was.

"What are you?" Riva asked.

"A Waverley," Bay said.

"No, I mean, what is your costume?"

"I'm my great-grandmother, Mary Waverley. She used to throw parties in the Waverley garden dressed as a garden nymph."

"Nice."

"Blind Melon bee girl?" Bay asked, pointing to Riva's antennae.

Riva made a face. "It wasn't my first choice. We all got together and came up with a theme, then we each took turns picking which costume we wanted from the list. I got to pick last, hence, the bee costume. I feel like such a Mavis."

This was the most Riva had ever said to her, and Bay wasn't sure what she was supposed to do. Finally, she said, "Mavis?"

"You know, like in *Are You There God, It's Me, Margaret?* The girls in the book formed a secret club and got to choose secret names. The other girls got names like Alexandra and Veronica, but Margaret got stuck with the name Mavis." Riva's eyes went to Phin, who was standing next to them, and frowned. He *was* standing a little too close, like he thought he was invisible. "Well, see you later."

"Bye."

"Nicely done," Phin said, back from being invisible. "You actually had a conversation with Riva Alexander. She's going over there to tell them."

"I don't care."

"You are such a liar. You like to think you don't care, but you do. There's this little thing called give-and-take. Some people you can be yourself with, some people you have to be less weird with. And guess what? Those people are all over the place. You can't avoid them. The world isn't just yours. Everyone has to live in it." Phin began to back away from her, slowly, like she wouldn't notice he was moving. "Now, if you'll excuse me, I'm going to make like a ghost and hover."

* * *

Over the next hour, Bay would catch sight of ghost Phin, hovering around different groups, listening to their conversations. He hung around Riva the most, and then would move when she started getting suspicious. He seemed to be ridiculously enjoying his anonymity.

Bay had lingered around the refreshment table for a while, and some people talked to her, complimenting her hair and dress. A Hamilton High boy dressed like a ninja had asked her to dance, but she'd said no. She'd spent the rest of the time with the awkward girls on the bleachers, watching Josh.

Phin had been right about word getting around about her. Riva had gone immediately and told her friends that Bay was there. But Bay wasn't the only news that night. Riley Asher had been sent home for wearing a nude body suit and long wig, saying she was Lady Godiva. There was a rumor that someone brought a flask of vodka. And some Hamilton High soccer players were saying rude things to the cheerleaders. With so much gossip going around, it was hard to keep track of which news was spreading where, but Bay knew exactly when Josh found out about her. She'd been watching him intently, waiting.

Someone from his team came up to him and punched him on the arm, saying something with a laugh. Josh shook his head. The teammate looked toward the bleachers and pointed at Bay.

That's when Josh's eyes met hers. She didn't look away, even though she felt her heart beat so hard in her chest that it made the gauzy parts of the dress flutter. He looked confused. He took in her hair and her dress, and his lips parted slightly.

This was it, she thought. She stood up. The awkward girls around her looked at her, then looked over to Josh, and for a moment she felt their hope, too, like it was contagious, like she was doing this for all of them.

His teammate punched him on the arm again, and Josh frowned at him and turned his back to her.

She slowly sat back down and the awkward girls looked away, dissapointed.

Well, that was it, she thought, her shoulders relaxing a little.

Josh had seen her. That was all she'd wanted. Well, that's not all she'd wanted, but she'd accomplished what she came here to do.

It was done.

Now she just had to wait for Phin to stop floating around, eavesdropping on everyone. Then she could go home and finally try to stop loving Josh Matteson so much.

7

At some point during the next hour, Bay became aware that Josh had left the gymnasium. She'd never looked directly at him again, but she always knew where he'd been by the thin stream of smoke he left behind him. Until now. She was sitting on the bleachers, by herself now because the other awkward girls had decided to be even more awkward and dance in a group to slow songs in the middle of the gym. She was near the door, close enough to hear the word *fight* whispered as several kids snuck out.

She suddenly had an uneasy feeling as to where Josh might have gone.

There's a secret society in high school that most kids only find out about later, and then it suddenly makes sense when they remember the week all the popular girls went without makeup and all the popular guys dyed their jeans pink. It was their rush week, their formal induction into the upper crust. The exclusivity made them feel important and in control, and their gatherings were mostly harmless. But sometimes there were drugs. And sometimes fights.

Bay couldn't find Phin—there were too many ghosts at the dance, boys who would go home in ruined sheets to angry mothers—so she slipped out the door with the others, going to the faculty parking lot, which was almost void of cars.

The soccer players from Hamilton High were all out there. Bay broke through the crowd to find that the swellhead soccer star of Hamilton High was on the ground with a player from Bascom High. It took her a moment to realize she recognized the number eight on the back of his jersey.

Josh.

Bay saw Riva's bee costume and pushed her way over to her. "What happened?" Bay yelled over the din.

Riva's bee antennae were trembling. "That's Cobie from Hamilton High," she said, her voice high. "He and Steven were getting into it, so Josh stepped in to intervene. And then Josh just starts pummeling Cobie for no reason! He totally caught him off guard. But not for long. And now no one will help him!"

Bay's breath caught. Josh was quick and lean, but Cobie was much taller and heavier. He was trying to pin Josh to the hard pavement, sneaking in punches to his side as he did so.

If no one else was going to help, then she had to. She had to do something. They wouldn't hurt a girl, would they? They would part the moment she came up to them. Right?

This was the first fight she'd ever witnessed in real life. There was something primal about it, filling the air with a charge. She was caught up in it and scared, scared for Josh, and scared for herself, because she'd always thought of herself as the person who would step up to help, who wasn't like everyone else. But maybe Phin was right. Maybe she lived in a made-up world. Maybe in the real world, maybe deep inside, she was just like everyone else.

Suddenly, something flashed by her in a gust of wind, blowing her hair and making the hem of her dress flutter.

It happened so fast. In seconds Cobie was tossed into the air with a force that landed him on his backside, feet away. The breath was knocked out of him and the look on his face mirrored what they were all feeling. What on earth was *that*?

The crowd began to hum, and people turned to see teachers and parents appearing at the back door of the gym, their faces illuminated by the ambient security lights.

Everyone started to scramble. Cobie's Hamilton High teammates pulled him up, dazed, and dragged him away as he kept asking, "What in the hell just happened?"

In the chaos, Bay was jostled around and she fought against the surge, trying to find Josh. When she finally saw him, he was still on all fours, trying to lift himself up. Quick as a flash, she ran to him and helped him to his feet. Everyone else was running in a herd toward the security crossbar at the entrance to the parking lot, trying to make it around to the front of the building.

The problem was that it would be very easy to head them off at the pass, and several teachers and parents had already disappeared back into the gymnasium, presumably to do just that.

Bay put Josh's arm over her shoulder and headed in the other direction, one that led them away from the gym and toward the academic buildings. She guided him around the back of those buildings, through the field of dogwood trees that had been planted by the alumni association years ago. The wind was blowing, making the bare limbs clack and scratch eerily.

Josh was walking with a slight limp, favoring his rib cage on his right side. He had to lean on her as they finally walked up the far hill, the back way into the well-lit student parking lot. There wasn't anyone there, proof that most had, indeed, been stopped at the front of the gymnasium.

She looked around for the Pathfinder she knew he drove. If pressed, she could probably even recite his license plate, as many times as she'd watched him drive away.

"Where is your car?" she finally asked.

Josh's head jerked up from where he'd been watching his feet, each step a focused effort. He immediately stepped away from her.

He hadn't known it was her. The look on his face was as if someone had come up behind him and said, *Guess who?* And he'd turned, geared for a pleasant surprise, only to find that it was the last person he'd wanted it to be.

He looked around. She saw his relief that no one was there to see them together. She also saw his suspicion start to grow, as if she had planned this. "Why did we come this way?"

"Because we would have been caught if we'd gone the other way. Where is your car?" she asked again.

He stared at her for a long time. If she yelled *Boo!* he would probably jump a mile. "Over there," he finally said. "I brought my dad's Audi."

She looked at the car, then back to him, trying to judge whether or not he was capable of driving. "Can you make it?"

"Yeah. He got me in the ribs, but nothing's broken."

"How do you know?"

He rubbed his side. "I've been hit with soccer balls harder than he can punch."

Bay turned to go, not able to stand the way he was still looking at her, as if she would . . . what? Bewitch him? What on earth did that mean, anyway?

"Wait," he called as she walked away.

But she didn't. She kept walking, her hands fisted at her sides. Insufferable boy. He was foolish and hardheaded and, now that she thought about it, had horrible taste in shoes. How could she belong with him? Why did she love him so much? Why couldn't she just turn it off, like a switch?

"Bay, wait," he said as he galloped awkwardly after her.

"What?" she whirled around and said.

He wasn't expecting her anger. Frankly, neither was

she. They both looked a little startled. "At least let me take you home."

"No, thank you. Phin's mom is picking us up."

He pressed his lips together. His white makeup and painted mouth were smeared and blurred from the fight. He looked like he had been blotted out and some-one new was coming through. "So you and Phin . . . ," he said.

"Me and Phin what?"

"Nothing."

Bay turned away again.

"Wait. You have my blood all over you."

She looked down to see that the fake zombie blood he was wearing was smeared all over the side of her great-grandmother's beautiful dress. It made her want to cry. Her mom and aunt Claire were going to kill her.

"It's fake," she said, trying to keep her voice even. "I can tell everyone I was going for a Stephen King *Carrie* look."

"Let me take you home."

She was feeling tender, that was all. That's how she justified this moment of weakness. She pulled her phone out of her ankle boot and called Phin.

It took a moment for him to answer. It almost went to voice mail. He finally answered, sounding breath-less and shaky. "Hello?"

"Phin, it's Bay. Where are you?"

"I'm in front of the gym. My mom will be here any minute. Where are you?"

"In the student parking lot." Bay looked at Josh, then looked away. "I've got a ride home."

"Oh," Phin said, distracted. "Okay."

"Are you all right?"

"Yeah." He paused. "Yeah, I'm fine."

Josh was quiet on the ride to Bay's home. The inside of his father's Audi smelled like leather, corn syrup, and a fresh, cologne-y scent she'd first smelled when Josh leaned against her as she'd helped him walk to the student parking lot. It was on her clothes now, that Josh-scent, but it felt stolen, not meant to be there.

Being this close to him, in this confined area, made her chest feel quaky. The intimacy made her giddy, like when you've been awake too long or had too much caffeine. She found herself impressed by silly things. *He drives so well! Look how easily he steers! He doesn't even take his eyes off the road as he turns up the heater!* It occurred to her then that he'd mistaken her nerves for cold chills.

She focused on his hands on the steering wheel, willing herself to be still. He had nice hands, sun-browned and thick. His forearms were ropey, muscles tight.

Hopkins Dairy was a little out of the way, but every kid in elementary school had gone there on a field trip, so everyone knew where it was. She didn't have to tell Josh how to get there. The moment before she was about to tell him to turn right or turn left, he was already doing it.

It was over too soon, this bubble ride. As they neared
the turn to the dairy, Bay cleared her throat and said,
"You can stop at the entrance. I'll walk down the driveway to the house."

To which Josh said, taking the turn off the highway,
"That's okay."

As he drove down the bumpy gravel driveway, Bay
felt herself getting more uptight. It wasn't like he hadn't
seen the Hopkins farmhouse before. But it suddenly
seemed unbearable to her, with as little as he proved
he knew about her, for Josh to see the farmhouse and
think it was really where she belonged.

When she and her mother had fled from Bay's father in Seattle, they had stayed in the Waverley house
with Claire, but they'd moved to the farmhouse next
to Henry's dairy when Sydney and Henry married.
Bay liked the farmhouse. She knew the first time she
saw it that it was where her mother belonged, even
though her mother considered herself an urban soul
and didn't care for the quiet. It made her jumpy, like
back in Seattle, waiting for someone's temper to flare
and something bad to happen. But Bay didn't belong
there. She belonged at the Waverley house.

She wasn't embarrassed by the farmhouse. Not exactly. But she'd seen Josh's house, and she hated that
she felt even the slightest need to explain where she
lived.

He pulled in front of the small, white, two-story
house. The bare-bulb porch light was on. There was
also a light on behind the living room curtain.

She didn't get out immediately. She sat there and waited, thinking he was going to say something. This was what her parents did after going out. They came home, but then stayed in the car—engine off, windows down in the summer; engine on, heater running in the winter—and talked, something about being in a car at night provoking one last conversation, one last kiss, before getting out.

It was a date thing, she realized.

And this wasn't a date.

Josh stared straight ahead.

Without another word, Bay got out and walked stiffly to the door, telling herself not to look back.

"I can't believe I missed her going to her first dance," Henry said hours earlier, after Sydney came home from dropping Bay and Phin off at the gymnasium. Sydney had tried to reach him on the phone to tell him, but he'd missed the call.

Sydney had just swept in with a gust of perfumed air, her cheeks alight with happiness at this unusual turn of social events in their daughter's life. She'd bought Chinese on her way home, and she was now setting the takeout boxes on the kitchen table. Henry stood there, fresh from his shower, and rubbed a pink and white towel over his hair to dry it. Pink and white. Sydney said that she and Bay had slowly but surely girl-ified this place. But he didn't mind.

A house isn't a real house without a woman in it, his grandad used to say.

"I've been saving up all these things to say to Bay when she started dating," he said from under the towel. "I even wrote a few down. Seriously, I think I have notes in my office."

Sydney laughed, as if touched by this knowledge. "How about I send her to you first thing in the morning, and you can lecture her about how terrible boys are and how they only want one thing."

Henry draped the towel around his neck and sat at the table as Sydney put down plates. She touched his face before she sat across from him.

The first time Henry met Sydney was on the monkey bars at school. Some people come into your life and change it forever. Sydney did that with Henry. He'd loved her from the moment he set eyes on her. He became her best friend in elementary school. But she began to drift away from him as they got older. Hunter John Matteson had fallen in love with her, too, and actually had the balls to tell her. Henry had lost her in increments in high school, then lost her for good when she went away when she was eighteen. He'd never expected to see her again. His grandfather had still been alive then, though the stroke had slowed him down. He'd taken to spending his days trying to fix Henry up, wanting to see him settled and married. But nothing ever took. When Sydney came back, it felt like Henry had been running in circles, setting trees on fire, until there was nothing left but a barren landscape. Then she'd appeared and he finally stopped running in circles and ran to her like she was a cool, soft field.

That's what it feels like to finally find her, his granddad had said.

Henry didn't believe his luck at first, when they'd started dating. To this day, he would still find himself stopping in the middle of yet another story about his granddad (he knew he talked too much about him), thinking, How could someone like her find this remotely interesting? He wanted to give her the world. But even that didn't seem like enough. It paled in comparison to everything she'd given him, this life together, this family, these pink and white towels, this fifteen-year-old daughter who was now going to dances.

"How did this happen?" Henry asked, giving up trying to use chopsticks on his shrimp and snow peas. He picked up a fork. "How did she get to be fifteen? She'll be leaving us before we know it."

Sydney suddenly went still. Henry could feel by the change in the air what was about to happen, and he slowly set his fork down and waited for it. He could almost see new red streaks popping out in her hair. This had become a common occurrence lately. It was first frost anxiety. Henry and Tyler had compared notes long ago and realized it happened every year around this time, their wives always doing something crazy. This year, Sydney was all over him. Not that he minded. Anything to help. But he kept worrying over the whys of the thing. What was really going on in that mind of hers?

She dropped her fork and leaned across the table and kissed him.

She pulled him out of his seat, and they were all over each other, shirts off, pants unbuttoned. Then they were on the kitchen floor, where they squeaked against the floorboards and knocked against the cabinets. The world tilted and time flew. Before he knew it they were straightening their clothing and going back to eating, giving each other googly smiles over their Chinese takeout.

The pink and white towel, still damp from his shower, was forgotten on the floor.

Somewhere in the back of his mind, Henry wondered if this kept happening because there was something she wanted that he wasn't giving her, so she was forced now to take it.

He didn't like the thought. He would give anything to her. Anything he had.

All she had to do was tell him.

Sydney kissed Henry again before he went to bed. His internal clock always slowed his steps around eight o'clock every night, as if he were a wind-up toy losing speed. If he stayed up too late, Sydney would sometimes find him standing on the staircase, halfway upstairs, his hand on the railing, fast asleep with dust settling on his sharp cheekbones.

Henry smiled, sleepy and satisfied, as he walked to their bedroom. He had lines around his eyes from years of squinting against the sun. *The sun*. That's exactly what he felt like to her, giving her light and nourishment, always there, predictable. He rode out her restlessness and went wild with her when she needed it, but he always got up the next day the same man, the same heart, the same light.

Sydney waited up for Bay, not knowing quite what to do with herself. She finally put on her kimono, twisted up her hair with her unused chopsticks from dinner, then watched Molly Ringwald movies from the eighties on her laptop, the movies where the odd girl always got the happy ending.

When she heard a car come up the driveway, she slapped her laptop closed. Bay was right on time. Sydney had never had to give her a curfew before, so she'd made it ridiculously early, but Bay hadn't batted an eyelash. Grandmother Mary had never given Sydney a curfew, though there were times Sydney now wished she had. More often than not, she'd let Sydney sleep over at her friends' houses, where she'd always felt free to sneak out and meet her boyfriend at all hours of the night.

She got up quickly, thinking she should turn off the living room light so Bay wouldn't know she was waiting up for her. When she heard the car stop in front of the house, she realized it was too late for that. Maybe she should run to the kitchen and make hot chocolate so they could sit and talk about the night. No, Bay would hate that.

She hadn't heard a car door close yet, so she sidled

up to the living room window, leaned her back against the wall, and lifted the curtain slightly. It took her a moment to make out the car, a dark Audi. Not Phin's mother's Chevy. Who was that at this hour? The car seemed familiar, and she knew why when the passenger side door finally opened and the interior light came on. There was her daughter, getting out of a car driven by Josh Matteson.

Sydney's cell phone suddenly rang, and she jumped in surprise. She grabbed it off the coffee table and answered.

"Hello?"

"Sydney? This is Tallulah Young, Phin's mom. I'm sitting in front of the gym at school with Phin. Bay's not here. He said she already got a ride home. Did you know about that?"

"No," Sydney said as the front door opened, "but she just got here."

"Is she all right? Phin said there was a fight at the dance."

Sydney's heart kicked in her chest when she set eyes on her daughter. Her dress was smeared in blood.

"It's fake," Bay said quickly. "Fake blood. From a costume."

"She's fine," Sydney said to Phin's mom, not taking her eyes off Bay. "Is Phineus all right?"

"He's fine. He ruined my best sheets, though. It's coming out of his allowance."

"Geez, Mom, I said I was sorry," Phin said before his mother hung up.

Youngs may be the strongest men in town, but you should see their mothers.

"I can't believe you waited up for me," Bay said, taking the defensive before Sydney even said a word, which was Sydney's first clue that she was hiding something. When Sydney didn't say anything, Bay plucked at the dress. "It's fake. It even smells like corn syrup. Smell."

"I don't want to smell it. I want to know how it got on you," Sydney said.

"I helped someone who had fallen down. He was wearing a zombie costume. That's all."

"That's all? You got that much of his costume on you from just helping him up?"

"Yes! I wasn't *making out* with him, if that's what you think! I didn't do anything wrong. I just helped someone who had gotten into a fight."

"Josh," Sydney said flatly. "You helped Josh Matteson."

The look on Bay's face was priceless. "How did you know? Did Phin say something to his mom?"

"No," Sydney said. "I just saw Josh drop you off."

"You were watching?" Bay demanded. Sydney played the silent card again. "He offered me a ride home. Completely platonic. He drove the speed limit. We wore our seat belts. He barely said two words to me."

"Josh Matteson."

"Yes, Mom, Josh Matteson."

Sydney felt a sinking sensation as she remembered something Claire had said. *She's mentioned a boy once or twice.* "Oh, Bay, he's not the one, is he?"

"The one what?"

"Your aunt Claire said you liked a boy. It's not *Josh,* is it?"

Bay looked affronted. "So what if it is? What's wrong with Josh Matteson?"

Sydney bit her lip, not knowing where to begin.

"How can you expect me to tell you anything when you *never* tell me anything," Bay said, walking past her and up the stairs. Sydney followed her.

Bay's room was the first one at the top of the staircase. It was painted a dove gray that turned peacock blue after dark, as if the room absorbed the warmth of daylight and radiated with it at night. Bay didn't turn on her light. She stepped over shoes and books in the darkness, ripping all the wilted flowers out of her hair and tossing them onto her paisley-print rug.

Bay took off Grandmother Mary's dress and looked at it forlornly.

Sydney held out her hand and Bay walked over and gave it to her.

Bay kicked off her ankle boots, then crawled into bed, still in the long johns she'd worn under the light dress to keep warm.

Sydney stood silently in the doorway. "Are you dating him?" she finally asked.

"No. He doesn't like me." Bay turned on her side,

away from Sydney. "He doesn't even know me," she whispered, and Sydney realized her daughter was crying.

It all started, as these things often do, with a boy. Sydney blossomed in high school. And she loved it. She loved every minute of it. And she was so desperate to keep it that she separated herself almost totally from her family. She was rarely at home. Her grandmother Mary understood what it was like to have that kind of attention, so she let her youngest granddaughter bask in it. A little too much. Sometimes it felt like a push. *You go have fun. I remember what it was like to be you.*

Sydney was the belle of the ball, envied for many things—her beauty, her way with hair, but mostly because the most popular boy in school had fallen in love with her. Sydney and Hunter John Matteson had been inseparable. This was much to the distress of Emma Clark, who had loved Hunter John all her life, and who would end up marrying him, in the end. All she had to do was wait. What she knew, what everyone knew, was that Hunter John was only making hay while the sun shone. He could only dally with a Waverley while in school. As soon as he graduated, real life began, the life each Matteson father thrust upon his son.

In real life, a Matteson never married a Waverley.

Sydney didn't understand that at the time. She thought she and Hunter John would be in love forever. There'd been no warning when they graduated. He'd ended their relationship suddenly, leaving her stunned,

her heart shriveled to the size of a pea and her hatred
for this town building until it shed from her skin and
left angry blue flakes on her sheets when she got out
of bed in the mornings.

Bay never knew exactly why Sydney left Bascom.
She didn't know Sydney left because a Matteson broke
her heart and she decided to do what her own mother
had done, leave this stupid town and everyone in it.
Sometimes Sydney wondered, if Hunter John hadn't
played with her that way, would she have stayed? Probably not. But at the very least she would have left with
a bigger heart and a happier soul, maybe one that never
would have attracted the likes of Bay's father into her
life. Had it been her insecurity that had made her stay
with a man who had beaten her? She might never
know.

It was moot, in the end. It all happened the way it
was supposed to, because she got Bay out of it. And
when she returned to town, there was Henry, whom
Sydney had known as a child. Henry had watched her
with Hunter John, all while being in love with her himself, helpless to stop her from giving her heart away.

She would be damned if she would let another Matteson break the heart of another Waverley, especially
not her daughter. Josh wasn't as chest-thumping and
proud as his father had been, but his good nature only
meant he was going to do what he was told. He was
going into business with his father, just like his father
before him.

Sydney didn't know how Josh felt about her daughter

right now, but she did know that it's remarkably easy to fall in love with someone who is already in love with you. It's a little like falling in love with yourself. Sydney was honest enough with herself to know that's how it had happened with Henry. He had loved her long before she had loved him. And Bay was an extraordinary young woman. Beautiful, kind, mysterious. If Josh spent any amount of time with her, he would fall for her. Sydney knew that with a certainty as hard as flint.

So the obvious course of action was to prevent it from ever happening.

8

Monday afternoon, Bay sat outside on the beige stone steps of the main academic building at school and did her homework, waiting for the late buses, the ones that took the Wide Open Spaces kids home. They were the kids from the farthest edges of the city school district. They were a quieter crowd than the rest of the kids. Their lives weren't filled every minute with something. Most of their lives, it seemed, were actually spent on the bus. Bay was usually the first one off, at Pendland Street, which she could easily walk to when she felt like it. It wasn't that far away. But she needed the excuse to be here, because that's what she'd told Josh she'd do in her note. And giving up would mean conceding that she was wrong, even though at this point she knew she was.

She was just waiting for her heart to catch up.

Everyone loved an October afternoon. Even the Wide Open Spaces kids were more lively than usual on the sidewalk. It was the kind of day everyone thought of as a quintessential fall school day—crisp air, letter jackets, plaid skirts. Something everyone says they once read in a book.

She finished her homework, then brought out her copy of *Romeo and Juliet*. She'd read it hundreds of times. Now she just liked to turn the pages to words she enjoyed, rolling them over in her mind: *solemnity* and *pernicious, jocund* and *caitiff*.

Doff.

Rote.

Fray.

She heard someone clear his throat behind her, so she automatically scooted aside and moved her back-pack, thinking she was in the way of someone walking down the stone steps.

Someone did move by her, but then took a seat next to her.

She looked over, a little irritated because there were thirty-three steps from the sidewalk up to the rotunda, and this person still wanted her personal space.

But then she realized who it was.

"Hi," Josh said.

Every day she'd been sitting on these steps, waiting for him. And now that he was finally here, she had no idea what to say. She wasn't sure she wanted to say anything now. She couldn't help that she belonged with him, that every time he was near, she felt a pull in her stomach, as if something inside her was pointing to him and saying, *Home. Home. Home.* But she didn't have to try so hard. It wasn't changing anything but herself, changing herself into someone miserable and insecure, someone so *not her*.

"You left your phone in my car Saturday night," Josh said. He had his elbows on his knees, one hand casually holding her cell phone out to her.

"Oh. Thanks," she said, taking the phone and stuffing it in her backpack. So that's where it had been. She couldn't find it anywhere when her mother had demanded custody of it as part of her being grounded, as if Bay used it all the time and would feel its absence mightily.

She fumbled around in her backpack, thinking he was just going to get up and leave. But the longer she dug through her backpack, needlessly rearranging her books, the more she realized that he wasn't going anywhere.

She finally turned again to him. Josh was staring at her, sunglasses covering his eyes. He was wearing jeans and a rugby-striped sweater. She stared back, silent, raising her eyebrows. If this was going to be a conversation, *he* was going to have to make the effort.

"I'm sorry I was rude to you," Josh finally said. "I was having a bad night, but that was no reason to take it out on you." He looked at his hands, clasped together between his wide-splayed knees. "I'm glad you were there. I thought about it a lot this weekend. I realized I didn't even thank you. So, thank you."

"Okay," she said.

"Okay?"

"I accept your apology."

He smiled. "Very magnanimous of you."

"That's me. Magnanimous." Several minutes passed in silence. Bay finally said to him, "You're still here." It wasn't said rudely, but curiously, as if he might have forgotten.

"Yes," he said, nodding.

"Is this," she circled her finger in his general direction, referring to his presence, "a part of the apology?"

"No. But I understand why you would ask that. And, again, I'm sorry."

"Why were you fighting with that guy?" Bay asked, something she'd been dying to know, but figured she would never have the answer. Now that he was here, and wasn't going anywhere, apparently, she might as well take the opportunity to find out.

Josh shrugged. "He made a joke about how my dad couldn't buy my way into the state championships. We're a good team. My dad has nothing to do with it. Literally. He hates soccer."

"You're a great player. I've seen you play. I mean, we all have," she quickly added.

"There was a part of me that hoped I'd get caught. Someone even posted a video of the fight. I thought my mom and dad were going to be called back from vacation and I would get a lecture and they would tell me how disappointed they were in me. But the principal didn't so much as look at me today, even with this," he said, taking off his sunglasses and pointing to his black eye. It was purple and yellow today, melancholy colors. "They'll never know, unless I tell them."

"Why would you tell them?"

He shook his head. "Sometimes I just want them to know I'm not who they think I am."

It was such a strange thing to say that she automatically asked, "Who are you?" And it finally occurred to her that she really didn't know. She knew as little about him as he knew about her. She simply had the benefit of knowing, *knowing,* where she needed to end up.

"I'm Josh Matteson, nice to meet you," he said, putting on a big fake smile and holding out his hand as if he wanted her to shake it. She didn't. His smile faded and he put his sunglasses back on. "I don't want to go to Notre Dame, like my grandfather did. I don't want to go into business with my dad."

"That's not who you are. That's who you *aren't,*" she pointed out. "What do *you* want?"

He seemed flummoxed by her response. "I don't know," he said. "I get cold sweats when I sit in my car in the mornings, trying to make myself go to school. I go to sleep at nine at night because I'm so exhausted. Sometimes my cheeks hurt from smiling, from pretending I'm okay with where my life is heading."

The answer was so obvious that she thought he was playing with her at first. Then she realized he wasn't. "Then stop pretending," she said.

He gave her a look, like she'd said something cute.

"I bet you've never pretended a day in your life," he said.

"You say that like it's easy."

He shrugged. "Sometimes I daydream of mowing," he said. "I love watching when the soccer fields are mowed. It seems so soothing, to ride on a lawn mower, back and forth, for hours."

The late buses pulled in, and the Wide Open Spaces kids grabbed their backpacks and band instrument cases and started lining up.

Bay stood. "You could get a job at the soccer arena in Hickory. I bet they do a lot of mowing there. And playing. And teaching," she said.

Josh watched her as she shouldered her backpack. He looked a little bewildered, as if he had steeled himself for something unpleasant. Bay did a mental eye-roll. Did he really think just talking to her would be so awful?

"Would you like a ride home?" he asked.

"As thrilling as it was the first time, no, thanks. The buses are already here." She didn't mention she was grounded.

Josh stayed seated as she descended the steps.

"Will you be out here tomorrow?" he called.

"I'm here every day," she said as she got in line.

Just before she stepped onto the bus, Josh called, "Bay!"

She turned to him. He stood up, wincing a little, his hand on his side, favoring his rib cage. "Tell your friend Phin I said thanks."

"For what?"

"Watch the video," he said, then slowly walked up the steps and disappeared.

She tried to watch the video on her phone on the bus ride to her aunt Claire's, but her battery was dead and she needed to recharge it. It didn't matter anyway, because she had to give her phone to her mom when she got home.

The initial terms of Bay's inaugural grounding were as follows:

1. Sydney would take Bay to school in the mornings and pick her up at her aunt Claire's in the evenings.
2. Bay would surrender her phone, as soon as she found it.

Sydney said there might be more items to add to the list, she just hadn't thought of them yet. Bay had gone over the terms in her head, finding all sorts of loopholes. Like, there was nothing that said she couldn't actually sit on the steps of the school and talk to Josh, though the likelihood of such a thing happening was so astronomically slim that her mother probably thought it wasn't worth mentioning at the time.

Another loophole: Her mom didn't actually say she couldn't leave the house for specific purposes, although that was what a grounding implied.

Her mother seemed to be playing this by ear. This

surprise grounding, which happened a full twenty-four hours after the alleged crime, was supposedly because Bay didn't ask permission for someone other than Phin's mother to take her home. At least, that's what Bay's obviously confused father told her, trying to make her mother's decision make sense.

But Bay knew there had to be more to it than that.

Because as many times as Sydney had encouraged Bay to get out and meet people and date, the moment Bay told her she liked someone, she reacted like *this*. Which led Bay to the conclusion that it wasn't the crime her mother had a problem with. It was the boy.

Bay's mother didn't like Josh Matteson. And Bay had no idea why.

"Claire, you need a website," Buster said as Bay entered the kitchen in the Waverley house a half hour later.

Claire smiled at Bay. Bay gave her a faraway look in return, perhaps a little too content for someone who had just been grounded for the first time.

"Who doesn't have a website?" Buster continued. "I can't believe you still fax."

"I don't know how to make a website," Claire said as she stirred the large copper pot of sugar and water and corn syrup, waiting for the mixture to boil. Once it boiled, she would watch the food thermometer rise until it was time to add the flavoring and coloring. Lemon verbena again today.

The labels on all the lemon verbena candy jars read:

> *Lemon verbena essence is to soothe,*
> *producing a comforting quiet.*
> *Wise is a voice with nothing to prove.*
> *Everyone should try it.*

Buster looked around furtively, then whispered, "Okay, don't tell anyone this, but there's a top-secret profession called *web designers* who will do it all for you. I'll hook you up, but you have to swear to secrecy."

Claire shook her head at him. She'd met him last summer at one of her catering jobs, where he'd been a waiter. Later, out of all the applicants from Orion's cooking school looking for part-time work, she'd chosen him. Sometimes she doubted this decision. He never shut up.

"Okay, forget the website," Buster said. "You need to accept the offer from Dickory Foods. That business advisor you consulted said you should sell within a year, before you lose momentum. So, you sell the business, but still stay in charge of it. Think of it: expansion, advertising, the plant in Hickory. Can you imagine? Not having to stir every day? Not having to put labels on jars? Not having to assemble mailing boxes? No more of those biodegradable packing peanuts stuck to my butt with static when I leave this house?"

"You like when the packing peanuts stick to your butt," Claire pointed out.

"I do enjoy the attention."

"Just crack those molds and get to work."

The doorbell rang and Bay went to get it. She hadn't said a word since she'd arrived.

"What's with her?" Buster asked.

Claire just shrugged.

"You have some visitors," Bay said, smiling as she walked back into the kitchen with Evanelle Franklin and her companion Fred. Evanelle was eighty-nine now, tethered to oxygen and wearing thick glasses that made her rheumy eyes look huge. Fred, calm and pressed, was always beside her, carrying her portable oxygen container like a purse. He let her do all the talking, content to be her straight man.

Fred had lived with Evanelle for years, and Claire knew he loved the tiny old woman as much as Claire did. He'd become a fixture in their family over the past ten years. He'd been shy and uncertain when he'd first moved in with Evanelle, coming to parties in the Waverley garden with some trepidation, as if worried he might be asked to leave.

Evanelle and Fred went everywhere together now, and most people referred to them as a single entity, EvanelleandFred, which tickled Evanelle.

"Evanelle, I didn't know you were coming by!" Claire couldn't leave the pot, but she wanted to go hug her. Evanelle was like a favorite story she didn't want to end. She'd known Evanelle, a distant Waverley cousin, most all her life. Her childhood memories were full of strange gifts Evanelle would give her that Claire would always need later, and of how Evanelle and Grandmother Mary would sit in the kitchen and share stories and laugh. It was the only time Grandmother Mary ever laughed, with Evanelle.

Evanelle's health had been declining lately, and every time Claire saw her she seemed smaller, like she was slowly burning away and soon Claire would hug her and step back with only ash in her hands.

"I have something to give you," Evanelle said, holding up a paper bag. "It came to me the other night."

"Would you like some coffee?" Claire asked Evanelle and Fred. "I can get Bay to make some. I don't think her mind's on candy today, anyway." Bay had been staring at her shoes, a slight smile on her lips, but looked up, blushing, when Claire said that.

"No, that's okay," Evanelle said. "We were just on a drive and thought we'd stop by. Fred said I needed to get out of the house for a little while, that I needed airing out."

"I never said that," Fred said.

"Okay, I added the airing-out part," Evanelle amended.

"How was your doctor's appointment last week?" Claire asked.

"He gave me some bad news. I'm old."

That made Buster laugh. He walked over to Claire and took the spoon from her. "I'll take care of this. You visit with Evanelle."

Claire lifted off her apron, then took the bag from Evanelle, finally getting to hug her. She smelled like Fred's cologne, which always amused Claire. Evanelle said it was just because she spent so much time with him, but Fred and Claire had a theory that she would dab some on her neck when Fred wasn't looking. She always said she liked the way men smelled. "Come to the sitting room with me, Evanelle. Bay, you come, too."

"Stay here and talk with Buster," Evanelle told Fred when he started to follow them. She took her portable oxygen purse from him and stage-whispered, "He's a cute one. You should flirt with him."

"Evanelle!" Fred said. "He works for me at my market!"

"I'm just saying it can't hurt. You're a little rusty."

"I'm currently in a short-term relationship with someone in my bread class, but you can practice on me," Buster said. "I don't mind."

Fred clasped his hands behind his back awkwardly, not looking at all happy. "So this is what you do before you come to work at the market in the evenings," Fred said, eyeing Buster warily. "You said you couldn't work afternoons for religious reasons."

"Candy is my religion."

Claire led Evanelle out of the kitchen. Once in the sitting room, Bay went to the window and stared out as Claire sat beside Evanelle on the couch. As small as Evanelle was becoming, her large tote bag containing things like paper clips and plastic flowers and red ribbon and vinegar, all things she might feel the need to give someone, seemed huge now in comparison, like it was now carrying *her*. She set her tote bag and portable oxygen on the floor with a sigh.

It seemed like just yesterday the old woman was energetically walking around the college track every morning, ogling fine male posteriors, then stopping by for coffee and cake here at the Waverley house. That was before the Year Everything Changed, when Claire met Tyler, when Sydney came home, when Fred moved in with Evanelle. Claire wouldn't trade her life now for anything, but sometimes she thought fondly of that time before. Things had been so much simpler, clearer, than they were these days.

"Go on," Evanelle said, pointing to the paper bag. "Open it."

Claire opened it and pulled out an old wooden-handled spatula.

"That belonged to your grandmother Mary," Evanelle said. "She gave it to me one of the times she tried to show me how to cook. When she was younger, she didn't want anyone to compete with her in the kitchen, even though she was so talented no one could compare. She was mesmerizing, wasn't she? The way she would pour and stir and chop. It was like music. She even danced to it, remember?"

Claire smiled, staring at the spatula. "I remember."

"In her later years, she didn't mind so much, sharing what she knew. I think it was a little vanity on her side. She wanted to pass her gift along, so she would be remembered. But I didn't care for cooking, so she liked having you in the kitchen with her, to teach. I had a dream about Mary the other night. I knew I had to give that spatula to you."

"Thank you, Evanelle. I'm sure it will come in handy," Claire said, though she knew it wouldn't, not right now, with all this candy. Maybe later, when everything calmed down. "You know, I was thinking recently, why didn't Grandmother Mary ever do anything big with her talent? Why did she keep it at the back door?"

"Mary didn't do big because it would have been too much work," Evanelle said with a smile. "She just wasn't motivated. She liked when things were easy."

"So she never thought she needed to prove anything?" Claire asked. *Like me.*

Evanelle's eyes, magnified by her glasses, blinked twice, as if a memory had suddenly come to her. "I wouldn't say that. She had her share of insecurities, especially after her husband left."

"But she never cared what people thought of her," Claire said. "She was confident in what she could do, right?"

Evanelle shook her head. "She thought *too* much about what other people thought. That's why she became such a homebody."

Claire was skirting around what she really wanted to ask: *But her gift was real, wasn't it? Not some hoodoo she used to trick locals into thinking she could affect their emotions by using flowers from her gar-*

den? Not something she kept small, because her se-
cret could stay small that way?

But she didn't ask. It would sound ludicrous, and it
might even offend Evanelle and Bay, two of the most
clearly gifted people she knew. Of *course* Waverley
gifts were real. At least, theirs were.

Evanelle looked over at Bay, silhouetted in the
window. "How's your mama, Bay? I need to make an
appointment with her to get a perm." Evanelle patted
her frizzy gray hair.

Bay turned and smiled at Evanelle. "She's fine."

"Bay went to her first Halloween dance on Saturday night," Claire told Evanelle. "She dressed as
Grandmother Mary. She wore one of the old dresses
from Grandmother Mary's fairy picnics. We found
some old photos. Why don't you go get them, Bay?"

Bay left the room and went upstairs.

"What's wrong with her?" Evanelle leaned over and
whispered in her loud nonwhisper.

Claire turned to make sure Bay was already up the
stairs before she said, "She's in love, and her mother
isn't happy about it."

"Why not?"

"Because it's Josh Matteson."

"Hoo-boy," Evanelle said. "He's a cute one. But
that's tough luck for her. Mattesons and Waverleys
have never been a good combination."

"I know," Claire said unhappily as Bay brought the
shoe box downstairs and handed it to Claire, then went
back to the window.

"I remember these," Evanelle said as she and Claire went through the box. "Your grandmother was so pretty. All these men loved her. They were her boarders. She had a waiting list a mile long." Evanelle hesitated when she saw one photo. She took it out of the box and held it up. "There's Karl. Never thought I'd see him again."

"Who is he?"

Evanelle made a clicking sound with her false teeth. "He's your grandfather. Didn't you know that? Mary got rid of him when she was pregnant with your mama. Cheating son of a gun. She was never the same after that. He changed her."

"Changed her? How?" Claire took the photo from her and looked at it. Karl was standing outside the garden gate. There were apples at his feet, as if the apple tree had been throwing them at him. He was smiling, his hands in the pockets of his striped suit. He looked jaunty and a little smug. As many times as she'd seen this photo over the years, finding the box of photos always when looking for something else, she'd never known.

"People like us will never really understand," Evanelle said. "We fell in love with the men we were supposed to be with right off the bat. But women with broken hearts, they change."

Evanelle took a few deep breaths through the tubing at her nose. A slightly alarmed expression came over her face, the way she always looked these days when she thought she'd been out too long and might run out of oxygen.

"I should go home. Fred?" Evanelle called in an airy voice.

In a few steps he was there, as if he'd been waiting close by. "I'm here."

"Did that boy teach you a thing or two?" Evanelle asked as she stood.

Fred took the portable oxygen tank from her. "Evanelle, I'm forty years older than he is."

"I'm just saying you need practice."

Claire set the photos and the spatula aside, then she and Fred walked Evanelle to the front door. The air was as sharp and cool as lime ice when they stepped onto the porch, and they all stopped with the invigorating shock of it.

"It's getting colder," Evanelle said, pulling her fuzzy black coat up around her neck. "First frost should be here soon."

"On Saturday, according to the almanac," Claire said. "Halloween. I've been going out to check the tree every day. I think it's almost ready."

"Are you going to have a party?" Evanelle asked.

"Of course."

"I can't wait. You know, I'm a little antsy this year." Evanelle shivered. "I don't know why. Have you had any unexpected visitors?"

"No," Claire said. "Why?"

"Autumn winds bring strangers. That's what my

daddy used to say. He wasn't a Waverley. He was a Nu-guet. Nuguets know their weather," Evanelle said as Claire and Fred helped her down the front steps and into Fred's Buick, parked at the sidewalk.

"I worry about her," Fred said, once they'd gotten her inside the car and closed the door.

"I know you do," Claire said, folding her arms across her chest against the chill. "She's getting a little off track. But still doing great for eighty-nine."

"I don't know what I'll do without her," Fred said pensively. "It's like I miss her already."

Claire waved good-bye and waited until the car was out of sight before finally going back inside. Bay was still at the window and followed her to the kitchen.

"It's about a boy," Buster announced when they entered.

Claire looked at Bay, who had just washed her hands and was putting on clear plastic disposable gloves to funnel the hard candies into jars. "You told him?" Claire asked with surprise.

"She didn't have to," Buster said, shaking his head. "I always know when it's about a boy."

"You know that old man in the gray suit I saw a few days ago?" Bay said, changing the subject quickly. "I just saw him again when I was standing at the window."

9

"Mr. Zahler?"

There was a small tap at his door that night, and Russell's eyes flew open. He was lying on the bed in his room in the inn. Only a single bedside lamp was on, cutting through the soft, warm darkness like a moonbeam. It was one thirty in the morning. The digital radio that came with the room was playing something light and classical. He didn't know much about music. Most of his life, his ears had been stuffed with the tinny sounds of carnival rides. But this was nice. It had lulled him to sleep when he'd only meant to nap for a while before meeting Anne in the kitchen at midnight for food, as had become their custom.

He slowly rose, his joints popping. He took his old magician's robe from where he'd carefully laid it at the bottom of the bed and put it on to cover his old pajamas as he walked to the door.

Anne Ainsley was standing in the hallway, holding a plate that contained chicken salad, potato chips and a pickle. She had a cold, unopened can of beer in her other hand. "For when you get hungry," she said, handing him the plate and drink.

She wasn't upset that he'd stood her up for their midnight meeting. Hers was a life that accepted disappointment as inevitable. She was bored, and he entertained her. It was her curious streak that had led her up here with the plate she'd prepared for him, nothing more. She'd been drawn to his door to find out what was wrong. Perhaps she thought she might find him dead in his bed. That would certainly give her the excitement she was looking for. He wondered if she would mourn him, if that happened, if she would feel genuine sadness.

He wondered if anyone would, which was a new thought to him, and he took a moment to examine its weight and its edges. He didn't like this new thought, he decided, yet seemed incapable of tossing it away.

"Please, Anne, call me Russell," he said as he took the things from her. "I'm terribly sorry. I must have fallen asleep."

"You're tired. You've been doing a lot of walking lately," she said. "Listen, I'm sorry to remind you, but the original reservation for this room, the one I canceled for you, is through Friday. New guests are coming in that day for the room. They're regulars who come every year, so I can't cancel without my brother hearing about it from them."

"I understand," he said genially. "Truthfully, I wasn't planning to stay this long, but I found I enjoyed the company. I'll be gone by Friday, for sure."

"Where are you going?" she asked, leaning against the doorjamb.

All he wanted to do was go back to that soft, warm bed. But, don't bite the hand that feeds you, and all that jazz. "Florida. I spend my winters there every year."

She smiled. The lipstick she'd just applied was smeared on her yellow front teeth. "That sounds nice."

Nice wasn't what he would call it. "It's warm, at least."

"It was unusually hot for October around here before you came. I guess you brought the cold with you," she joked.

"That's not the first time someone has said that to me."

She laughed, then looked down the hall, afraid she might have woken the other guests, asleep in the night.

"Anne, you've made this old man more comfortable than he expected to be here. Your kindness has not gone unnoticed. Thank you," he said, politely telling her to go away.

"You're welcome, *Russell,*" she said, as he closed the door on her.

The fact that she'd been snooping in his room when he was out had not gone unnoticed, either, but he didn't mention that. He always kept a strand of hair draped over his folded clothes, a strand from a long, blond lock that one of the peep-show girls named Bountiful Belinda had given him. It was his way of telling if someone had been looking through his things. Anne had been meticulous about putting things back, except for the strand of hair.

And, of course, the Great Banditi flyer she'd taken.

He kept waiting for her to put it back, not because it was dangerous for her to know who he was, but because he only had those three flyers left. They were his only mementos of his carnival days, along with his deck of tarot cards, his hypnotizing crystal and his robe. He had his memories, of course, both good and bad, and he never forgot *anything,* his mind like a movie on a screen, constantly running. But it was nice to have things he could touch, too, things that reminded him that it had all been real. The line between real and story was a very, very thin one sometimes.

He walked back to his bed and sat on the edge. He put the plate on his lap and ate, enjoying each bite.

Five days, he thought with wonder. He'd been here five days.

Two days—in and out—was how it used to be. He'd been quicker back then, after he'd left the carnival. The stakes had been higher back then, too. He'd had bigger marks and there'd been more money involved, so leaving quickly had been a necessity. These days he was strictly small-time. He had fewer files, and they were worth less money, so the sense of urgency was almost gone. Food was his main motivating factor these days. Food, and a soft place to sleep.

Luck had been with him when he'd met skinny, sneaky Anne Ainsley. He hadn't realized how tired he'd been until he had this pillow-top, queen-sized bed to sleep in. The purple room was quiet and luxurious and he felt almost . . . dare he say it? *Safe* here.

Which meant he had to leave. Anyone who had ever worked the carnival circuit in his day knew that feeling safe meant sloppy, and sloppy led to bad things.

So he would get money from Claire Waverley, and be on his way.

Florida was waiting.

The campground where he spent his winters was called the Circus Tent, a place where retired circus performers who were down on their luck could stay for a few months at a time and get free meals and medical care. It had been founded by a former circus performer who had struck it rich later in life. It was for old circus and freak-show folks, mainly, but carnies were welcome, too. Only a few from Sir Walter Trott's group were left. Russell would see a barker or a mechanic from the old crew every once in a while down there, and they'd smile and nod at one another. They all knew what had happened to the original Banditi in that field in Arkansas. A lifetime of keeping tabs on people, stockpiling secrets until he could make a buck or two off them, and yet the one secret that could ruin *him* everyone else kept.

Sometimes it's difficult to tell what side of the moral compass we are all on. There are so many things to factor in.

No one knew what the original Banditi's real name had been. Rumor had it that he'd been there from the start, at the Chicago World's Fair. His skin had been as tough as leather and he'd had one glass eye, but he'd been oddly handsome in an exotic way. He'd been a big draw for the ladies, who had liked when he leaned in close to get secret clues about them, what they'd last eaten, what tiny initials were engraved on their lockets. He'd always given them just enough for them to believe he really was a seer, then he told them what they all wanted to hear: that their futures were filled with jewels and beautiful children.

Despite the attention, the Great Banditi's sexual preferences had run in an entirely different direction. His eye, his real eye, had always been on the young boys who helped assemble and disassemble the booths, the ones who cleaned the midway at night and picked pockets for the owner, Sir Walter Trott himself.

Russell had been one of those boys, left at the carnival by his mother the snake charmer, after she herself had been charmed by a local man with some money. No one had been surprised when she'd left Russell behind—he'd been a wild boy with a mean streak, and she hadn't been what anyone would have called nurturing—but everyone had been absolutely *stunned* that she'd left behind her beloved snake, an old albino python named Sweet Lou, who had slithered away a week later.

The Great Banditi had lured Russell into his trailer with kindness and taffy the night after his mother left and Russell had no place to sleep. Russell never dwelled on the details of that night. Or on the many details afterward. Almost ten years' worth.

But when Russell had been seventeen, he'd seen the Great Banditi, drunk in that field in Arkansas, and something had snapped. The aging magician was with one of the orphans they'd picked up in Mississippi, a pretty boy with tan skin and dark eyes and no idea what was coming. It was dark and quiet, the rides shut down for the night, and most of the boys were cleaning the midway and feasting on discarded popcorn and half-eaten candy apples, glad at least it wasn't them in that field that night. Russell had followed him into the field, for no reason he could ever explain.

When the Great Banditi had been found in the field in the morning, it looked like he'd gotten fall-down drunk and hit his head on a rock. The tan-skinned boy had run far away. Perhaps he was still running.

Everyone knew what had happened, but no one said a word. The original Banditi had been a horrible man, one who had cast a pall over the entire carnival, making it a bitter, fearful place to everyone on the inside. He raped and he stole and he cheated, and the owner could do nothing about it, because Banditi had something on him. What, no one would ever know.

Out of unspoken gratitude, Sir Walter Trott, a tiny man with very large ears, who said he'd been born in a logging camp in Oregon and that all his brothers were tall and strong and could fell trees with a single swipe of an ax, had offered Russell the position of the new Banditi. The original Banditi had taught Russell many tricks, after all, most he wished he'd never had to learn.

Russell Zahler had no heart, and very little conscience, but he'd never physically harmed another human being after that night. He was just a simple con man now, old and dreaming of soft beds as he stole from people who had enough to spare.

He was not the best person in the world, of course.

But, as anyone from Sir Walter Trott's Traveling Carnival could tell you, he was far from the worst.

Sydney's wayward receptionist, Violet, didn't show up at work the next morning at the salon. Sydney tried to call her several times, but got no answer.

Vexed because yet another teenager was taking the wrong path no matter how hard Sydney tried to steer her in the right direction, Sydney hurried through her last appointment and told Janey to close up, then she drove out to Violet's place before Sydney picked up her daughter. Part of Bay's punishment was no extra time between working at Claire's and coming home with Sydney in the evenings. No extra time to spend with Josh. And no phone to talk to him, either.

All day Sydney had felt dark and off-kilter. One of her clients today, Tracey Hagen, who had wanted a style to make her Tupperware sales go up, ended up with a style that made people too afraid to say no to her instead of charming them into buying. The end result was the same, but not exactly what she'd wanted. Sydney bought a sandwich keeper from her out of guilt.

The sun began to set as Sydney left the city limits.

There was a difference between provincial and rural, a fine line you don't even know you cross until you're on that road. And everyone knows that road, the one leading out of town into a deep green expanse of pastures and old farmhouses, which at first makes it seem like you're entering a fairy tale, something sweet and old-fashioned and lost in time. But, like all fairy tales, the beginning is always beautiful, a ruse to draw you into something you aren't anticipating. That long stretch of farmhouses turns into a barren landscape of trailer parks, rusting and decaying slowly from the rain and leaves in the gutters.

Sydney knew the area well, from long rides with Hunter John Matteson in high school, a daring sort of excursion to see just how far they would go, in more ways than one, before turning back.

She'd tried calling Hunter John today, too. There was part of her that was almost too proud to do it, because she knew his and his wife Emma's inevitable disappointment in Josh would mean they didn't think her daughter was good enough for their son. But if their parental intervention would nip this thing in the bud, then that's all that mattered. Her daughter's heart would stay a big, red, beautiful, joyful thing, full of love for someone who deserved her. She tried Hunter John's workplace first, then his home, where she was informed by the housekeeper that Hunter John and Emma were on an anniversary cruise.

Sydney felt both disappointed and relieved. Probably a little more relieved than disappointed. In the ten years she'd been back, she'd barely said a passing hello to either of them. That is, when they weren't completely ignoring her. She remembered vividly, one of the first weeks she'd been back in Bascom ten years ago, Hunter John confronting her and telling her that he loved his wife and wasn't leaving her. Apparently, the whole Matteson family had been in knots about it, thinking Sydney had returned to try to get him, and his money, back. It had amused her. As if you can do what he did to a Waverley heart and expect it to go unchanged.

The trailer park where Sydney's headstrong receptionist lived was appropriately called Wild West, with road names like Wyatt Earp Drive and Doc Holliday Court. She stopped at an old white trailer with a faded green and white awning over the front door. The yard was tidy enough, with some concrete gnomes and painted toadstools decorating it.

She went to the door and knocked. It was opened by an overweight, elderly man wearing only boxer shorts. The heat emanating from inside the trailer rushed out at Sydney, blowing at her like opening an oven door. It had to be ninety degrees in there.

The man looked Sydney up and down in her black tights and black heels, her short plaid trench coat, and her hair pulled up into a doughnut bun. "What do you want?" he asked over the blare of the television.

"Who is it?" a woman who was either seventy, or a very old-looking fifty, asked from her recliner.

"I'm here to see Violet," Sydney said. "She wasn't at work today."

"Violet!" the old man yelled.

A door off the living room opened. "What?" Violet said angrily, then saw Sydney standing in the doorway. "Oh. Come on in here," Violet said, hurriedly waving Sydney into her room.

Sydney crossed the living room.

"Sorry it's so hot in here. Roy and Florence like the furnace turned up," Violet said as she closed her bedroom door. The single window in the room was open and the cool air coming in clashed with the hot air from the heating vents, creating a swirling breeze that made the room feel like it was in motion. Violet was wearing only a tank top and shorts. "Charlie kept me up all night. Sorry I couldn't come in today."

"You should have called," Sydney said, going over to Charlie, who was sitting on the floor, playing with old plastic blocks. Sydney went to her knees in front of him. She put her hand to his forehead as he put a block to his mouth and looked up at her with those beautiful dark eyes. "Hey, baby. Are you sick?"

"He feels better now," Violet said quickly, as if maybe there had been nothing wrong in the first place.

Sydney looked around the small bedroom. There was a bare mattress on the floor, covered with an old Native American blanket. No furniture. Toys and clothes were scattered everywhere.

There was a set of matching blue luggage behind the door. It was the only thing in the room that looked like it had been treated with any sort of reverence. "What's with the luggage?" she asked.

"It's for when I leave. This isn't my home. I'm not treating it that way. This is temporary. It's always been temporary."

"It's not so bad," Sydney said. "You're just in a rut. Everyone gets in a rut. Ever thought of beauty school?"

Violet sat on the mattress and scooted back to the paneled wall to lean against it. "Maybe."

"I could help you out with a work-study program. And you could probably get a scholarship."

"Maybe. But if I do go to beauty school, it's going to be somewhere far away." She held up her bare, skinny arm so her hand could feel the cool air coming from the open window above her.

"Bascom is actually a pretty nice place."

"You left," Violet pointed out.

"I came back."

Violet shrugged, bringing her arm back down, her hand in a fist, as if she'd caught the cold air inside it like a bird. "Maybe I will, maybe I won't."

"When I left, it was just me. And that was fine. It was my time to learn, my mistakes to make. When I had Bay, everything changed. It was no longer all about me. I came back so she would have a stable place to grow up, where I had a support system."

"Charlie is a good baby," Violet said. "He won't give me any trouble."

"I know he's a good baby," Sydney said, smoothing down his thick, dark hair. "But the challenge is to raise him into a good boy, then a good man. You think you can do that when you don't have a place to live? What exactly do you think is going to happen once you leave this place? That you're going to find the perfect job, the perfect home, the perfect man?"

"Yes!" Violet said. "I *know* I will. Because I've already looked here. They're not here."

"Everything will be the same, no matter where you are, if *you* don't change first."

Violet scooted off the bed and walked around Sydney and picked Charlie up in front of her. "Am I fired?" she asked, putting him on her hip. He started fussing. "Because I need this job. I almost have enough to buy Roy's old Toyota."

Sydney stood. "No, you're not fired."

"Why are you so nice to me?" she asked, bouncing Charlie when he started to cry. Sydney resisted the urge to take him from her.

"Because I was you, once," Sydney said.

Violet snorted. "You have no idea what it's like to be me."

"Are you coming in to work tomorrow?" Sydney asked.

"Yeah, I'll be there."

With one last look at them, Sydney left the bedroom. The older couple in the living room watched her with suspicious eyes as she crossed in front of the televison toward the front door.

Once back in her Mini Cooper, Sydney sat in the cold, feeling frustrated because, no matter how hard she tried, she knew she couldn't catch someone who didn't know they were falling.

*   *   *

When Sydney arrived at the Waverley house, it was already dark. She hated these shorter days. She jogged
up the steps to the door, pulling her trench coat around
her in the chilly breeze. She was going to have to bring
out her heavier coats soon. She wondered if Violet had
a winter coat, or if Charlie had winter clothes.

Stop it, she told herself.

There was only so much she could control.

But that was just it. She was trying so hard because
she felt so *out* of control. Violet could have a baby at
the drop of the hat, and Sydney couldn't. How was that
fair? It had been so easy to get pregnant fifteen years
ago, something so unconsciously done that it had been
like waking up, something her body did naturally,
telling her it was time. Now it took such effort, such
energy.

Claire had warned Sydney about this. About her
attachment to Charlie. Sydney told her sister everything. Too much, probably, but Claire was always there,
always listened, always said the right thing, whether
Sydney wanted to believe her or not. Sometimes Sydney felt like she took too much from Claire. When
Claire called *her,* it was simply to ask how Sydney was
doing. Claire never asked for help, never seemed to
have problems she didn't already know how to fix. As
much as Sydney loved Claire, that could be pretty frus-
trating. It would be nice if, every once in a while,
Claire could have a problem, too. It wouldn't have to

be a big one. Just something small that would allow Sydney to show up triumphantly with a bottle of wine and say, "I know just what to do!"

Sydney reached the front door and tried to open it. It didn't budge. She got out her Waverley house key and tried to unlock it. It still wouldn't open. She tried the doorbell, but it didn't ring. Confused, she crossed the porch and looked in the sitting room to see Bay and Mariah watching television. The curtains closed on her suddenly, leaving her in darkness on the porch.

Oh. Now she understood.

Sydney went back to the door. She looked over her shoulder to make sure no one could hear, then she whispered, "I don't care if you're unhappy that I grounded her. I'll come back and paint you an ugly green color if you don't open right now," she said. She felt ridiculous, as she always did when she had to face this kind of Waverley stuff.

But the door opened.

The house had always been a little vain.

As soon as she walked in, she heard Tyler yell from upstairs, "I forgot. What was I supposed to do up here?"

Claire called from the kitchen, "Caulk around the attic vents!"

"Right, right," Tyler said.

Sydney went to the sitting room and said, "Ready to go?"

Bay nodded and stood.

"I'll be out in a minute," Sydney said, walking to the kitchen.

Claire was taking fried chicken out of a box Tyler had obviously brought home. She looked up from setting the pieces on a plate when Sydney came in.

"KFC? This is a new low," Sydney joked, walking over to her. "Start cooking again, *please*."

"I'm thinking about it."

"Really?" Sydney said, surprised. This was the first she'd heard of it. Everyone in the family had been trying to get her to start cooking again, and not just because they loved to eat. Well, that was most of it. But something about Waverley's Candies was turning Claire inward again, and that was never a good thing. Sometimes Sydney feared if Claire went inward too long, she might not ever come out again, like their grandmother, who'd hidden under the staircase when someone knocked on the front door, not wanting anyone in her house.

"Evanelle stopped by today and gave me a spatula. Maybe it's a sign." Claire shrugged, and Sydney knew that was that. Claire wasn't going to say any more.

Sydney turned and leaned against the counter. "How is Bay?"

"Why don't you ask her yourself?"

"I should. I *will*," Sydney said with resolve. "There are things I've never told her that I need to say. I just don't know how to say them."

Claire wiped her hands on a nearby towel. "Speaking of things we were never told, Evanelle told me today that Grandmother Mary's husband was named Karl." Claire walked into her small office attached to the kitchen and came back out and handed Sydney an old photo. "As in *this* Karl, from the photos we found on Saturday. How did we not know that?"

"We never asked, I guess. You can tell he's trouble. Look at that smile." Sydney looked closer at the black-and-white photo. "Mom had his chin."

"You do, too. Karl is the name on this kitchen journal we found, too," Claire said, holding it up. "The one all blacked out."

"Looks like you've stumbled upon a mystery."

Claire started to say something, then paused and looked at Sydney, tilting her head curiously. "Is your hair getting more red?"

She'd put her hair in a bun, hoping to make it less noticeable. "I swear I'm not doing it," she said, touching the bun. "Every morning I wake up and it gets worse. I'm going to try to dye it tomorrow. I can't wait for first frost. Everything will calm down again then."

Claire nodded. "Five more days."

"You seem to be faring pretty well," Sydney said. "No first frost trouble for you?" That was the thing about Claire, you never really knew for sure. You had to rely on her to tell you. Sometimes Sydney wished she could contain herself as well as her sister, so that everything didn't spill out. Then again, she knew the price her sister paid for those walls.

"Don't jinx it," Claire said.

"Don't go looking for it, either," Sydney said

pointedly, handing the photo back to her sister as she left the kitchen.

That next day at the salon, Violet still hadn't turned up as noon approached, which irritated the stylists because they had to take turns answering the phone and making appointments, which took forever, keeping their clients with wet hair dripping in sinks or in foils that needed to be checked.

"You said Violet would be in today," Janey said, as she checked out her client at the reception desk.

Sydney walked into the sunlit reception area where Bea McConnell was waiting on the white couch next to the windows. "You can go on back, Bea. I'll be with you in a minute," Sydney said to her. Then she turned to Janey. "I went to see her yesterday, to make sure everything was all right. She said she'd be here."

"She's trouble," Janey said, sitting back in the swivel chair at the reception desk. "My little sister was in school with her, before Violet dropped out. She was rough. She would steal. And not just other girls' boyfriends, although she did plenty of that."

"Those Turnbulls breed like bunnies and steal like magpies," Bea McConnell said. Sydney turned to see that Bea was still in the reception area, not wanting to miss out on this piece of gossip.

"She's only eighteen," Sydney said, guiding Bea to the back. "No one is set in stone at eighteen."

An hour later, Sydney was trimming Bea's newly touched up and highlighted hair when Violet walked in. It made Sydney feel triumphant, because it meant she'd been right about her.

"Violet," Sydney said, wanting to draw everyone's attention to her. "Would you mind changing out the coffeepot before you sit down? Where's Charlie today? At the babysitter's?"

"He's in the car. I'm not staying." Violet was wearing tight, dirty jeans and a sweater so big it fell off one shoulder, revealing her bra strap. She stood there and nervously chewed on a fingernail.

"Excuse me for a moment, Bea," Sydney said, palming her scissors and walking to the reception area. "What car?"

"I bought Roy's old Toyota. I told you. I just need a little more money. I told him I'd give the rest to him today."

"I don't understand." Sydney went to the window. "Is Charlie out there alone?"

Violet stood beside her and pointed. "I'm parked at the hydrant. I can see him from here. Can I have an advance on my paycheck?"

Janey was still at the reception desk, since her next appointment wasn't until three. She was listening with interest. "I can't do that, Violet," Sydney said.

"At least give me the money from the days I've worked."

"You got your check on Friday. You've only worked Saturday so far."

"Then give me that!"

Sydney paused for a moment, using silence the way

she did with her daughter, as a reset button. "What's going on?" Sydney finally asked her.

"I'm leaving. I'm tired of this place. I'm tired of everything. I'm tired of Roy and Florence. I wake up almost every night and Roy is watching me. It's creepy." Violet started chewing her nail again. "I'm not putting up with that shit. Not again."

Again? Sydney thought, feeling a shiver. "If it's that bad out there and you need a place to stay, you and Charlie can stay with me."

Janey, who had been taking a sip out of her water bottle, choked when Sydney said that.

"I'm not staying with you," Violet said, as if Sydney had suggested something farcical. "I know where you live. I'm not staying at a *dairy farm*. I want to be someplace where there are lights and *people*."

"So you're leaving town, just like that?" Sydney asked.

"If you give me my money, yes!"

"Does Charlie even have a car seat?"

Violet rolled her eyes. "Pay me for Saturday, plus my tip. Then I'll go. That's my money."

Sydney managed to look confused. "What tip?"

"Everyone here gets a tip. I always give myself one at the end of the day. From the cash register. It's only fair."

"Can I say good-bye to Charlie?" Sydney asked, hoping to take this outside. The entire salon was watching now.

But Violet wouldn't budge. "He's sleeping."

Without another word, Sydney gave Violet some money out of her hip apron and Violet left.

"She was stealing from you?" Janey asked.

"I don't want to talk about it," Sydney said, not turning to her. She didn't want to talk about the fact that she'd known for weeks now, but she'd been hoping that her persistence, her unfailing belief in Violet, would turn things around.

But Violet really was set in stone, deep down, where Sydney couldn't see. Sydney could only see the outer layer, which was young and malleable. And even that would harden with age.

As much as that upset her, the fact that Violet was taking Charlie hurt even more. Charlie, that sweet, innocent boy. Sydney stood at the window and watched Violet pull away from the curb in a beat-up gray Toyota Corolla.

And she felt an ache, a hollow, so large it brought tears to her eyes.

That evening, Sydney came home to a quiet house. She'd been hoping for a distraction: Henry in the kitchen burning corn cakes, which he would make at least once a month, because his grandfather used to; or Bay, ready to do battle over her grounding.

But there was nothing. The house was so quiet that the silence actually hummed.

Sydney walked to the staircase and called up to Bay, asking what she wanted for dinner. Claire had taken her home because Sydney had been slammed at work today, thanks to Violet. Bay called back flatly, "I ate at Claire's."

They hadn't talked much, or at all, since the dance Saturday. Bay seemed to be taking her grounding well, too well, as if her compliance was just another way of making Sydney feel like she was getting it all wrong.

Sydney walked into the kitchen. There was a small grease board by the refrigerator, so old that years of messages scribbled and erased still made faint impressions under the surface, like words deep underwater. Henry had written that he was still at the dairy, working late on some machinery that had broken down that day. Like Bay, he never used his phone. She was living with a couple of Luddites.

Still in her coat, her purse still over her shoulder, forgotten, she opened the refrigerator door and looked inside. She wasn't hungry.

She closed the door and reached for the kitchen phone.

"Am I interrupting?" she asked when Claire answered.

"No," Claire said. She always said no. "How was your day?"

"Horrible. Bay is in her room and Henry isn't home yet and I'm feeling . . ." *Barren,* she wanted to say.

"Have you talked to Bay?"

"No."

"Have you talked to Henry?"

"No."

"If you don't explain things to them, they're not going to understand," Claire said, even though Claire herself was never one to explain anything to anyone, sometimes not even Tyler. Tyler was so often lost in his own thoughts. But that was what Claire needed, someone to float around in her life, to tease her and make her look up and out of her own world. Sydney had always needed someone to settle her down, someone grounding. Henry.

"I know."

Sydney stared out the window above the kitchen sink, listening to the busyness of Claire's house. It sounded like Claire was in her kitchen, too. She thought she heard the rattle of some dishes, the spray of water. Mariah's laughter somewhere in the background. The sound of Tyler's footsteps.

"You know if you ever need me, I'm here for you, too," Sydney finally said.

"I know you are. I love you."

"Love you, too." Sydney hung up and went out the kitchen door to the back porch. She sat in one of the two old cane-back chairs there.

The back fields were so dark she couldn't tell where the fields stopped and the night sky began. It had been hard to get used to a world without streetlights, but she liked how it made her and Henry closer. They used to sit out here every evening when they were first married. Henry said his grandfather and grandmother used to do the same, which is why he'd kept the chairs. He said sometimes he could still see them here, see the way his grandmother used to drop her hand to her side and his grandfather would pick it up and hold it.

She wasn't sure how much time had passed, but her cheeks were starting to tingle from the chill when she heard Henry's footsteps in the kitchen. The kitchen door opened and he called, "Sydney?"

"Yes."

He stepped out and closed the door behind him.

"What are you doing out here?" he asked, taking a seat in the chair beside her. The rope seat creaked with the cold. He was still in his work clothes. She knew she should go in and fix him something to eat. He worked so hard. It was the least she could do. But she couldn't make herself move.

"I don't know," she said. "Thinking."

"What's wrong?" he asked, stuffing his hands into his barn coat.

"My receptionist Violet quit today. She's leaving town and taking Charlie with her. She's been stealing money from work."

He was silent, processing it, knowing all that she'd been trying to do for Violet, knowing how much Charlie meant to her. "I'm sorry," he finally said.

"I want to go back and be that age again, knowing everything I know now."

Henry shook his head. "Being young is overrated."

"I don't want Bay to make the mistakes I made," Sydney said. "Bay. Violet. I want to help *someone*."

"You can't fix things that aren't broken yet. You're only making yourself miserable. What's going on, really?" Henry asked. "Talk to me."

"It's been on my mind lately, why I can't . . . I mean, we've been trying for a while." Sydney stopped. Her eyes were suddenly blurry with tears. "I think it's my fault. I lived a hard life before I came back. I was with a hard man who did hard things to me." Henry knew about David, of course, but Sydney never mentioned him by name anymore, as if that might finally erase the memory of him. Yet somehow he was still there, like an accident she'd had long ago for which there would always be a scar. "Sometimes I wonder if that's the reason I can't have more children."

She heard, more than saw, him turn to her. "Is that what this has been about? The red hair and the visits to me in my office?" he asked. There was an undeniable relief in his voice, now that he understood. "*The kitchen floor?*"

"I want to give you a son." Her voice faded to almost nothing, just a thready hush. "You deserve a son. Maybe I don't deserve it, but I know you do."

"You gave me Bay," he said, without missing a beat. "I don't care if we can't have more children. I've never cared about that. Sydney, sweetheart, you've been holding on to this for too long. It's time to forgive yourself. It's long overdue."

Sydney nodded in the darkness, licking the tears where they were resting at the corners of her mouth. He was right, of course. There had always been a small part of her that didn't think she deserved the life she had with him, that she deserved to be happy.

Silence settled over them. Sydney realized, oddly, that her purse was still over her shoulder, like she was ready to leave instead of coming home.

Henry broke the quiet by saying, "This feels like a good time for one of my granddad stories."

Sydney gave a snort of laughter.

"I remember how devastated my granddad was when my grandmother passed away. He wouldn't get out of bed for weeks. When he finally did show up for breakfast one morning, he was so thin I could see right through him. He sat down at the kitchen table and said, 'Nothing will ever be the same because she isn't in the world anymore.'" Sydney turned to look at his silhouette. "That's how I know, how I've always known, that losing what you have is worse than getting anything new. You're my world, Sydney."

When she smiled, she felt the tightness of her tears, freezing on her skin.

She dropped her hand to the side of the chair and it dangled in the air between them. And, like it had been perfectly choreographed, Henry reached over and took it.

10

"So how do you know exactly where things belong?" Josh asked on the steps after school Wednesday afternoon. He was peeling an orange and a fine mist of citrus dusted the air around them.

She shrugged. "I just do."

"So if I point to a person, any person, you'd be able to tell me where they belong?" Josh pointed to a red-headed junior sitting on his trombone case on the side-walk, waiting for the late buses. "Tim Brown."

Bay laughed. "It doesn't work like that."

"Then how does it work?"

"I don't know. It just comes to me. I walked into my friend Kennedy's house for a play date in third grade, and her mother said Kennedy had to put away the laundry before we went to her room. While Kennedy argued with her mom, I just picked up the towels and went right to the linen closet upstairs. I knew where they belonged. That play date didn't last long," Bay said wryly. "With people, I can sometimes pinpoint where they're supposed to be or who they're supposed to be with. Sometimes it's a very clear picture in my head.

Dakota Olsen belongs at Princeton. I know it, just like that." Bay snapped her fingers. "But with Tim Brown, I can't see anything. It's easier to tell where people *don't* belong, because it's an uneasy feeling, like when you lose your balance and you're about to fall."

"That's pretty amazing," Josh said, setting the orange peel in a neat pile beside him on the step, then breaking the orange in two. He gave her half, which she took like he was giving her gold.

"I've been this way all my life. It's just who I am."

"Do you know where I'm supposed to be? What I'm supposed to do with my life?"

She took a moment to answer, wondering if that was why he was here with her again today. "No."

"I don't either. And you know what? It's nice to talk with someone who doesn't have a clear opinion about where I'm going to college or where I'm going to work when I graduate."

"I don't have the answers you're looking for." She'd had people befriend her before, wanting her to tell their futures, or whatever it was they thought she did, but they'd always walked away disappointed.

"That's okay," Josh said. "I think I need to find them out myself anyway. I envy you, you know. Your contentment."

She shook her head. "I'm not content."

"No?"

"I know where I belong, that's all."

"That's not content?" he asked.

"I guess it is. But, as my friend Phin pointed out,

I'm not the only one who lives in my world, and I can't convince everyone where they belong. I can't make people believe anything they don't want to believe. And that bothers me." She looked at the orange in her hands. "It shouldn't. But it does."

Josh seemed to mull that over, maybe thinking of her note. He finally nodded as he ate a section of orange. This felt so weird and intimate, *eating* with him.

"Did you tell Phin thanks for me?" Josh asked.

"Not yet. I only see him at the bus stop, and my mom has been taking me to school lately. Why are you thanking him?" She finished her half of the orange and wiped her hands on her jeans.

"Have you seen the video?"

"Not yet."

"You'll understand when you see it." The late buses began to pull in. "I guess you don't want a ride home?"

"No, thanks." She stood and grabbed her backpack.

"I won't be here tomorrow afternoon," Josh said, eating the last of his half of the orange, then picking up the peel he'd set beside him. "I have a student council meeting."

"That's okay," she said, winking against the sun now in her eyes. "I have to admit, I'm kind of confused why you're out here at all."

"I told you, I like talking to you. I don't know why I waited so long." He stood. "Do you want to come hang out at my house tonight? My parents aren't home, but our housekeeper, Joanne, is there."

Bay thought of how she had run through the woods

only last week, just to spend a few moments watching him with his friends. She would never fit in there like that. "I don't really know your friends that well."

"Oh, they won't be there tonight. That's why I asked. My parents call on Wednesday evenings. It puts their minds at ease when they don't hear a party going on in the background."

"Don't take this personally, but I don't belong at your house."

"Let's go out then," he said. "I mean, private. But not *private*. I can get some takeout and we can eat on the green downtown after dark."

Keep her a secret, he meant.

But the strangest thing was, she didn't mind. Because she wasn't the secret. The fact that he felt happy about something was. And, for whatever reason, Josh wasn't ready to let other people know it yet.

"Okay," she said, for purely selfish reasons, ones that concerned eating with Josh and talking after dark, which she considered a date, even if he didn't. Her breath quickened at the thought of something so simple, yet so incredibly wonderful. Eating and talking after dark. Maybe there would even be snow flurries tonight, like the image of how she first saw herself with him that would make things perfect, settled, real.

But then this simple, wonderful thing suddenly hit a snag. Because that's when she remembered she was grounded.

But just as quickly, she decided it didn't matter. *Rules* didn't matter, she found herself thinking.

Not when they were wrong.

Right?

It was cloudy and cool that night, with the moon behind the clouds. It was even darker and cooler on the ground behind Horace J. Orion's head on the green but, truthfully, Josh didn't feel it. He and Bay had on jackets and gloves and hats, and they were laughing too much to truly feel the chill.

Josh finished his sandwich and leaned back against Horace. Bay was sitting across from him, cross-legged, the coffee he'd brought her in her hands. He told her the story of the time he'd almost run away from home because his parents had let his older brother, Peyton, stay up to watch televison, but not Josh. Their housekeeper, Joanne, had caught him and had taken him back to his room before his parents ever knew. "I never tried again," he said. "Joanne had me convinced there was a camera on me at all times and I could never leave without her knowing. I showered in my shorts for months. I don't think I've ever told anyone that before."

"I'm glad," Bay said, laughing. "It's pretty embarrassing."

He watched her in the shadows. He knew she liked him. And he was certainly fascinated by her, to the point of fixation these days, but he wasn't sure his feelings ran romantic. Then again, he'd never felt that

way about anyone, so how would he really know? He'd
kissed girls before. And he'd almost gone all the way
with Trinity Kale in eleventh grade, before she'd
stopped them and said they should just be friends. He'd
agreed so quickly that he'd hurt her feelings. Sometimes he wondered if something was wrong with him.

What was he really doing out here? Did he really
think this sweet, odd, fifteen-year-old had all the answers? He wanted so much for it to be true. Even if it
wasn't true, Bay made him believe in the *possibility*
of it being true, which was more hope than he'd had in
a long time. She made him feel happy and safe and
excited. He'd even begun to look forward to spending
time on the steps with her at school. He'd driven by the
front of the school on his way home every day for
months now, specifically to see if she was really going to wait for him, like she said in her note. This was
something he was choosing to do, these were steps
he was taking on his own. It felt so strange. He didn't
trust it.

Josh stretched his leg out and tapped her foot with
his own. "So what are you going to do with your life,
Bay Waverley?"

"I'm going to end up at the Waverley house. That
much I know," she said, without hesitation. "I like decorating. Maybe I'll do something like that. I'll know
when I get to college."

"You did a great job at the dance," he said, suddenly
remembering the moment he saw her on the bleachers. She'd stood up in that dress, with those flowers in

her hair, looking like a dream he'd had when he was a boy, and all he could think of was getting out of there so he wouldn't have to face the fact that he couldn't live in that dream, that he'd never actually gotten anything he'd really wanted. And none of what he had was really his to keep, anyway. "You looked amazing that night. I should have told you. By the time I thought of it, you were covered in zombie blood."

She straightened her shoulders and gave him a proud look. "I thought I carried the look pretty well."

"Yes, you did." He stared at her a long time, so long that even she, who was a consummate starer, looked away.

"So how does this thing work?" he finally asked. "This belonging together?"

She laughed and scooted over next to him, to lean against Horace's head and look up at the cold night sky, like she was expecting something to fall. She had on a pink knit ear-flap hat, the strings from the flaps falling from either side to rest on her shoulders. "I don't expect you to kiss me or anything," she said, still looking up.

"No?"

She shook her head. "No. This thing between the two of us right now, how this feels, this talking and laughing, and sometimes the quiet, too? *That's* how it works. My aunt will call my mother and sometimes they'll just sit and not say a word to each other. That's how it works."

He felt unexpectedly emotional hearing that. It was

a relief. She was such a relief to him. Belonging, she seemed to be saying, shouldn't take so much work.

"Do you think it will snow tonight?" she asked, bringing her gaze back to him, and finding that their faces were unexpectedly near to each other. She smelled like cold air and roses. She'd told him she'd been making rose candy at her aunt's house that afternoon. When she'd gotten into his Pathfinder earlier that evening, it was like she'd brought the entire month of July with her.

Their faces were so close now they were almost touching. His eyes went to her lips.

And that's when his phone suddenly rang in his pocket.

They both jumped. Bay spilled her coffee on her jeans and she immediately stood up, trying to brush it off. He reached for the phone in his jacket pocket, confused when he saw the screen. "It's you. How did you do that?"

Bay stopped wiping at her legs. "Do what?"

He turned the ringing phone around and showed her the screen. It had BAY WAVERLEY on it. He chuckled. "You're calling me."

Bay suddenly felt around in all her pockets. "I must have dropped it outside when I . . ." she didn't finish her sentence.

"If it's not you, then who's calling me on your phone?"

"Wait—"

But it was too late. Josh answered. After a few seconds, he handed the phone to her.

"It's your mom."

"I'm sorry," Bay said as they sat on a bench on the green, side by side, looking straight ahead.

"It's okay."

"I mean *really* sorry," Bay said.

"It's partially my fault. I knew something was up when you met me at the road instead of in front of your house."

Bay looked at him in his scull cap and his North Face jacket, calmly waiting for the consequences. He had retreated back into misery, that slow burn curling off his skin again. His problem, she was gradually understanding, was that he was numb with indecision and fear. The only thing he could feel was miserable, until someone offered him an alternative, and then it was like giving him oxygen when he was suffocating.

They were just getting to the gist of this. Why did her mother have to call when she did? She was making this hard, when it didn't need to be hard.

Her mom was so bad at the grounding thing that she'd forgotten to ask Bay for her phone again. Bay had put it on vibrate and, after Josh had called to tell her he was on his way to pick her up with sandwiches and coffee, she'd put the phone in her pocket and crawled out her bedroom window. She met him at the road, telling him her dad went to bed early and she didn't want

Josh's car to wake him up. Which, to her credit, was true. But she must have dropped her phone when she'd climbed down the tree (which was harder to do than it sounded). Josh's number was the last one that had called her, so when her mother had found the phone under the tree when she'd discovered Bay missing, she'd hit redial and voilà! Here she was.

Bay watched sullenly as Henry's king cab truck circled the green and came to a stop. Henry got out wearing jeans, a T-shirt and his barn coat. Her mother got out wearing her red kimono robe. She hadn't even changed.

Bay covered her eyes with one hand, as if she could make them disappear.

They silently crossed the green toward them.

"Come over here with me, Josh," Henry said as they approached. "We have some things to discuss."

"Dad!" Bay said, outraged that they thought Josh had done anything wrong.

"It's okay, Bay," Josh said as he got up.

"You're overreacting," Bay said to her mother when Sydney came to a stop in front of her and just stood there, glaring at her.

"Do you have any idea how scared I was? I went to your room tonight *to call a truce.* I had two cups of tea and a box of Mallomars. I was going to put an end to this once and for all because we've both been miserable and we needed to talk it out. But I opened your bedroom door *and you weren't there.* Your window was wide open. I thought you'd been kidnapped!"

Oh, God. Mallomars. She'd brought Mallomars. Truce food, they always called it, because no one could argue over Mallomars. There wasn't anything her mother could have said that could have made Bay feel more guilty at that moment. She'd snuck out on the night her mother was going to call a truce. A truce. It sounded so good. She was tired of everything being so hard.

"I called your aunt Claire, asking if you were there. That's when she told me about this strange man you told her you'd seen on Pendland Street."

This was just getting worse. "He looked like a salesman," Bay tried to explain. "Just sly and fake, not dangerous."

"So you're saying I shouldn't have worried when I walked into my daughter's room and discovered she was missing?"

"I wasn't missing." She looked over to where Josh was standing with Henry. Henry was leaning in toward Josh, his arms folded over his chest. Both their heads were low. Henry was saying something Bay couldn't hear.

A van drove around the green and parked behind Henry's truck. Claire, Tyler and Mariah all got out. Claire was at least dressed. But Tyler and Mariah were in their pajamas, too.

"What are they doing here?" Bay moaned.

"I called Claire and told her where you were," Sydney said. "She was worried, too."

"Is Evanelle going to show up next?"

"Maybe."

"Bay! Hey!" Mariah said, running up to Bay. "What are we all doing here at night?"

"Sydney?" Claire said as she approached. "Sydney?"

Sydney finally turned her evil eye off of Bay.

"Did you leave the lights on in your salon?" Claire asked.

"No."

Claire pointed across the green to the White Door, where lights were shining, forming lemon-yellow squares on the dark sidewalk in front of the salon. "Then I think something's wrong."

"I didn't bring my keys with me," Sydney whispered as they all approached the salon cautiously, like a band of cat burglars really bad at their jobs.

"I don't think you'll need them," Henry said, trying the door and finding that it swung wide open. Henry had left Josh on the green with orders to stay there. And he did. Josh was sitting on the bench, watching their odd little family with an expression Sydney found curious. He didn't look embarrassed or amused or superior. He looked like he wanted, more than anything, to join them. She hadn't expected him to be so nice. She hadn't expected him to take his share of the blame, even though her daughter was clearly the one who had made all this happen. She hadn't expected to see what her daughter so evidently saw in him. Someone lost.

She hadn't wanted to like Josh Matteson.

After Henry had done a tour of the salon and hadn't found anyone there, the rest of them entered.

"Are you sure you didn't just forget to turn out the lights?" Tyler asked, which was such a Tyler thing to say. He forgot everything. He got lost going to work. He was on his fourteenth pair of reading glasses this year. And he was currently wearing two different shoes. Sometimes Sydney completely understood how he'd gotten past her sister's walls. He'd obviously gotten lost looking for a way in, and had stumbled onto a secret passageway. That was the only way to get to Claire, those secret passageways, the vulnerable places: family, acceptance, longevity.

"I was the last to leave," Sydney said. "Even if I forgot about the lights, I'd never leave the door unlocked."

"Who else has a key?" Henry asked.

That's when it hit her. Sydney went immediately to the reception desk and found the safe under the cash register open, and empty.

"You've been robbed," Claire said from behind her. "We should call the police."

"Oh, that's just great," Bay said, throwing her hands in the air. "Josh is going to think you're having him arrested!"

"I don't care what Josh thinks," Henry said. Bay wouldn't meet his eyes.

"We're not calling the police," Sydney said. "I know who it was, and she's long gone by now. Let's all just go home."

They filed out. Sydney closed the safe and followed

them. Before she turned out the lights, she looked over to her station.

Violet had taken the money, but left the bouncy swing.

When Sydney, Henry and Bay got home, Bay went immediately to her room.

"Go to bed," Sydney told Henry as they wearily climbed the stairs together. Parenting was tough. Maybe she was crazy to want to do it again. "Get what sleep you can. I'm going to talk to her."

"You don't need me in there?"

Sydney shook her head. "You did the boy stuff. I'll do the girl stuff."

"Good night," Henry said, kissing her. He walked down the hall, but then stopped at their bedroom door. "Was Tyler wearing two different shoes tonight?"

"Yes."

"I should have thought of that. I don't think we embarrassed Bay enough."

Sydney smiled as she opened Bay's door.

"It wasn't Josh's fault," Bay immediately said. She was sitting on her bed, hugging a pillow. "I didn't tell him I was grounded. We just talked. That's all we do."

Sydney walked over to her. The box of Mallomars and the two cups of tea, now cold, were on the bedside table where she'd left them earlier that night, when she'd discovered Bay missing. Her first thought had been that someone had taken her daughter and the panic had made the room pulse in time to her heartbeat. Until she'd found Bay's phone outside, it had never occurred to her that Bay would sneak out on her own. Bay never snuck around. She was too upfront. But Bay had entered the Matteson world before Sydney could stop her. *Upfront* wasn't in their vocabulary. "That's funny, because as of last Saturday he didn't even know who you were, according to you."

"We just started, you know, hanging out on Monday. I wrote him a note earlier this year, telling him if he ever wanted to talk, I would wait outside school in the afternoons."

"You wrote him a note?" *A note.* There was no time in your life when the power of a note was this strong, how writing down what you felt made it real somehow, how awaiting a reply felt glacial, like eons passing.

Bay tossed the pillow aside and slid down the bed, staring at the ceiling where she had taped old covers of tattered paperbacks she'd bought at a library sale years ago. She would read a book hundreds of times, carrying it with her until the pages were torn and the covers were falling off, then she'd paste the covers to the ceiling where she could stare at them, like remembering a good dream. "The first time I saw him, really saw him, was the first day of school, and I knew I belonged with him."

Of all the things she could have followed in Sydney's footsteps, it had to be this. "Oh, Bay."

"I don't know what's so wrong about it."

Sydney sat on the bed beside her. She took the pillow Bay had tossed aside and tucked it behind her back. She paused to compose her thoughts, then said, "I dated Josh's father in high school."

Bay immediately sat back up.

"Not just casual dating. We were inseparable, together for three years. I loved him more than I had ever loved anyone at the time. But I also loved what being with him meant, that I belonged to that group, that I was accepted. We talked about marriage. I would go on and on about the wedding and about living in the Matteson mansion."

"What happened?" Bay asked.

"He broke up with me on graduation day. Do you know what he said? He said, 'I thought you understood.' Matteson sons follow in their fathers' footsteps. They go into the family business. They marry girls from the right families. I wasn't one of those girls. That's why I left Bascom. He broke my heart, but more than that, he broke my dream of being normal. I figured, if normal wasn't here, I was going to find it somewhere else. But I never did."

"*That's* why you left?"

Sydney nodded.

"Why didn't you tell me?"

Sydney reached out and touched Bay's cheek, which was still red from the cold, making her look like a china doll with painted circles of blush. "I guess I thought that why I left was less important than why I came back."

Bay looked at Sydney as if seeing her for the first time through adult eyes. Bay was so close to that shore it almost brought tears to Sydney's eyes. She was too damn emotional these days. "There's so much I don't know about you," Bay said.

Sydney knew this day would come. She'd just been hoping to put it off for another few years. Say, twenty. She said with resignation, "Ask away."

Bay crossed her legs yoga-style and settled in. "Was Hunter John Matteson your first?"

"Yes. Next question."

"How old were you?"

"Older than you. Next question."

"What was your mother like?"

Sydney wasn't expecting that one. She thought about it and said, "I don't remember her very well. She left Bascom when she was eighteen, too. She came back for a while. She was nine months' pregnant with me and Claire was six. A few years later, she left again for good. She was a troubled person. Evanelle once said that it was because she ate an apple from the tree in the backyard and saw what the biggest event in her life would be. She saw how she would die in a horrible car pileup, and that's the reason she went so wild, like she was trying to make something even bigger happen, so it wouldn't come true."

"She ate an apple?" Bay grimaced involuntarily at the thought of it. "Waverleys never eat the apples!"

"I don't know if it's true, sweetheart. I've never put much stock in it. It's like a lot of things when it comes to our family. Rumor. Myth. I think she might have had mental problems. What I remember of her was manic, and when she wasn't manic, she was depressed. And Grandmother Mary tried her best with me and Claire, but she was a peculiar lady."

Bay started playing with the ends of her long hair, making tiny braids. "What was your mother's Waverley magic?"

"Claire and I have talked about it. We don't really know." Sydney shrugged.

"Is that *all* you remember of her?"

"I have one strange memory of her. It's funny, I don't think I've ever told anyone this," Sydney said with a laugh. "I was young, maybe three or four, and I was sitting in the grass somewhere, maybe the garden, sweating and crying because I'd fallen and scraped my elbow. My mother knelt in front of me, trying to tell me it was all right. That didn't work. The more attention I got, the more hysterical I became. I was a little . . . *dramatic* as a child."

Bay smiled, as if not much had changed.

"Anyway, I remember her saying to me, 'Watch this.' She opened her hand in front of me, but nothing was there. But then she blew on the palm of her hand and sparkles of ice flew into the air and landed on my face. It was so soft and cool." Sydney put her hand to her face, remembering. "I'll never know how she did that. It was the middle of summer. I was so startled I stopped crying."

Bay was transfixed, like Sydney was telling her a fairy tale. Which she supposed she was. The Waverley version. "Who is your father?"

"I don't know," Sydney said. "She never told me. Claire doesn't know who her father is, either. But we're fairly certain it's not the same man."

"What did Grandmother Mary think of you dating Hunter John Matteson?" Bay asked, dashing Sydney's hope that they wouldn't get back to that.

Sydney took a deep breath, trying to remember something she'd tried so hard to forget. She reached for the Mallomars. She took one and handed one to Bay. "She liked it. I think she was a little conceited when she was younger, and she liked to think of me marrying into the Matteson family as her coup. A little like how teaching Claire to be such a good cook was her coup. We are her legacies, for good or for bad."

"Josh is different," Bay said with absolute certainty.

Sydney looked her daughter in the eye, the serious look, the one that said *pay attention*. "I've always challenged you to explore more, to look outside of this Waverley legacy, because I never wanted you to limit yourself. But you've always challenged me right back. There's never been a time in which you weren't absolutely certain of who you were and where you belong. I never, ever want a boy to take that away from you. I don't want anyone to ever make you believe you're someone else, and then take it all back and say, 'I thought you understood.'"

"I can't make him feel what I feel for him. I know that," Bay said. "But I do know, without a doubt, that I'm meant to be in his life in some way. And he's meant to be in mine."

"If you're meant to be in his life, why is he sneaking around with you?" Sydney pointed out. "Why not just be open about it?"

Bay was silent, that stubborn tilt to her chin a familiar sight to Sydney. She always looked like that when someone disputed her sense.

"Bay, I can guarantee you one thing: Josh knows about me and his father. He knows, and he's doing this anyway. And while his parents are *away*."

"He's not like that," Bay said again.

"We'll see," Sydney said. "But no more sneaking around."

Sydney made a move to get off the bed, but Bay stopped her and said, "Will you stay with me for a while?"

Sydney smiled at her daughter, who had this amazing ability to turn from woman to child in a matter of seconds. She sat back and welcomed Bay into the crook of her arm.

And that's where they stayed, until late into Thursday morning, Bay having slept through her first classes and Sydney through her first appointment.

It was the phone that woke them up, Claire on the other end, hysterical.

The Waverley first frost woes, it seemed, had finally decided to pay Claire a visit.

11

It happened earlier that morning when Claire was in her kitchen office, taking a break from the stove to check her orders. Her mornings were usually spent alone. Buster and Bay came in the afternoons, then Tyler picked Mariah up from one of her dozens of after-school activities and brought her home in the evenings, and that's when everything became lively, the air becoming light, like it was dancing across her skin. But mornings, like this morning, were quiet, save the bubbling of syrup in the kitchen and those particular creaks and sighs old houses occasionally made, as if complaining about their bones.

The doorbell rang.

Claire turned in her desk chair, startled, when she heard it. The chime started out strong, but then faded, like a plug being pulled. Maybe the bell was broken. Or maybe the house was just reminding her to go back to the kitchen and watch the sugar pot boil before she burned the entire place down.

A knock followed the chime.

No, someone was there. A delivery, maybe? She wasn't expecting anything.

She got up and walked through the house to the front door, but it stuck when she tried to open it.

"Stop it," she told the house. "I'm not in the mood for this."

But it still wouldn't let her open it.

"Is everything all right in there?" a muffled voice called from the front porch.

"Yes, fine," Claire called to him. "I'll be with you in a moment."

Claire turned on her heel and walked back through the kitchen and left by the screen door on the back porch, which never stuck because it was a new addition.

She rounded the driveway to the front of the house. She was wearing her yoga pants and one of Tyler's old dress shirts, covered with her apron. She wished she would have grabbed a jacket because the morning was still chilly and slightly foggy, like the neighborhood was wrapped in wax paper.

The person at the front door turned when he heard her footsteps in the fallen tulip tree leaves. He crossed the porch and stood at the top of the steps and looked down at her.

It was the old man in the gray suit.

"Claire Waverley?" he asked in a voice as smooth as warm butter. "My name is Russell Zahler."

Claire tucked her hair behind her ears nervously, not taking her eyes off the man. It was *him*. The stranger, the specter who had haunted the edges of her life all week. "You've been outside my house for days," she said.

"It's a very nice house." He walked down the steps and stopped a few feet in front of her. He put his hands in his trouser pockets and looked at the house. It gave her time to study him, his closely cropped silver hair and his pale skin. His eyes were pale, too, a silvery gray like dimes. "You've done well for yourself."

"What do you want?" she asked.

He took a step away from her, as if to assure her. "I've scared you. I'm sorry. I didn't mean to do that. I had no idea how to approach you. I wasn't sure what to say."

"You were speaking to Patrice Sorrell and her sister Tara about me, weren't you?" she asked. "On Saturday afternoon, downtown."

He nodded. "I was just making sure I got the right person."

"The right person for what?"

He reached into his interior suit pocket and brought out a folded page that looked like it had been ripped from a magazine. "It's a long story, but it starts with this. I was waiting to see my doctor last month when I read this in a magazine."

He handed her the page, and she immediately recognized it. It was the article in *Southern Living* about her candy. She found herself smiling, because her initial thought amused her. Was this her first fan?

"I have this bad heart, you see. Oh, it's nothing

serious. I've got my pills for it. That's why I was at the doctor's office. My kids always make sure I go to my appointments. I saw this story about you, and I knew I recognized your name. When I looked you up on my granddaughter's computer, I found this, too."

He took another page out of his pocket, this one a photocopied interview Claire had given to a popular foodie blog called "Sweet Baby Mine," right after the *Southern Living* article hit the stands. She'd given a lot of interviews back then, giddy with it, before everything got so busy, so complicated.

He had not one but two features about her? Who was this person?

"I'm an old man now," Russell said. "Before I die, I had to set this straight. I had to come see you. You see this quote, right here? If you'll allow me," he said, taking the page of the blog interview back from her. "You say here, 'If I weren't a Waverley, then these candies wouldn't sell. Because what I'm selling is my name, my heritage. Waverley women are mysterious and magical women with a long and well-known history in the South. These candies are *their* candies, made from their secrets. Their blood flows through me. That's what makes the candy special. That's what makes *me* special.'"

Claire raised her brows at him when he finished reading.

"This article, you see, it's all wrong," he said.

"What do you mean?"

Another reach into his pocket. Another paper pulled out. This time a photograph. He handed it to her.

It was a photo from the 1970s of four people sitting in a curved booth the color of cinnamon. There was a full ashtray and a half-dozen beer bottles on the scarred table in front of them. Russell Zahler, forty years younger, was sitting next to a pretty young woman with light hair and a restless look in her eyes. He had his arm around her. A dark-haired man and woman were with them. The dark-haired woman was holding a toddler.

Claire felt light-headed. She walked to the porch steps and sat down. Russell Zahler followed at a respectful distance, lowering himself slowly to the step beside her.

Claire had precious few photos left of her mother. Sometimes she couldn't even remember clearly what she looked like. The sound of her voice was completely lost. This felt like a little piece of her coming back to her. She pointed to the light-haired woman in the photo, the one sitting next to Russell Zahler, sitting next to him like Claire was doing right now. "That's . . . that's my mother."

Russell Zahler nodded.

Claire used her finger to trace over the toddler the other woman in the photo was holding. It was Claire, scraggly brown hair and big brown eyes, in the arms of a stranger. She had her thumb in her mouth and was staring into space, going to that quiet place that used to soothe her, while the rest of them laughed as though there was nothing wrong with a child her age being around booze and cigarettes. Claire could barely remember that time in her life, but she remembered her quiet place. Her mother had never let anything bad happen to her, but there had always been that danger. Claire had always hated the danger. But her mother had lived on it.

"Lorelei and I dated, years ago," Russell said. "I was working in Shawnee, Oklahoma, just passing through. So was she. We were like meteors colliding. She was a wild one, that Lorelei. Not easy to forget."

Claire felt her fingertips go numb. Claire was born in Shawnee, Oklahoma. She had never said this to another living soul, not even her own sister, but Claire had dreamed about this happening most of her life. That must be why this man seemed so familiar to her, why she felt she knew him. This photograph explained why she smelled what she did when he was around, the smoke, the beer, her mother's lip gloss. Those few scents were ingrained in her memory of her mother. Claire had spent more time in bars the first few years of her life than she had for all the rest of her years combined as her mother had carted her around the country, restless as the wind, before Sydney was born, before Lorelei brought them to Bascom.

She turned to Russell and studied his face. Although probably in his eighties, which was twenty years older than her mother would have been, the years had been kind to him. But the folds of his skin made it hard to decipher his bone structure. Was there *anything* of him in her? she wondered.

She asked in a small, dry voice, "Are you my father?"

He shook his head. "No, honey. I'm not your father."

She gave a shaky nod, embarrassed for some reason, for letting that little bit of desperation out.

"And Lorelei Waverley isn't your mother, either," he added.

"Your real mother was named Barbie Peidpoint," Russell Zahler said from the other side of her office desk. The house still wouldn't let him in the front door, so Claire had led him around back and into her office. Distracted, she'd left the pot of slow-boiling sugar and water and corn syrup on the stove, and she'd served him coffee because that seemed like the polite thing to do. He'd come all this way, from Butte, Montana, he'd said. She thought maybe he was travel-weary, or slightly addled. She wondered if he had family or friends she could contact, because this story he was telling didn't make sense. He'd mentioned his children. How could she contact them?

"Barbie was a sickly woman," he continued. "You can see how skinny she was, holding you as a baby. She died about three years after that photo was taken. Something was wrong with her heart, apparently. Your dad there was Ingler Whiteman. We worked together for a while. He died, too, a couple of years later. Got hit by a train."

Claire shook her head and told him what she'd been telling him all along. "My mother was Lorelei Waverley, not this woman."

But Russell kept circling, very subtly but persistently bringing his point home. "I was surprised that you were here in this town," he said. "Lorelei always hated this place. Bascom, North Carolina. Too small. Too weird. She was always trying to escape herself, escape this *legacy,* as she called it, how all the women in her family had these talents no one could explain. I never thought she'd come back."

Claire conceded that he did seem to know a lot about her mother. But that didn't mean he was right. "She didn't come back. Well, she came back for a while. Then she left me and my sister here."

"She had wings that couldn't stop flying," Russell said.

"She died. A long time ago," she said, as gently as she could, thinking maybe he was hoping to find her.

"I know. I read it in the paper when it happened. That big pileup in Tennessee. It made national news. Lorelei Waverley," he said with a nostalgic sigh. "I hadn't thought of her since. Not until I read about you in that magazine. I recognized the name Waverley, and then the name of this town. That's when I realized *you* were Donna. That's your real name. You're the baby in that photograph."

The smell of sugar just before it burns, a sweet, smoky scent, filled the air. The pot she'd left on the stove. Claire wanted to go to it, but she couldn't seem to move out of her chair. "I admit that I don't have any photos of myself before I was six, so I can't say for sure. But the time line fits, and this does look like me. But just because this other woman is holding me doesn't mean she's my mother. You've gotten this all wrong."

"You can't deny the resemblance," he said, looking at her over his coffee cup as he took a sip. He'd never taken his silver eyes off of her, watching her every expression, her every tick.

Claire looked at the photo she was holding again. Yes, the woman had dark hair and eyes like Claire, and, yes, the man had a long nose like her. "It doesn't mean we're related," Claire said. "What would my mother be doing with another woman's child? She didn't even like children."

"They weren't model citizens, Barbie and Ingler. Maybe Lorelei thought she was saving you. Or maybe she just wanted something to steal. One night she was gone, and so were you. They looked for you for years before they died."

"You've obviously traveled a long way for nothing, Mr. Zahler."

"Oh, not for nothing, I assure you," Russell said, crossing his legs.

She held out the photo across the desk for him to take, but he didn't. She was beginning to get a bad feeling. He wasn't addled. She could see, too late, that he knew exactly what he was doing.

"You're getting national exposure. Your business is growing. Everyone I've talked to in town has mentioned your candy business, how things are only going to get bigger for you. But building something on reputation alone has its drawbacks. If the foundation is weak, everything falls down like a house of cards."

The air around her turned anxious and electric. The overhead light dimmed slightly, then brightened, like a power surge.

"Proof can be gotten," Russell said, brushing imaginary lint off his pant leg. "There's no doubt about that. I'm guessing your mother forged your birth certificate. It would be pretty easy to tell these days. And I've been asking people here about your family. Excuse me, I mean the Waverleys. You have a sister and a niece and an old cousin. They all have something about them that people talk about with awe. They are magic ones, aren't they? The ones Lorelei talked about. A quick DNA test would be able to tell you with certainty that you aren't related. But you don't have to do that, do you, Claire? You've always known. You aren't any more special than I am. Although I must say, we're both good at faking it."

It felt like she was falling, but there was no place to land. "What do you want?"

"You know what I want. Your financials are public record. I'll come back tomorrow for a cashier's check. I'm sure that will give you enough time." He stood and smiled at her, taking a small piece of paper from his pocket and setting it in front of her. On it was the amount he wanted. It wasn't an easy amount to part with—there went her summer profit—but she *could* afford it. "It doesn't have to be this hard, Claire. Cheer up. I could tell you all about your real mother and father, to give you more of a sense of who you are. Everyone needs to know who they really are, don't they? You said you don't have a photo of yourself before age six? Keep that one. I have copies. I have copies of everything."

She heard him leave by the back door. She could almost feel the floorboards under her tremble with tension.

She remembered the blog reporter for "Sweet Baby Mine" asking her, "If you didn't have Waverley blood in your veins, would this venture be as successful?"

And she had answered, without hesitation, "No."

Because if she wasn't a Waverley, then none of this was real, *she* wasn't real.

The burned sugar smell was getting stronger. She finally got up and went to the stove. The candy syrup had not yet burned all the way down, but it had turned dark brown, like toast.

She had to save the large pot. She had several, all rotated around the stoves in various candy-making stages, but they were expensive, so she removed the candy thermometer and took the pot to the sink, holding it by one side with a potholder. That's when she realized that she hadn't thought far enough ahead. She was left holding the pot, but had nothing to scrape out the burned syrup. It had to be done while the

mixture was still warm, or it would harden to the
pot like cement. She saw the spatula Evanelle had
given her, sitting on the kitchen windowsill, and she
smiled in relief, like someone had thrown her a rope
into a dark cavern.

Things weren't all bad. She'd saved the pot.

She scraped the syrup out and immediately got to
work on another batch of candy. She would focus on
Russell Zahler later. This had to be done first. It had
to be a sign that Evanelle's gift had been nearby. It
meant she should work. It meant, *Don't think about it
now*.

But everything she touched for the next hour
scalded, broke or gave the wrong measurements. A cup
of sugar poured out only a teaspoon. Stove dials turned
on the wrong burners. Her despair was filling the
kitchen, threading into everything she touched, making it wrong, off, singed.

She was losing it. *Losing it*.

She slid her back down the cabinets and sat on the
floor, close to tears.

What was she supposed to do now?

The answer came to her suddenly. It had been there
all along—ever since the Year Everything Changed—
waiting for her to finally realize it.

Call your sister. She almost heard the words out
loud, like steam hissing softly.

She wasn't alone. She had to stop acting like she
was.

She lifted herself up and went to the phone.

12

Claire paced the floor after she called Sydney, allowing herself now to go over everything Russell Zahler had said. It all made sense. Every insecurity she'd ever had about not being born here, about not being a real Waverley, rose like sweat on her skin, and she was now drenched with it. All the doors upstairs were opening and closing worriedly.

She was in the sitting room when she heard footsteps on the porch. She ran to the front door and opened it to find not only Sydney, but also Bay, Evanelle and Evanelle's companion Fred.

"I brought wine!" Sydney said, holding up the bottle as she walked in.

"And I'd just made this casserole when Sydney called us," Fred said as he breezed past her wearing oven mitts and carrying a foil-covered baking dish.

"He made way too much of it, like he knew we were going to need it," Evanelle said, handing Claire her portable oxygen tank and walking to the sitting room, giving Claire no choice but to follow. "I said to him, 'Why are you making all of that? It's just the two of us.' Then Sydney called about you needing us, and it made sense."

"What is all this?" Claire asked, confused. She'd expected her sister's somber face, and then a serious discussion about the possibility that Claire wasn't a Waverley and what that would mean. Somewhere along the way, Sydney would probably encourage Claire to call the police, then Russell Zahler would be taken into custody. They would discuss what they would say to the local paper when contacted for a piece they would write, which would probably have the headline LOCAL FOODIE FAKE. Tyler and Mariah would probably want to leave town for a couple of weeks, maybe to spend some time with his parents in Connecticut until this all blew over. Tyler would say to her, *I knew it all along. This magic was all in your head.*

"I called Evanelle," Sydney said. "I thought she should be here to celebrate."

"Celebrate?" Claire tried to remember what exactly she'd said to her sister on the phone. It was all a jumble of emotion, tumbling out before she could catch it. "Someone is trying to *blackmail* me."

"Oh, we know," Sydney said, putting the wine bottle on the coffee table and falling back onto the couch. She was wearing old jeans and one of Bay's T-shirts that read, EITHER YOU LIKE BACON, OR YOU'RE WRONG. Claire was gratified at least that she hadn't taken the time to get all dolled up, that she'd hurried right over. But still. "We're celebrating that you called for help.

Even though, in this case, you don't really need it. The fact is, you asked. No matter how hard we've tried over the years, we've *never* been able to get you to do that."

Bay came from the kitchen with plates and forks.

"What are you doing here?" Claire asked Bay, completely confused now. Had Bay been on the porch when she'd opened the door? She couldn't remember now. If she hadn't been, then what had Bay been doing in the kitchen? Claire looked at the clock on the mantle. It wasn't time for school to let out, not time for her shift to begin. "Why aren't you in school?"

"I overslept. This is better than school." Bay put the plates and forks on the coffee table. "What happened in the kitchen? It smells like you set a bouquet of roses on fire, then tried to put it out with sugar. It made me think of J—" Bay stopped herself from saying what Claire knew she was going to say. Josh. "It made me think of something I don't know how to fix."

"I was having a little trouble with the candy."

"You tried to work after he left?" Sydney asked. "Whatever you do, don't give what you made to anyone!"

"I threw it in the trash," Claire said.

"Good. Because the last time you made something when you were upset, we all cried at the slightest provocation for weeks."

Fred began to scoop the casserole with its creamy sauce onto the plates, as if Claire had asked them all over for tea.

After a few moments of silence, Claire reminded them, "A man just walked into my life and told me I wasn't a Waverley."

"That's nonsense," Sydney said, taking a plate from Fred. "Out of all of us, you are the *most* Waverley. This looks great, Fred."

"Thank you. It's hash browns and ham casserole. I've had the recipe for years."

"I'm not the most Waverley," Claire said. "Grandmother Mary taught me what I know, and it's not even half of what she could do. Now that I think about it, why didn't she wait for a Waverley trait to show in me? She just started teaching me. Recipes to memorize. Steps to take. Do you think she knew? Oh my God . . . Mariah." Claire suddenly felt sick. She sat down beside Sydney on the couch as Fred pushed a plate into her hands. "If this is true, then it explains so much."

Claire had watched Mariah all her life, waiting for her gift. While she was doing homework, Claire would wonder, *Is she better at it than anyone? Did the answers just appear to her on the paper?* When she would draw, Claire would watch to see if the image changed overnight. Did the tigers move around? Did they look fatter, as if they'd caught prey while no one was looking? Were the deer in the landscape painting in the sitting room missing? Grandmother Mary had once mentioned a great-aunt who could only draw the truth, which made her an in-demand, if terrible, portrait painter. People kept coming to her, knowing she could paint something beautiful, but only for people beautiful on the inside. But, while Mariah's drawings were pretty—her father was an artist, after all—they weren't magic.

As she got older, Claire held out hope that maybe Mariah's gift would present itself when she was a teenager, when everything dormant rose to the surface, like a pot of soup left to boil, all the ingredients sitting at the bottom until there was enough frenzy to roll them to the top.

Now she wasn't so sure.

"Stop it. You're being ridiculous," Sydney said. "Our mother didn't want children in the first place. Why would she steal one?"

"She was always trying to do something big, dangerous, drastic," Claire pointed out.

"Because she ate an apple?" Bay asked, obviously enjoying this as she forked mouthfuls of casserole into her mouth, not taking her eyes off the sisters.

"Yes," Claire said, at the same time Sydney said, "No."

"Wait, did she or didn't she?" Bay asked.

"We don't know if seeing how she would die made her the way she was," Sydney told her daughter. "We'll never know. I think it might be interesting to talk to this man, just to ask him some questions about Mom. We never even knew what her Waverley magic was. You said he's coming back tomorrow? Maybe I could meet him."

"No!" Claire said immediately. "No one is talking to him."

"Where is the photo he gave you? I want to see," Sydney said, making a give-it-here gesture with her hand.

Claire reached into her apron pocket and handed it to her. Sydney grabbed it and studied it in detail.

"Oh, look how young she was," Sydney said, passing it around like it was a baby photo.

"Evanelle, did Mom or Grandmother Mary ever say anything to you about me not being her real daughter?" Claire asked.

"This is the first I've heard of it," Evanelle said, passing the photo to Fred, who smiled and passed it to Bay, who secretly put it in her pocket. "She loved you, Claire. You were her own."

"But you don't sound surprised," Claire said. "Do you think it's true?"

Evanelle shrugged. "It could be true. But it doesn't matter. Of course you're a Waverley. It's in you, no matter where you came from. I tell Fred that all the time. He has my gift of anticipation. It's been in him all along. He just hasn't realized it yet. He's so fixated on me not dying, he can't see what's right in front of him."

Fred eyed her sadly as she said that. He took another bite of casserole before putting his plate down and reaching into his jacket pocket. "That reminds me, Sydney, I was sorting through some of Evanelle's things and I came across this. I thought you might need it." He handed Sydney a night-light, no bigger than a small flashlight. "When you turn it on at night, it reflects stars on the ceiling."

Sydney smiled indulgently. "Thank you, Fred. If ever I need stars on the ceiling, I'm all set."

"What did I tell you?" Evanelle said proudly, clicking her dentures. "He's just like me."

"I'm getting out of the candy business," Claire announced, more dramatically than she intended, but this was getting out of hand.

"Well, I'm glad for that. I miss our Sunday dinners. Remember those?" Sydney asked everyone. "We used to sit around like this for hours."

"I loved those Sunday dinners," Bay said.

"Speaking of food, this casserole is delicious," Sydney said.

"I'll email you the recipe," Fred said. "It's just hash browns, cubed ham, sour cream and Cheddar cheese. The secret is cream of chicken soup. My mother used to say that every good Southern casserole had cream of chicken soup in it."

With a clatter, Claire set her plate on the coffee table and stood. "Did you all happen to miss the fact that my livelihood is at stake, that my entire identity is being questioned?"

Sydney rolled her eyes. "Your identity isn't being questioned. What's yours is yours. No one can take that away from you. You can only give it away. Are you going to give it away to some stranger?" Sydney leaned over and took Claire's hand in hers. "Claire, listen to me. You're being conned. I know what that looks like. Why do you think this man has been asking around town about you and the family? He saw an article about you, recognized your name and the town, and remembered a photo he had of Mom that he could use. He mentioned your financials. That means he did his research. He found out all he could about you, which means he found your vulnerabilities. But he had *nothing,* until you believed him. Then you gave away your magic, just like that."

"No. It started happening before that. I stopped using flower essences from the garden in the candy, and no one noticed." Everyone but Bay, who had known all along, seemed vaguely surprised, but again, not like Claire expected. "I don't understand it, I don't understand how people can say they're still affected by what I do when it's not from the garden."

"That's because it's you, not the garden," Sydney said. "It's always been you."

Claire sat back down. She looked at each of them, one by one, then covered her face with her hand. She felt drained and abashed, like when you completely overreact to something—a spider, a misunderstood comment, someone walking up behind you.

"Tell this man to go, and he'll blow away like smoke," Sydney said. "You'd be surprised how much is bluster."

"How do you know all of this?" Bay asked her mother suspiciously.

"That's a story for when you're older," Sydney said.

"He said my birth certificate was probably forged. He said if I had to take a DNA test, it would prove I wasn't who I say I am."

Sydney, Bay, Evanelle and Fred all exchanged glances. And, well, yes, when Claire said it out loud, it did sound a little absurd. But he'd been so convincing. Magnetic. He'd known exactly what it would take to get her to buy what he'd been selling.

"Claire, don't take this the wrong way," Sydney said. "You make beautiful candy, but you didn't come over on the *Mayflower*. No one cares about your DNA."

Claire rubbed her forehead. "I was really scared," she admitted.

Sydney shook her head and looked at Claire fondly. "Then you should have asked for help sooner."

"Who would ever believe Claire wasn't a Waverley? That's ludicrous," Fred said, buckling himself up behind the wheel of his Buick and starting the car.

"No one," Evanelle said as he pulled away from the curb. She was holding the empty casserole dish in her lap like a pet. "But those girls are always trying to prove something, prove that they're worthy of the happiness their mother and grandmother didn't have, like being miserable is the only way to be a Waverley."

After a few minutes of driving, Fred adjusted the heat to the level he knew Evanelle liked, then said, "What did you mean when you said I had your gift of anticipation?"

"I meant just that. You've got my gift."

"I'm not a Waverley."

"Sure you are. You're one of us."

That made Fred smile.

"And being a Waverley means you have to find someone who loves you just as you are, like my husband did with me," Evanelle continued, not missing a chance to critique his love life, or lack thereof. Next to watching sci-fi movies, it was her favorite pastime. "I'm leaving you my house, you know. You'll have your own home and your own business. You'll be quite a catch."

Fred shook his head. It had taken him a long time to realize that the best relationship he'd ever had was with *her*. "I spent thirty years with James before he left me. I've known for a while that I wasn't going to do that again. Fall in love. I'm not good at it. I've been happier by myself, living with you, than I have in my entire life. That's the biggest gift you've ever given me."

She gave him a skeptical glance, one of her sagging eyebrows lifting. "Better than the mango splitter I gave you?"

"Better."

"Better than the colored pencils?"

"Better."

"Better than that tarp I gave you before the big snowstorm? The one you used to cover your car so all you had to do was take off the tarp and all the snow was gone and you didn't have to scrape your windows?" She laughed to herself. "Ha! That was a real handy gift, if I do say so myself."

"Nope. Even better than that. You're my best friend, Evanelle Franklin."

Ten years ago, after his breakup with James,

Evanelle had picked him up and brushed him off and had ultimately convinced him that, if he could choose to be like anyone, it would be Evanelle. He would choose to be the person who knew what you needed and gave it to you and didn't expect to be thanked. He would choose to be accepting and funny and he would take in old gay men when they had their hearts broken and would mend them with peals of laughter and long talks at the kitchen table.

"I don't think I've ever had a best friend before," Evanelle said thoughtfully.

"Me, either."

"Well, aren't we a pair?" she said, reaching over to knock his knee with her bony knuckles.

Fred drove home, feeling that awful sense that she was fading away, right before his eyes, and he had no power to stop it. He pulled into the driveway and cut the engine, then sat there as the car ticked as it cooled. He turned to Evanelle and said suddenly, "Don't leave me, okay?"

Evanelle just smiled, making no promises.

Then she got out of the car.

Evanelle walked to her bedroom and sat on the bed. Fred came in and exchanged her portable oxygen for her at-home oxygen.

"Thanks, BFF," she said to him, a term she'd learned from Mariah. Evanelle pronounced it *Biff*.

That made Fred smile. Then he left her alone for her nap.

Evanelle took off her shoes and rested her head on the pillow, all thoughtful now, her thoughts zipping back years and years.

She couldn't get her mind off her Mary, how it had all turned wrong, how all this Waverley unhappiness had started with her.

Mary and Evanelle had been only a few months apart in age. Being a Waverley female, growing up in that house, Mary had always had something magical about her. It was expected. But Evanelle's gift was, frankly, a surprise. She was from a distant line of Waverleys from across town, with no special talents to speak of, until the day young Evanelle gave the postman a stick of Blackjack chewing gum before his wife unexpectedly showed up to say hello to him at work. He'd told his wife he'd stopped smoking and the gum helped mask the tobacco odor. Then Evanelle gave a spool of dark thread to the preacher's wife a week before she tore her dress sneaking out the window to go dancing in Hickory.

Evanelle walked to the Waverley house on Pendland Street every day for years to see Mary. They grew up together, Evanelle always making the effort, and Mary slowly growing used to the fact that Evanelle would always be around. At one point, Mary even referred to the two of them as fig and pepper, which was what she always called any two opposite things that made perfect sense together. The truth was, Evanelle was Mary's only friend, because Mary was arrogant about her looks and her talent, and often treated others callously, but Evanelle was never one to get her feelings hurt easily. She'd learned that early on. You can't be a giver of sometimes unwanted presents and be sensitive about it.

Mary grew up to be as beautiful as Evanelle was plain, the kind of beautiful that made you stare too long, as if in disbelief. Women stayed clear of her, and told their husbands to do the same, though the women always came to her back door when they wanted something to make their parties special, to make them the envy of their friends, something made with marigold and dandelion and sometimes rose petals hidden in pats of butter. Mary was not only a beauty, she had a pretty Waverley gift, too, working with flowers and food. But if the women who wanted her goods were nasty, or spoke down to Mary, there was always a catch to what she gave them—a dish that was supposed to make other women at parties jealous also made them resentful, and the more they ate, the less they wanted to be friends; a dish that was supposed to make a husband more affectionate also made him unable to lie, so all past discretions would be revealed.

Mary's brothers all died in the war and Mary was left alone in the house. Her back-door business was small, eventually only the truly desperate showed up, so she took on boarders to make ends meet. Evanelle still walked to the Waverley house every day. After her husband left for work at the phone company, Evanelle would go help Mary clean and do the wash, generally keeping an eye on things and making sure none of the male boarders got fresh with Mary. She didn't have to worry. Mary's boarders fawned over her and couldn't do enough for her. They even attended those silly fairy picnics she liked to give, when she dressed up in flowing dresses, flowers in her hair, calling herself a garden nymph. Men treated her special, and she believed she was.

Until Karl came along.

The right men make all the difference in the world. But the wrong men do, too.

And Karl was very definitely the wrong kind.

He started out as one of Mary's boarders. They all loved her, those men she took in, but she just played with them. She knew she was exceptional. Prettier than most, and magic in the kitchen. In her glory days, women were all jealous, and men were all in love. But Karl was the one who got to her because he acted like she was nothing special. He never attended her picnics, never told her she was pretty. There's no better way to get a vain woman's attention than to ignore her. So she got rid of her boarders and she stopped cooking. It was only when her hair lost its luster and she served only cold meat and cheese for dinner that he finally said, "I guess I have to marry you. No other man would want you now." He started a handyman business. Oh, he was handy, all right. Handy with the ladies. The apple tree hated him. It threw apples over the fence at him all the time.

Evanelle would still visit every day, even though she knew Karl didn't like her.

Mary would always say, *Stay with me while I do this,* each time she decided to make him go. So Evanelle would stay while they fought and broke things and slammed doors. It always ended with Karl packing a suitcase and leaving and Mary crying herself to sleep. But, sure enough, when Evanelle would come the next day, Karl would be back, as if nothing had happened.

Eventually, Mary did get rid of him, but it took having a baby to do it. Evanelle knew that Mary was pregnant before Mary did. She woke up one morning with the overwhelming need to give Mary a baby bed, the dark wood one in her attic she'd been saving for when she and her husband got pregnant, which, as it turned out, they never would be.

She had her husband help her take it to Mary, and the look on Mary's face when she opened the door was one Evanelle would never forget. It was like she blamed Evanelle for it happening.

Evanelle sat while Mary told Karl. They argued about it, then he left with his suitcase like always. But he never came back. And Mary was never the same. He'd done a number on her heart. It takes a lot for a Waverley heart to grow back. And broken hearts cast long, dark shadows. Evanelle always thought that Mary's daughter, Lorelei, was sad and restless from the womb, because of Mary's heart.

Evanelle knew the old, reclusive Mary for much longer than the young, vivacious Mary. She seemed to turn old the moment she realized Karl wasn't coming back. Still, it was the young Mary who invariably came to mind when Evanelle thought of her cousin. Young Mary, her long hair sparkling in the sun, standing in the garden, her whole life ahead of her like a bowl of fresh berries waiting to be devoured.

Evanelle went to sleep that afternoon, lulled by the hum of her oxygen machine, thinking of how we always remember those we love when they're the happiest. She hoped that when her family thought of her, they would think of her at this moment, warm in her bed, clear air in her lungs, happy that she'd had this life, this strange, beautiful life full of strange gifts, given and received.

She wished she had told Mary that it could be like this. It would have saved everyone a whole lot of trouble. She wished she had known back then.

Known that happiness isn't a point in time you leave behind. It's what's ahead of you. Every single day.

13

"Claire?" Tyler asked, walking into her office late that night. She'd told him she'd be up to bed in a few minutes, but that had been three hours ago. She often worked late on Thursday nights. Fridays were the days she normally shipped her orders, so she liked to double-check everything. Buster had come in to work that afternoon, perplexed that there had been no candy in production. She'd instructed him to box and label the orders, then sent him off to the shipping store a day early in her van that still had WAVERLEY'S CATERING on the side of it. She'd never gotten around to changing the lettering. Or maybe she just hadn't wanted to.

When Buster had come back from mailing the orders, she'd told him he could take tomorrow off, that she had some personal matters to tend to.

"Personal?" Buster had asked, intrigued. "Do tell."

"Not a chance," Claire had answered.

"Fine. Have it your way." Buster had handed her the keys to her van and walked away with some packing peanuts stuck to the seat of his pants.

"Claire?" Tyler asked again.

She looked up at him from her chair at her computer. He was standing next to her now, wearing only his pajama bottoms, heat radiating from him in such a comforting way that she reached up and put her hand on his chest just to feel it. "Sorry. I must have lost track of time."

"I thought you were still working," he said, nodding to her dark computer screen. "But you're still thinking about that journal you found, aren't you?"

Among other things. There was no denying that she was holding the *Waverley Kitchen Journal* she'd found last weekend, having flipped through its blacked-out pages hundreds of times now. "There's so much she didn't tell me. This one may contain the most important thing—maybe it was about my mother, maybe it was about why Grandmother Mary never made her back-door business bigger—but she blacked it all out."

"Maybe she blacked it out because she didn't think it was important, ever thought of that?" Tyler kissed her, then walked away. He knew something was wrong, but he didn't press her. "Come to bed soon," he said.

She got up and walked to the opposite wall in her small office, where her bookshelves were. All her cookbooks were there. One shelf was dedicated entirely to Grandmother Mary's journals. The journals were all small and thin, more like hand-sized notebooks. And all the covers were black except for a few red ones Claire assumed Mary had bought when the store happened to be out of black. They were all numbered on the inside flap, so Claire knew the order they

were supposed to be in, a chronicle of her grandmother's life in recipes and gardening tips, and occasionally observances about the weather or on what Mary
happened to be wearing that day. She never wrote
about people, but Claire could glean certain big events
in Mary's life by what she wrote about cooking. For
instance, in journal number sixty-four, she began to
write about jelly and chocolate cake and poultices to
ease the itch of chicken pox, so Claire knew that was
around the time her two granddaughters had moved in.

Claire looked in the flap of the Karl journal. Number seventeen. She counted her way from the left on
the shelf and slid it in with the others. She ran her hand
along the thin spines. There were one hundred and ten.
Numbers three, nine, twenty-seven and sixty-one were
still missing—along with any others over one hundred
and ten—presumably still hidden around the house
somewhere.

Her hand went back to the Karl journal, wanting to
pull it out again and try to figure it out, but instead she
pulled out the journal next to it, the next one in chron-
ological order. Journal number eighteen, if she remembered correctly, contained simple recipes, nothing
from the flower garden, no tulips or violets or angelica,
just things anyone would have around the house. Claire
had always thought of it as Mary's back-to-the-basics
journal.

She opened the journal and there, on the very first
page, was the recipe for fig and pepper bread.

Claire smiled, because it made her think of her

sister. And Sydney's words earlier that day suddenly made sense. *It's you, not the garden.*

Food is just something you grow and recipes are just words written in notebooks.

They are nothing until the right person comes along.

And that's when the real magic happens.

Claire had been baking since before daylight that next morning. Dough was rising in bowls everywhere, and the more she baked, the more the loaves seemed to multiply on their own. Every time she opened the oven, she took out more than she'd put in. The air in the kitchen was flecked with flour and scented with yeast.

Claire was kneading roughly chopped figs into a mound of dough when she heard a tap at the back door telling her Russell had finally arrived.

"Come in," she said, shaping the dough into an oval and setting it on a baking sheet. Then she cut three straight lines into the top of the dough.

Russell opened the door slowly. He was wearing the same gray suit as yesterday. It was a little threadbare, she now realized. He looked around cautiously, to see if anyone else was there. He must be wondering, *Had Claire told anyone? Had she changed her mind?* This, she thought, was probably the hardest part of the game for him, the most dangerous. Now that she could view the situation more objectively, she was beginning to understand why her mother had associated with him, however briefly. Lorelei had always loved the wild ones, the ones who balanced themselves on moral cusps. It had made her feel alive.

"I was wondering," Claire said when he finally entered, "when you were asking about me around town, did anyone ever tell you about my grandmother?"

"Your grandmother?" Russell repeated. "No, not in detail."

"When you knew my mother, did she ever talk about her?" She put on oven mitts and leaned over to pull a baking sheet with two more loaves out of the oven.

He skirted the question by saying, "Now, Claire, Lorelei wasn't your mother."

Claire took the loaves off the baking sheet and set them on wire racks to cool with the others. "My grandmother Mary once sold a woman a bottle of her snapdragon oil, and the next day the woman found her family's lost emeralds, buried in a bean tin in their backyard," Claire said, as she slid off her oven mitts. "There are all sorts of stories like that about her. I'm actually surprised you haven't heard them."

"Smoke and mirrors," Russell said.

"Maybe in your world, but not mine."

Russell was confused, and Claire could tell he didn't like it. "Do you have my check or not?"

"Not yet," Claire said.

"Today. I said today."

Claire went to the knife block and slowly pulled out a bread knife. "First, you need to satisfy my curiosity about something." She took one of the cooled loaves of bread on the counter and cut a thick slice of it. "You read about my candy business, but did you ever actually taste the candy?"

"I don't have a sweet tooth," Russell replied.

"That doesn't surprise me. I'm thinking you could have saved us both a lot of trouble if you had." She put the slice of bread on a blue plate. She even put a pat of butter beside it. "Here, try this," she said, sliding the plate in front of him, where he was standing at the end of the kitchen island.

Russell's eyes briefly fell to the plate, then he focused back on Claire. "Thank you, but I'm not hungry," he said.

"Maybe I didn't make my terms clear. Try this, or we have nothing to discuss."

He didn't take his eyes off her, but his feelers were twitching. "You do realize that trying to poison me would just draw more attention to what you don't want anyone to know?"

"I'm not trying to poison you," Claire said with a laugh. "That's fig and pepper bread, made from staples I already had in the cabinets." She sliced off a piece from the same loaf and took a bite. The crust was hard, but the bread was moist, and the sharp spice of the pepper was a strange complement to the exotic sweetness of the fig. She chewed and swallowed, making a production of how good it was.

But Russell said, "I'm still not eating it."

Claire smiled. "What do you think this bread will do to you, Mr. Zahler? Change your mind? Make you forget? Make you ashamed? Because I'm capable of making all those things happen. That's how good I am. That's how well my grandmother taught me." She leaned forward and whispered, "Take a bite. I dare you." She could feel it tingling under her skin, her gift, her intent. It made her feel powerful and grounded. *Rooted.*

Russell shifted his weight, just slightly. "As I said, I'm not hungry."

Claire leaned back and shook her head. "I have to admit, the DNA test and forged birth certificate were nice touches," she said. "But I'm calling your bluff."

Russell stared at her with those silver eyes, waiting her out, but she simply stared back. He seemed to be using the silence to search for another angle. But suddenly, for whatever reason, Russell decided to break eye contact. He lost his bluster, and it was almost a physical transformation, making him a size too small for his suit. "I left you with too much time to think about it." He put his hands in his pockets and paced a few steps away. He paced back and said, "If I had demanded the money yesterday, you would have given it to me. I could tell. What happened?"

"I talked to my sister," Claire said simply. "You underestimate the power of family, Mr. Zahler. I almost did, too."

"But, Claire, as I said, Lorelei wasn't your—"

"Don't insult me again with that, Mr. Zahler."

Without another word, he turned and walked out. Maybe he decided she wasn't worth it. Maybe he was tired. Maybe he had bigger fish to fry somewhere else. How he ended up here, with the story of Lorelei, she would never know. His departure was so sudden, she thought of going after him. She wanted to ask questions about her mother, what he really knew about her, what relationship they really had. Small things that might make Lorelei more solid to her. But she didn't. In the end, she decided she could live with all she would never know about her mother and grandmother. She could live with not knowing what was in the Karl journal. The one true thing was that these women were a part of her life, a part of who she was.

And who she was, was a Waverley.

Anne Ainsley was washing the dishes from breakfast (her brother said an automatic dishwasher was out of the question for his fine china) when she thought she smelled something burning. She stopped and turned her head, making sure the oven was off. Earlier, she'd cracked the window over the sink to let out some of the hot air from breakfast preparations. She sniffed at the window a few times. It was coming from outside.

She left the dishes in the sink and opened the kitchen door.

Drying her hands on her jeans as she walked out, she looked around and saw smoke coming from her private alcove. Was the heat pump on fire? Oh, great, she thought. She'd lose her one private spot outside.

As she jogged closer, though, she realized that the

smoke was coming from the ground, where there were papers burning on the large metal lid from the garbage can. Russell was sitting in one of the chairs in her alcove, tossing papers onto the fire one by one, watching each of them burn.

He didn't acknowledge her as she sat in the chair opposite him.

She watched as he burned the magazine article about Claire Waverley and her candy business. Then copies of Claire's tax records. Anne's knee bounced anxiously, thinking she would have *loved* to have had a closer look at those. Next, he burned copies of death certificates for two people named Barbie Peidpoint and Ingler Whiteman.

Last, he tossed two identical photos onto the pile (but there had been three copies, Anne remembered, from the suitcase). At the last moment, he reached in and snatched one of the photos back. He shook the singed photo quickly, cooling it off. Then he put it in his interior jacket pocket, where thin tendrils of smoke escaped from his buttonholes.

Russell hadn't stayed long at breakfast, like he usually did. For a slender man in his eighties, he sure could put it away. But this morning he'd seemed in a hurry. He'd only taken coffee and a few slices of bacon. Then he'd disappeared. Anne thought at first, since this was checkout day, that he'd left without so much as a farewell. She'd even gone to his room to make sure.

But his suitcase had still been there, and she'd felt unaccountably relieved.

"What was all that?" Anne asked, after the flames had died down.

"A ritual of mine," Russell said, still staring at the smoldering ash. "I'm tying up loose ends before I go."

"Was that one of your files?" she asked, because by now he'd surely known she'd snooped. As good as she thought she was, not much escaped Russell's attention.

He didn't respond.

"The file on Lorelei Waverley?"

He finally nodded.

"What are you doing here, Russell?" Anne said, leaning forward. "I can't figure you out, and it's driving me crazy."

His eyes lifted to meet hers. Instead of answering, he said in his most polite voice, "You have my thanks for the most comfortable stay I've had in a while. Checkout is at eleven, correct?"

She sat back in her seat, disappointed. She'd spent the past few nights staring at the carnival flyer she'd taken from his suitcase, staring at the photo of him from when he was young. He'd been a handsome devil. She'd tried Googling Sir Walter Trott's Traveling Carnival and the Great Banditi, but nothing came up. What a life he must have lived. Her skin itched at the thought of all his secrets. She couldn't imagine the stories he could tell. The burning sausage and pepper stand. Catching the robber. That was just the tip of the iceberg. She couldn't believe he was leaving. Nothing, *nothing* was ever going to be this interesting.

But, then, disappointment was nothing new. She stood. "Take some water from the hose over there and make sure this is out before you leave. Andrew will have a fit if something gets damaged."

She caught a look of sadness on his face, like her leaving him triggered a sense of loss. He wanted her to be fascinated by him. He wanted her attention. But, stubborn as men were, he wouldn't tell her. She turned and walked away.

"I was here hoping to blackmail Claire Waverley," Russell suddenly called after her.

She turned back around and gave him a grunt. "I could have told you that wasn't going to end well."

He held his hands out, palms up. "My options are limited these days."

She walked back to him. He seemed smaller, frailer, sitting there as she stood over him. "What are you going to do now?"

"I told you. I'm going to Florida."

"How are you going to get there?" She glanced at his polished shoes with the holes in the soles.

"By bus."

"I have a car. I could take you," she said, the words out of her mouth before she realized she'd said them. But once they were out, she thought they sounded *wonderful,* like the first time you hear what will become your favorite song.

Russell shook his head. "I don't have a heart anymore, Anne."

"And I don't have expectations anymore. What?" she asked with a laugh. "You thought I wanted a love affair? You're old enough to be my father."

He clutched at his heart dramatically. "I'm wounded."

She scoffed as she sat back down. "Hardly."

He considered her for a moment. "If not a love affair, then what?"

"*I want stories,*" she said. "And I don't care if they're lies. I'm tired of picking around in other people's lives, making things up on my own. I want to hear everything you have to say. I've lived here all my life, and all the stories are the same. Every one of my husbands, the same story. But you've been everywhere, haven't you? I want to follow you where you go, and see what you do. I think you've been on your own for a while, haven't you? At some point, you're not going to make it on your own. I could be there for you. I'm a decent cook. I could take early retirement and get a little money in the mail every month. And there's over six thousand in the inn safe that my brother won't miss until he discovers I'm gone."

He hesitated for just a moment. Then he shook his head dismissively. It was ridiculous, but she was offended, offended that she wasn't deviant enough for him. "Too messy," he said. "He'd call the police."

"In case you haven't noticed by now, I'm nosy," Anne pointed out. "That's how I know my brother has flash drives full of video chats he's recorded, showing him having virtual sex with some woman in Finland who calls herself Karma-licious. He spends hundreds of dollars a month on her. I could take one of the flash drives and then leave one in the safe so he'll know I know. He won't call the police."

That tempted him. She could tell. Food. Money. Those were his weaknesses. He took a deep breath and exhaled with a long, drawn-out sigh. He stared into the smoldering ash of his failed attempt at cash. "Oh, Anne, it's not as glamorous as you think it is. You have a good life here. I'm going to a charity camp for retired circus workers."

"Do I look like someone who wants glamour? I think that sounds *fantastic*." She reached into her jeans pocket and brought out the flyer she'd taken from him. She unfolded it and showed him. "What do you say, Great Banditi?"

He studied the flyer, looking at the old photo as if through a telescope pointed back in time. "You can keep that, if you'd like. But on the condition that you remember me fondly. There are so few people who do."

"I find that hard to believe. Who could forget you?"

He smiled derisively. "Oh, many people remember me. But not *fondly*."

Anne pushed the flyer into his hands. "I'm not keeping it. I'm going with you. Meet me in front of the inn at five o'clock, after tea. All the new guests will be checked in by then. My brother won't know I'm gone until the morning."

She felt her nerves tingling and her stomach jumped with excitement as she walked away, even though

Russell called sadly after her, "It's been a pleasure, Anne."

"Checkout is at eleven, Mr. Zahler," Andrew Ainsley said, sitting at the front desk like a large, lazy sentinel.

"Thank you. I am aware. I'll be down shortly," Russell said as he walked up the staircase after making sure the ashes of his Lorelei Waverley file were cool. He reached his room and closed the door behind him. He'd left the curtains open and warm autumnal sunshine was covering the bed, making it glow. He wanted to lie down, to absorb the softness of the mattress one last time.

But he didn't. Instead, he sat on the edge of the bed and waited for sounds of other guests leaving for checkout. He would sneak out behind them and avoid Andrew Ainsley at the front desk.

He took the photo out of his pocket, wondering why he had saved it at the last minute. He certainly didn't like being reminded of his failures.

He was usually good at reading people, and he'd been almost certain Claire Waverley wouldn't tell anyone about his visit to her, that she wouldn't immediately call her family for support. Everything he'd learned about her had pointed to a singular, contained person who liked her mysterious air. She wasn't the kind of person who would risk others thinking there was nothing special about her.

He'd obviously pegged her wrong.

And then there was the moment she'd leaned in and

said, *Take a bite. I dare you.* He'd had such a clear image of Lorelei that it had startled him and he'd felt a cold chill go down his spine.

He hadn't expected that, either.

But in everything else, in every other detail, he had been meticulous. It should have gone so smoothly. He'd spent countless hours in libraries over the past few decades, when he couldn't find a place to stay in towns he'd drifted to. He would charm librarians into helping him search for information. Because of his time with the carnival, there were thin lines connecting him to so many people that, if the lines were visible, Russell's life would look like a string map. He stored away secrets and collected photographs, always on the lookout to add to the folders he'd amassed on people he'd once known. Stories formed this way. Angles.

He looked at the photo of himself, Lorelei, Ingler, Barbie and the child. It all made perfect sense, the story he told. Barbie and Ingler and their solemn little girl. Lorelei and her wild streak, stealing the baby away. Russell an innocent bystander, watching the drama unfurl forty years ago. Naming the child Donna had been a nice touch.

But that was all it was. A story.

The truth was, Russell had met the beautiful, tragic Lorelei at that bar in the photo the very night the photo had been taken. She'd waltzed in with her child, a daughter, Claire. No one told her to leave, to take the baby out of the bar. Lorelei could charm anyone. Russell had bought her a beer and invited her to sit with him and his new friends Ingler and his wife, Barbie. They were drifters, newly hired at the carnival as ticket takers. Barbie had wanted to hold the toddler Lorelei had on her hip, so Lorelei handed her over, and at that moment the bartender had taken a photo with the new camera he'd been showing off.

Later that evening, Russell had taken Lorelei back to his travel trailer. She'd smiled as she'd shown him the camera she'd stolen from the bartender. For the three weeks the carnival was in town, Lorelei had stayed with him, her quiet little girl sleeping in a corner. Russell often forgot she was there. He and Lorelei had fun. She was sly, with a sleight of hand that impressed even him. She was also beautiful and charming and could make everyone love her. She was just the kind of restless soul, the misfit, the society runaway that carnivals attracted. She could have stayed and fit right in. But Russell knew she wouldn't. At the time, she had been too young to realize you can't outrun your demons.

On the day the carnival broke camp and hit the road again, Lorelei disappeared with her silent daughter in tow. She stole a few hundred dollars from Russell, but left the camera for him.

In some ways, she had been no different from the many women he'd picked up to share time with in every town. But in other ways, she'd been wholly unique.

He remembered once, one night when they'd gotten drunk in his trailer, she'd told him the story of her strange North Carolina family and their apple tree and the vision she'd had when she'd eaten an apple. He remembered her reaching over and grabbing an apple he'd had on a small plastic table. She'd touched it, and a thread of white frost had snaked over the apple, eventually covering the entire thing. She'd then tossed the cold apple at him with a laugh. "Take a bite. I dare you."

And he remembered thinking, *Everything I make up is nothing compared to her reality.*

They'd woken up the next morning, hungover, and she'd never said another word about the incident. Sometimes he wondered if he'd dreamed the whole thing.

He heard some voices in the hallway, the shuffling of luggage. The couple in the room next to his were walking downstairs to check out.

Russell tucked away the photo, then picked up his suitcase and looked around the room, making sure he hadn't forgotten anything.

He thought of Anne Ainsley, and he really did hope she would think of him fondly. That was unusually important to him right now. For once in his life, maybe he would leave something good behind, a few conversations and stories she'd remember with a smile, the Autumn the Great Banditi Came to Visit.

He took out the folded carnival flyer she'd given back to him and he set it on the bed.

Then the Great Banditi did what he did best.

He vanished.

14

Before homeroom that Friday morning, Bay went to the main office in the rotunda to drop off a note from her mom, confirming that she knew Bay had missed school yesterday, that way Bay wouldn't have an unconfirmed absence in her file. No one liked going to the main office. It smelled like feet, and the secretary, Ms. Scatt, was unfriendly and put too much white concealer under her eyes and everyone was afraid to tell her how unnatural it looked.

Bay had just walked out of the office when she heard Phin call to her, "Hey, Bay!"

She looked down the hallway to see Phin at an open locker, his backpack at his feet. She walked over to him. She hadn't known his locker was on this floor. Then again, almost no one in school knew where their lockers were, which was why everyone had such heavy backpacks. In every building, the lockers on the left side were painted red, and the lockers on the right side were painted black—the school colors. But, over the years, the red lockers had faded to an unmanly pink, so none of the boys liked to have those lockers, and they traded with girls who didn't like the black lockers, and everyone eventually forgot where they were supposed to be.

"Hi, Phin," she said, enjoying the oddity of seeing him out of context. She almost never saw him in school. They didn't have any of the same classes or even share the same lunch period.

"You haven't been at the bus stop all week," he said, closing his locker, which was pink because he obviously couldn't get anyone to trade. "What's going on? There's some ridiculous rumor about you and Josh being caught on the green on Wednesday."

She leaned against the lockers beside him. "My mom grounded me because I caught a ride home with Josh the night of the dance. Then I went out with him without her permission on Wednesday."

Phin eyed her flatly. "With Josh Matteson."

"It's not what you think."

He shouldered his backpack, which was heavy enough to make him lose his balance a little. It probably weighed more than he did. "If he's leading you on, he'll have me to deal with."

That made Bay laugh. "Phin? Seriously?"

"Yes, seriously."

She sobered as she pushed herself away from the lockers. "I don't think that will be necessary. Apparently, he owes you a debt of gratitude. Something about a video of the fight at the Halloween dance."

"Have you seen it?" he asked.

"No. My mom has my phone, and now my laptop.

Because of Wednesday. What's on this mysterious video?"

"Nothing." Phin looked over her shoulder. Pink blotches appeared on his cheeks and neck.

Bay turned around to see Riva Alexander walking down the hall. She was one of those girls who looked good with weight on them, although she wouldn't know it until she was older. The scarf around her waist today had tiny bells on it that made a *ting, ting, ting* sound as she walked. Seniors generally kept to the senior building, where most of their classes were, so it was unusual to see her here.

Instead of walking by them, on her way to somewhere else, she stopped in front of Bay and Phin. "Hi, Phin. Am I interrupting something?"

"No," he said immediately, which made Bay smile.

"I saw the video. I just wanted to give you this," she said, handing him a folded piece of paper. "I wrote you a note."

"Uh, thanks," he said, taking it from her.

Riva walked away, head high.

"What was that all about?" Bay asked.

"I have no idea," Phin said. "Is it just me, or is everything getting weird around here?"

The warning bell rang for homeroom, and everyone scattered.

"It's not just you," Bay said with a smile as she backed away, then ran to homeroom before the final bell.

*   *   *

The first buses had just left and Bay was sitting on her familiar step in front of the school that afternoon, when she heard a car horn. She looked down to see her mother's Mini Cooper pull in front of the school.

So much for waiting to see if Josh would appear. She hadn't seen him since Wednesday, when her family had shown up en masse on the downtown green, which was enough to scare anyone, let alone a poor eighteen-year-old who had done nothing wrong. She had no way of contacting him and, short of going to hang out in the senior building, she didn't know how to talk to him at school, either. She'd only been in the senior building twice. Once on her first day of school, when she'd gotten lost and had seen Josh for the first time, then when she'd gone back to give him her note.

Bay trudged down the steps and got in her mother's car without a word. Her mother was wearing her hip apron, which meant they were going back to her salon.

"Claire said she wasn't working on candy today, so I thought I'd pick you up," Sydney said, pulling away from the curb, making someone honk at her for darting in front of them.

"Oh," Bay said, feeling a little guilty for acting so surly. "I thought this had something to do with Josh."

"We'll figure out Josh some other time," Sydney said.

"How is Aunt Claire?" Bay asked, thinking about yesterday and how seriously Claire had taken the question of her heritage. If someone had ever said to Bay that she wasn't a Waverley, she would have laughed.

She never would have taken it seriously. But that was because she'd never been left to figure things out on her own, with only a few clues to lead the way.

"She said she took care of it," Sydney said.

"What does that mean?"

"I'm not sure. But I trust her."

They passed the businesses and offices that shared the same thoroughfare as the high school, then Sydney took the highway loop that led downtown, which was quicker than cutting through the neighborhoods. Bay could close her eyes and still know where they were. She knew this place by heart.

"Did you mean what you said yesterday, that you wanted to meet that man just because he might be able to tell you more things about your mother?" Bay asked. "Even if they were bad things?"

"Yes," Sydney said. "She will always be a big mystery to me. But I think she's an even bigger mystery to Claire. I'd want to know, if just for Claire."

As Bay looked out the passenger side window, she said, "I'm sorry for the way I've been acting. I have you and Dad, and that's more than you and Claire ever had. I know you came back so I could grow up here, even though you didn't want to. You never left me, or let me believe I was anything but myself. I'll never have the doubts or questions you and Claire have. You've done a good job, you know that? You and Claire both. You've done a good job." Bay felt herself getting choked up, which embarrassed her.

"Wow," Sydney said, turning her head briefly to look at Bay. "Thank you."

"You're welcome."

"But you're still grounded."

Bay leaned her head back against the seat and smiled.

Once they got to the beauty salon, Bay manned the phones, figuring, since she'd lost her candy job with Claire, this was going to be her after-school employment until her mother found another receptionist.

She sat behind the desk and tried to read *Romeo and Juliet,* but the book was falling apart. She hated when this started to happen. She hated letting go. But it was time to put the cover of the book on her ceiling, and start something new.

She reached down and stuffed the book into her backpack. That's when she noticed the photo that the old man had tried to blackmail Aunt Claire with. Bay had kept it with her.

She took it out and studied it in detail, then she looked up and stared out the salon's window, mulling things over. The day was growing darker, sending shadows across the green. Horace J. Orion's head looked like he was about to take a long winter's nap.

It had been at this time of day when she'd first seen the old man standing on the green, a suitcase by his side, no form of transportation nearby.

A suitcase.

The next time she'd seen him, he'd been taking a stroll down Pendland Street.

There was an inn within walking distance of the Waverley house on Pendland Street.

He'd been staying at the Pendland Street Inn.

Bay immediately stood up and hurried to the door. "I'm going to stretch my legs," she called to her mother. "I'll be right back!"

Parked in front of the inn, Anne Ainsley sat and waited behind the wheel of her old Kia SUV, a relic from her last marriage, but at least it was paid off. It was well after five o'clock now. She'd almost been late because she'd forgotten that Halloween was tomorrow and Andrew had wanted her to buy candy, the expensive kind, so they'd have it for the trick-or-treaters that always came to the inn. Anne had raced to the nearest drugstore, bought the candy, and had arrived back with three minutes to spare.

But she'd been waiting in her car ever since.

Russell wasn't coming.

She leaned over to look up at her old family homeplace, and she knew she couldn't go back in. She'd packed all her clothing and her few belongings. Then she'd taken some things from the inn she thought they might need. A card table and folding chairs from the basement. Some of the good linens, pillows and towels. A digital radio. Some cookware. In addition to the cash from the safe, she'd also taken a few good pieces of her mother's jewelry, pearl necklaces and ruby earrings, to sell in case she needed to. Andrew kept them in a cigar box in his closet. He'd probably forgotten about them. The only reason he kept them was because he hadn't wanted Anne to have them.

She thought about Russell Zahler's suitcase and how little he carried with him. How little he needed. She wanted to be like that. She wanted a life not full of things, but stories, so many stories that, if they'd had weight and heft, they wouldn't have fit into a *thousand* suitcases.

With one last look at the inn, she started the engine.

She was about to put the car in gear when the passenger door suddenly flew open, and Russell Zahler got into the seat beside her, his suitcase on his lap.

"So you were going to leave without me?" He nodded. "I approve. It's much less pressure on me, not being the reason you're going. Next time, don't wait so long." He stared out the windshield.

Her mouth fell open. A test? Really? "You were watching?"

"I've been sitting in your alcove all day. I wanted to see if you'd really do it."

She stared at him, her mouth still agape.

He seemed to grow uncomfortable with her silence. "Okay, I left through the back door this morning, but then I sat down in one of your chairs and I couldn't make myself get up again." He paused. "I'm tired, Anne. I'm very, very tired."

"Maybe I don't want you to go with me now," she

said, a little put out with him. "Maybe I want to do this alone."

Russell straightened his shoulders, still staring straight ahead. "I'll give you a story a day, in exchange for a ride to Florida. A story a day, for meals, and care, if I ever need it. But I require a promise that you'll always remember them. If you remember the stories, you'll remember me the way I want to be remembered. That has become curiously important to me."

"What happens when you run out of stories?" Anne asked.

A corner of his mouth lifted. "That will never happen. Trust me."

So this was it, Anne thought. She was escaping her bubble and flying loose in the air.

"Put on your seat belt," Anne said, pulling away from the curb.

Immediately, she heard someone yell, "Wait! Wait!"

She and Russell both turned in their seats to look out the back windshield. Bay Waverley was running down the sidewalk toward them, waving her arms madly to get their attention.

Anne turned back and hit the gas.

"No," Russell said. "Wait. It's me she wants to see."

Anne braked. "She's going to get my brother's attention."

"It will just take a moment," he said, lifting his suitcase into the backseat, then reaching for the door handle.

* * *

When Bay caught sight of the old man getting into the SUV with his suitcase, she'd taken off into a full sprint, yelling for them to wait.

She'd gotten this close. She *couldn't* just let him go without some answers.

She kept yelling as she ran, but the SUV pulled away.

Bay slowed to a stop, the photo clutched in her hand.

Then, to her surprise, the vehicle suddenly stopped, and the old man got out. "We're in something of a hurry, child," he called to her in that smooth voice she remembered.

Bay ran up to him on the sidewalk. "Do you have any more photos of her?" Bay asked breathlessly, holding up the photo and pointing to Lorelei's image. "My name's Bay. I'm a Waverley. Lorelei was my grandmother."

"I know who you are," he said. "And, no. I just have a copy of that one. Nothing more."

"What did you know about her?" Bay asked quickly, gulping air. "Is there anything you could tell my mom or aunt Claire about their mother?"

He sighed impatiently, then looked up and squinted his silver eyes at the darkening sky. "I met Lorelei in a bar in Shawnee. I was working the carnival there. We had some fun. That was it. I only knew her for three weeks."

"But Claire is Lorelei's real daughter, isn't she? Lorelei didn't steal her."

He looked down and met her eyes. He let some

tension build, like it was a reflex. "As far as I know, yes, Claire is her real daughter."

Bay wanted to jump on that, to ask *why* he would lie about such a thing, why he decided to come to town and disrupt the lives of perfectly decent people. But a few day-early trick-or-treaters appeared down the street and Russell turned quickly at their voices. She sensed his unease. Her time with him was short, so she didn't linger on judgments.

"Then who are these people?" She pointed to the dark-haired couple in the photo.

"Friends of mine from the carnival. They had nothing to do with Lorelei, or Claire. That was just a moment captured in time. It was the only time they met, I believe. And that's all I can tell you," he said, making a move to get back into the SUV.

Bay leaned down to see who the driver was. It was Anne Ainsley, the sister of the owner of the inn. Strangely, that made sense. Bay had caught glimpses of her over the years, and it always struck her that this wispy, rail-thin woman who flitted around the Pendland Street Inn like a ghost didn't belong here. Anne belonged in the wind, not confined to a house.

"Wait!" Bay said before he could get back inside.

Russell turned, his hand on the car door. "What is it, child?" he said. "We really need to go."

Bay hesitated. "What was her Waverley magic?"

He didn't pretend not to understand. A strange look came over his face. "Lorelei Waverley was very fond of the cold."

Bay felt her shoulders drop. "That's not magic."

Russell smiled. "It is when you can touch an apple and cover it in frost in the middle of the hottest summer on record. She could have made a fortune on the carnival circuit. But she kept it to herself, for reasons she never told me." Russell lowered himself into the passenger seat and closed the door without another word. As Anne drove them away, Russell rolled down the window and called out blithely, "My sincerest of apologies for any trouble I may have caused."

After Russell left her house that morning, Claire was a cooking fool. She finished making fig and pepper bread, and started in on soup. Simmering soup on a cold day was like filling a house with cotton batting. The comforting scent of it plumped and muffled and cuddled. She went on to make egg custard tarts for dessert, longing for pansies to place on top to decorate them.

That night, Claire served the homemade vegetable soup, fig and pepper bread, and tarts to her slightly perplexed husband and daughter. She understood their confusion. It had been a long time since she'd spent the day cooking real food for them, let alone set the table in the small dining room, where they ate with real silverware and cloth napkins.

They should use the dining room more often, she decided. When Grandmother Mary died, Claire used her life insurance to remodel the kitchen, which ended up taking most of the dining room where Mary had once served her boarders. But it was just the right size now for the three of them.

"That was delicious, Claire," Tyler said at the end of the meal.

"Yeah, it was great!" Mariah agreed. "But don't use potatoes in the vegetable soup next time."

"Why not?" Claire asked.

"My best friend doesn't like them."

Good old Em. They couldn't get through a meal without Mariah mentioning something about her. "How did Em know we were having vegetable soup?" Claire asked as she stood to gather the empty dishes.

"I don't know." Mariah shrugged. "She just knew."

"Did you call her?"

That made Mariah laugh. "Why would I call her? She's right here."

Claire and Tyler exchanged glances. "What do you mean, she's right here?" Tyler asked.

"She's here. In this room with us."

"Why can't we see her?" Claire asked as the curtains fluttered slightly.

Mariah shrugged again.

"Can *you* see her?" Tyler asked.

"Sometimes. Mostly I can only hear her."

"So Em isn't a friend from school?" Tyler asked.

"No. She doesn't go to school. She says I should go to my room now, that you two need to talk. May I be excused?"

Claire nodded and they both watched Mariah shoot up the stairs, taking them two at a time.

"Em is imaginary!" Tyler said. He slapped the table and laughed. "You know what? I'm *relieved*. I thought I was missing something. I kept thinking to myself that if *you* had been taking her to school and picking her up, you would have known who Em was. You would have known her parents and what they did for a living and their favorite food."

Claire was still holding the empty dishes, still staring at the staircase. "She's a little old for imaginary friends, isn't she?"

Tyler got up to help her clear the table. "She's choosing her own path," he said, walking to the kitchen. "I look at her sometimes and can't *wait* to see what she becomes."

The curtains were still fluttering. A gust of air shot by Claire and up the stairs after Mariah. Then the curtains went still.

Together in the kitchen, they loaded the dishwasher. Tyler was rinsing the bowls before handing them to Claire, when she suddenly said, "I'm getting out of the candy business."

Tyler didn't miss a beat. "You finally decided to sell to Dickory Foods in Hickory?"

"No. I'm just ending it. It wouldn't be the same if someone else made it. It wouldn't be . . . Waverley."

"Okay," Tyler said amiably. He turned off the faucet and dried his hands. "Is that why you actually cooked tonight? Is this a preview of coming attractions?"

Claire closed the dishwasher with a firm click,

confused by this reaction. She'd tried to think of ways to tell him all day, fearing she was letting him down in some way. "That's it? What about what this means for our finances? It's going to take a while for me to get my catering business back to what it was. What about Mariah's college fund? I thought you were worried about it."

"I had no idea you'd taken those words to heart. Candy has been very good for her college fund, but we were doing fine with it before." He put his hands on her waist. "I know you haven't been happy with the candy business for a while. We'll manage."

"Was I that obvious?"

"You think I'm not paying attention when I'm staring into space?" he asked as he brought her closer.

"I know I worry too much."

"It's a tough job, but someone has to do it."

"Exactly!" she said, looking up at him. "Will you please tell that to my sister?"

"No way. She'll cut my hair into a mullet, like the last time she did when she got angry with me. I had bad luck for weeks after she did that. Three flat tires before my hair finally grew out."

Funny how easily he accepted Sydney's gift, but not her own. Tyler began to nuzzle her neck when she asked, "Have you ever believed I could do special things with food?"

"Of course I believe it. But there's so much more to you, Claire. Sometimes I think I'm the only one who can see *that*." He kissed her like he meant it, leaving her breathless against the cabinets. "I'll meet you up-stairs."

After tidying the kitchen, Claire walked upstairs and found Tyler in the hallway, lost in thought as he rearranged his paintings hanging there, a series he called "Claire's World," which he'd painted when they first married. She wasn't actually in the paintings, he wasn't a portrait painter, but they were beautiful stud-ies in light and color—leafy greens, black lines that looked like lettering, bright apple-red dots. If she stared at them long enough, sometimes she thought she could make out a figure, crouched among the greens. Claire wondered, not for the first time, what she did to deserve this man, her husband. She'd done everything in her power to dissuade his interest in her when they first met. She had been fine alone. She used to think that if she didn't let anyone in, she wouldn't get hurt when they left, because everyone she'd ever loved had left her. But, that was just it, she had no power over him. None of the Waverley kind, anyway. He loved her for every other reason but that one. And she still didn't know why.

She was just glad he did.

Tyler stayed awake long after his wife had gone to sleep. She was turned away from him in bed, her bare back lovely and smooth. He ran his finger down her spine and felt her shiver, goose bumps breaking out on her skin. He tucked the blankets around her, even as he kicked them off of himself.

Within the dynamics of their marriage, he knew he couldn't be the one who fell down the rabbit hole. His job was to stand at the top of the rabbit hole in order to lure the rabbit out.

But, secretly, yes, he knew all about the tricks this house played on him. And he knew Claire could do magical things with food. And, if forced to admit it, he knew damn well that apple tree threw apples at him. But his job was to let Waverleys be Waverleys. Not be a Waverley himself.

There were times, though, when he needed to jump down the hole. Times like tonight.

He rolled out of bed and put on his clothes. He walked out of the bedroom, got distracted by the paintings in the hallway again, and spent some time rearranging them. Then he went downstairs, where he got distracted by the tremendous amount of bread in the kitchen. Real food in the house again. That made him smile. Claire wasn't going to make candy anymore, for reasons he might never know. But it was remarkably clear that she was happier now that she'd made the decision. And that was all that mattered. Truthfully, it was going to be nice to leave the house not smelling like sugar and flowers anymore. The scent of his wife's candy-making followed him to work and filled his office, where it attracted dozens of hummingbirds that tapped at his office window every day, trying to get in.

Tyler took a slice of the fig and pepper bread, then he went outside to the garden.

Experience had taught him that getting too close to

the tree was not a good idea, even if it was dormant. He'd never trusted that thing. He opened the garden gate and stood at the threshold in the cold, eating the piece of bread, realizing he'd forgotten to put on shoes. He'd also forgotten to caulk around those vents in the attic, like Claire had asked him to do. He was about to turn to go back inside, when he remembered the reason he was out here in the first place.

"Listen, tree, you better bloom tonight," he said to it. "They've had enough."

Claire woke up on Halloween morning with a deep breath, as if floating out from under water. She didn't remember what she'd been dreaming of, only that it was cold and sweet. The sun was just rising, and she knew, knew before she even looked outside, that the first frost of the season had finally arrived. She got out of bed, careful not to disturb Tyler, sleeping on his stomach and probably dreaming of warm things like embers and cocoa. She pulled on her nightgown, which had been on the floor, then put on her slippers. As she left, she grabbed Tyler's blazer where it was hooked over the door.

She walked through the house, through the darkened kitchen, onto the back porch. Sure enough, icy stars were covering her van, and a fine layer of crystals made the bare honeysuckle vines covering the gate shimmer.

Her breath formed clouds in front of her as she hurried across the driveway to the garden gate. The neighborhood was quiet in that way only the cold could make it, as if freezing sounds before they hit the ground.

She fumbled for the key in the vines, her hands shaking. First frost was always exciting, but this year it meant even more, this season, this renewal. There was some small part of her that was almost afraid it wouldn't happen this year, that there was no more magic, that it was never really hers to begin with.

She slowly opened the gate, holding her breath.

There, at the back of the lot, the tree was in full bloom. Tiny white flowers had burst onto its branches, turning it from bare to lush overnight. The tree was shaking as if in celebration, and white petals floated to the ground in waves, making a sound like pouring sand. Already, the garden was covered in white, like snow. Claire walked in, her palms up, and caught some petals in her hand. She walked all the way across the garden, up to the tree, petals now sticking in her hair.

"Welcome back," she said.

"Mom?" she heard from the garden gate. Claire turned and saw her sleepy daughter had followed her. Mariah was standing at the gate in her nightgown, her hair a tangled mess of curls. She was Tyler made over.

Claire walked back to her and put an arm around her. She rubbed her shoulder to warm her.

"The tree finally bloomed," Mariah said.

"It did. Just in time."

Mariah smiled. "It's beautiful."

They watched the tree for a while, which it enjoyed. The blossoms began to accumulate on the ground. "I love you," Claire said softly to Mariah, putting her lips to her daughter's head and speaking into her hair, making her scalp warm. "You know that, don't you? For all the wonderful things you are, for all the wonderful things you're going to be."

"I know," Mariah said.

"Do you want to hang out with me in the kitchen today?" She now rested her cheek on her daughter's head. "I know you don't like cooking. But we could spend some time together."

Mariah pulled back. "I don't like cooking, but I love spending time with you! I just get in your way when you're making candy."

"Oh, baby. No, you don't. I was in my own way. It had nothing to do with you. Come on," Claire said, leading her out of the garden. "There's a first frost party to prepare for! We have to call everyone, too."

Tyler got up and started raking the footpaths in the garden, which had to be done every hour because the blossoms kept piling up. He would come in periodically for food and drink, blossoms covering his hair and jacket, and sometimes he'd have a small scratch on his face from when he'd gotten too close to the tree and it would reach out one of its limbs and hit him.

Bay showed up after Claire had called Sydney with a grocery list. Bay lugged in the bags and boxes of food and said her mom had dropped her off because she had a small errand to run, but that she'd be there soon to help out.

Buster arrived a short time later, looking groggy and confused.

"I never work on Saturdays. What is this?" he asked, looking around at all the food littering the countertops, where candy usually was. "Am I dreaming? I am, aren't I? I'm dreaming."

Claire had called him to help with the party preparations, but also because he deserved to know. "This is first frost," Claire said. "I'm quitting the candy business and focusing on my catering again. I thought you should know."

"It's about damn time," he said. "Who knew you could do all this?"

Claire smiled and looked around the kitchen. "My grandmother Mary."

15

Dear Josh,

I know we've never talked before, but you probably know who I am already. I'm Bay Waverley, the girl who knows where everything belongs. Nice title, huh? It makes me sound like a neat freak. Which I am, a little. But that's another story.

Anyway, have you ever had the feeling that you were waiting for something? I have. I feel that way all the time. I feel like I'm always waiting for things to fall into place, to fall where they belong, so I can finally take a deep breath. When I saw you in the hallway on the first day of school, I got that feeling. I don't know how, or why, but I know I belong with you in some way. I just wanted you to know. I'm not going to hang around you and demand your attention. I don't expect anything from you. But we spend all our lives looking for puzzle pieces that will give us a clearer picture of ourselves, of where we're supposed to go and who we're supposed to be. And I found you. I can't explain what a relief it is. Isn't it a relief? Out of everything uncertain in our lives, at least we know this. I'll be here for you if you ever need me. I'll be waiting outside on the school steps in the afternoons for as long as I can, if you want to talk.

　　Sincerely yours,
　　Bay

Josh had read the note so many times that the fold creases were getting thin and were about to tear. He was lying in his bedroom, which was still decorated in that pretentious way his mother had designed when he was younger: white clapboard bed frame, nautical blue-striped comforter, the large letter *J* above his bed. If it weren't for his messy computer desk and the soccer posters and trophies, it would look like something you'd see in a real estate listing.

You probably know who I am already.

Of course he already knew her. Josh had been given the "Don't Even Consider Her an Option" speech a long time ago. First from his mom, then from his dad, who didn't know his mom had already said something. So, yeah, he got it. Mattesons don't mix well with Waverleys. Like glue and ketchup, his dad, the king of bad similes, had said.

All his life he'd seen her around town, her hair as dark as storm clouds, always flowing behind her because she always seemed to be running. But he kept his distance, and Bay never seemed to notice him, not until her first day of high school. And then she had to blow everything out of the water with this note.

He'd told her more about his unhappiness than he'd ever told anyone. He couldn't believe he told her he went to bed at nine o'clock. But she didn't seem to mind. She was just so calm. Sitting next to her, the world kind of made more sense. Don't go to Notre Dame. Don't go into business with your father. Go to work at the soccer arena in Hickory if you want to. But don't define yourself by what you *don't* want to do. Define it by what you do want to do.

Was this why his parents didn't want him associating with a Waverley? Because they made you believe there really was a choice? Because they could bewitch you into thinking you could be happy?

He wished he could stay away. He knew that's what his parents would want him to do. But his parents weren't here. They were visiting Josh's brother Peyton at college, then they were going on an anniversary cruise. They were going to be gone for a whole month. They never would have left Josh's brother Peyton home alone. And proudly so. Peyton was rowdy and popular—not popular like Josh—*king-of-the-world* popular. If their parents had gone away for a month when Peyton had been in high school, Peyton would have thrown parties and broken into the liquor cabinet and gotten two hundred girls knocked up (his words). Their parents always called Josh the more responsible one. That irked him. It always had. His brother, who

was tall with their father's broad shoulders, once held
him down in the grass on their back lawn and kept
calling him "Mama's Pretty Boy." "Mama's Pretty Boy
does everything he's told. Mama's Pretty Boy should
be in a boy band, shouldn't you, Mama's Pretty Boy?"

Peyton had matured a lot since going off to college,
but they still weren't exactly friends. In fact, sometimes
it seemed Peyton knew exactly what he was doing
when, instead of going to Notre Dame like their grandfather, he went to Georgia Tech. And instead of studying business and taking over Matteson Enterprises like
their father wanted him to, he was going to law school
next year. He knew he didn't have to do it, because Josh
would.

It was all just assumed, and Josh had gone along
with it, until he'd interned at Matteson Enterprises over
the summer. He'd been miserable. The offices had no
windows. And, for the first time, it occurred to him
how crazy it was that they were constructing *entire
houses* inside a plant. It might have been different if
they built houses the traditional way, out in the sun.
But this was so . . . industrial. Everyone walked around
with their pale, industrial skin. He couldn't breathe.
The entire summer, he couldn't catch his breath.

There was a knock on his bedroom door. Josh hid
the note under his pillow as Joanne, their longtime
housekeeper, poked her head in. Her hair had turned
gray over the past few years, but it was still straight
and unmovable. Josh and Peyton used to think she
used furniture lacquer on it.

"There's someone at the front door for you," Joanne said.

"Who is it?"

Joanne wrinkled her nose. "A Waverley."

Josh got up quickly and ran past Joanne and down the staircase. He slid in his socks on the marble floor as he reached the front door and opened it.

Bay's mother was standing there.

She was wearing jeans and shearling-lined loafers that looked like slippers. Her hair was down and sparkled with odd red highlights in the cool morning sun.

"Mrs. Hopkins," Josh said.

"Call me Sydney," she said, not smiling.

He opened the door wider. "Come in."

"No, thank you." She took a step back and said, "Why don't you come out?"

Josh stepped out in his stocking feet, closing the door on Joanne, who was at the top of the staircase, frowning at him. "What are you doing here?"

Sydney put her hands into the pockets of her short plaid trench coat. "I don't know you, Josh. I don't know anything about you. I just know your dad and your mom from our high school days. And, I admit, what I think of them clouds what I think of you. Your dad hurt me in a way that I didn't need to be hurt. That's not going to happen to my daughter." She looked out over the wide front lawn, the grass still bright green and now free of leaves. The lawn management company had come by yesterday and cleared the whole neighborhood because today was Halloween and no one wanted trick-or-treaters falling in rich neighborhoods and suing people. Because how inconvenient would that be? "Bay doesn't fit into your world any more than I did. So don't even try to make that happen."

"I don't want to hurt Bay," Josh said, meaning it. He didn't. That had never been his intention.

"I believe that," she said, still looking out over the lawn. "I really do."

He found himself staring at Sydney, seeing so much of Bay in her. They had the same intense blue eyes, like something forged in flame. Sydney had seen more, though. Her eyes were narrower, more skeptical. Josh's mother had never liked Sydney. His mother was jealous of anyone who took any of his father's time or occupied any of his thoughts. His dad was her entire world. If she was in the middle of talking to Josh and his dad came home, she would stop midsentence and go to him, as if waves had swept her to sea. And his dad loved it, loved it the way his brother Peyton loved being king of the world. This was what men in his family did. They held court and they broke hearts and they didn't care. Bay was sweet and kind, and too young to be hurt in a way she would carry around with her years later, like her mother. She had her whole life ahead of her. An extraordinary life, he was sure of it. Josh had just been playing with the ideas she'd put in his head. He'd never really taken them seriously. Maybe he was a true Matteson, after all, with his selfish dalliances. There was no getting out of what he should do. He was eighteen now. It was time to man up, as his father would say.

"I won't see her again. I promise."

That made Sydney laugh. She turned to him and said, "Oh, don't be so melodramatic. Not seeing her again would just make everyone miserable. Including me and her father."

"I don't understand." Josh folded his arms over his chest in the chill. He was only wearing his practice shorts and a T-shirt.

"I can't make your decisions for you. And I can't make you or my daughter learn from my mistakes. What I can do is give you an option. There's another choice you can make. One your father never even considered. But you might."

"What choice is that?"

"Bay can't live in your world. But you can live in hers. If you decide you want to, then come to our first-frost party this afternoon in the Waverley garden. We're an odd family, but we're close. You're welcome to join us." She patted his shoulder. "Now, go inside before you freeze."

He watched her walk to her Mini Cooper. Before she got inside, Josh called, "Sydney? What made you decide to come out here?"

"There's not a lot I can fix for her anymore. Her Band-Aid and bedtime story days are almost over. This, I can fix with a simple *Welcome*."

She got in her car and drove away, and Josh found himself thinking, *Was it really that simple? Choosing a life?*

Maybe you don't have to be *led* into the future. Maybe you can pick your own path.

Maybe you don't *fall* in love. Maybe you jump.

Maybe, just maybe, it's all a *choice*.

Henry arrived at the Waverley house later that day and he and Tyler set up the large table and the mismatched chairs in the garden, far enough away from the tree that it couldn't knock them over.

Evanelle and Fred arrived as the afternoon wore on, and together they all took the food outside. Loaves of fig and pepper bread, of course. But there was also lasagna cooked in miniature pumpkins, and pumpkin-seed brittle. Roasted red pepper soup, and spiced caramel potato cakes. Corn muffins and brown sugar popcorn balls and a dozen cupcakes, each with a different frosting, because what was first frost without frosting? Pear beer and clove ginger ale in dark bottles sat in the icy beverage tub. They ate well into the afternoon, and the more they ate, the more food there seemed to be. Pretzel buns and cranberry cheese and walnuts appearing, just when they thought they'd tasted everything.

They laughed and talked about trivial things, because it was a relief to have the mood and the energy to talk about the small things now.

When night began to fall, trick-or-treaters gave the

Waverley house a wide berth, because who knew what candy Claire might give out? Something that would make the children embarrassingly honest, or something that would make them listen to their mothers? *No, thank you*, they all thought. Butterfingers and Snickers bars were much more preferable.

The family brought out lanterns and halogen heaters when it got dark, and put them all around the garden. They lit candles on the table, all while the apple tree shook and blossoms continued to fall. When the petals hit the flames of the candles, they hissed and popped into ash, leaving behind a scent that was so beautiful and sweet that it smelled like both yesterday and tomorrow.

Claire thought of all the raking she would have to do over the next few weeks, dragging large bags of apple blossoms to the curb every day, where they would inevitably be taken by women who thought if they bathed in the blossoms, their skin would glow; and men who thought if they stuffed their mattresses with the blossoms, they'd dream of money and fine sons and beautiful wives, all things men were supposed to want, but it really just made them dream of their mothers; and children who would build large white forts in their backyards with them and believe that they could live inside them forever and never grow up.

She was looking forward to the work. She'd missed this.

As things were winding down, they all grew tired of brushing blossoms off their hair and clothing, so they just sat there and let the petals accumulate on them, which the tree seemed to particularly delight in. After a while, they looked like they were frozen in time, covered in dust, like a cursed fairy-tale banquet, waiting for the prince to arrive and wake them up.

Tyler and Henry stood, grabbing beers and going off to the side to have one of their man enclaves. They shook the blossoms off their clothing as they walked, like patient parents or indulgent lovers who had held still and let themselves be decorated.

Evanelle kept checking her oxygen tank. She gave a look to Fred that it was almost time to go. Sydney kept glancing toward the garden gate, looking more and more disappointed until Bay finally asked her, "Who are you waiting for?"

Sydney put her arm around Bay and said, "Prince Charming, I thought. I was wrong."

And so first frost was almost at an end.

And Claire knew everything was going to be all right.

The lights of the candles flickered as the Waverley women talked at the table. The men watched from across the garden, watched in that way Bay envied, like they were rare birds. Somewhere on the street, children were laughing, their voices trailing on the wind like smoke.

"I have something to tell you," Bay said to her mom, the words suddenly bursting from her, seemingly without context.

Sydney stopped in the middle of saying something to Claire, and they both turned to Bay.

"That old man, I saw him yesterday afternoon," Bay admitted. She'd kept this secret for an entire day, but she had to let it out. And maybe if she admitted it now, she would feel that sense of letting go, the happiness that first frost was always supposed to bring. She hadn't felt it yet, and she'd been waiting all evening. Soon, they would all go home and first frost would be over and things were *always* set right by then. That's the way it worked. "I had an idea that he might be staying at the Pendland Street Inn, so I ran over there. He was leaving town with Anne Ainsley. I asked him about your mom."

"You *talked* to him?" Sydney asked. "Alone?"

"Just for a minute. He was in a hurry to leave. I asked and he said, as far as he knew, Claire *is* Lorelei's real daughter. Then I asked him about Lorelei's Waverley gift."

The sisters just stared at her, quiet now, and still, as still as stone.

"He said it was frost," Bay said. "He said she could turn things cold."

The barest of smiles reached Sydney's lips. But Claire looked confused. "Her Waverley gift was frost?" Claire repeated. "I don't understand. What does that mean?"

"I remember," Sydney said. "I don't remember much, but I remember that. The way she could blow flecks of ice off her hand in the middle of summer."

"Evanelle, did you know?' Claire asked.

Evanelle shook her head. Her entire body seemed swallowed by her big coat, like a heap of clothing sitting in the chair next to Bay. "Maybe it happened when she ate an apple. That tree always did love Lorelei."

Claire seemed bewildered. "Frost. That's pretty amazing, even for a Waverley."

Sydney looked at Bay and said, "You're grounded for another week."

"What?" Bay said, surprised. "Why?"

"Something I *know* I taught you. Don't talk to strangers."

Bay rolled her eyes and slouched into her seat. "Mom, I'm *fifteen*."

"Fifteen and grounded."

Evanelle chuckled. "I forget how much I like it here with you girls. I'm sure am going to miss this when I'm gone."

Fred suddenly got up, to stretch his legs he said, but they all knew he didn't like when Evanelle talked of dying. He walked over to Tyler and Henry.

A wave of melancholy hit them, until Mariah, who was by the tree making snow angels in the blossoms, suddenly laughed and said, "My best friend said don't be in such a hurry to leave, Evanelle. You still have things to do."

"We've recently discovered that Em isn't real," Claire explained to everyone.

Everyone at the table said, "Ahhh." Like it suddenly made sense.

"She is real," Mariah protested, seeming to be genuinely hurt by the statement. She stood and put her hands on her hips. "You just can't see her." The tree reached a limb down and fondly placed a crown wreath of blossoms on Mariah's head. Mariah didn't even seem to notice.

Bay, as she always did, took up for her cousin. "Tell us more about this Emily person," she said, waving her over.

"Who's Emily?" Mariah asked as she walked to the table.

"Isn't Em short for Emily?" Bay asked, putting her arm around Mariah. She loved this kid. No one was as good at being herself as Mariah, magic or no magic.

"No, her name is Mary," Mariah said. "I just call her M. Like the letter *M*. She says I'm named after her."

Everyone suddenly went quiet. The voices from the street even faded away.

"Grandmother Mary?" Claire finally asked. She looked over at Tyler, to see if he heard. He hadn't. "She's here?" Her voice had gone lower, as if wanting to keep this secret, this extraordinary new bond she shared with her daughter, just between them.

Mariah shrugged. "She said she's always been here."

Evanelle slapped her knee. "Nice one, Mary! You always could keep a secret."

Sydney leaned over and whispered to Claire, "And you were worried Mariah wasn't a Waverley."

"She says don't worry about the Karl journal,"

Mariah said. "All she wrote in it was how much she loved him, and when she didn't love him anymore, she crossed it out."

"Ask her to tell us which one of us is fig and which one is pepper," Sydney said to Claire, still whispering, elbowing her.

"Why don't you ask her?" Claire said to her sister, and they turned into bright, bickering little girls, right before Bay's eyes. "She's right here."

Sydney lifted her chin. "You're just afraid she's going to tell you that you're pepper."

"I'm *clearly* fig."

Bay smiled and decided that it was enough that everyone else was settled and happy. She could wait. This was enough.

"She's gone now," Mariah said. "She said there's someone at the gate."

Evanelle nodded as if this made sense. "Mary always did run and hide when there was company."

The tree suddenly began to sway its limbs back and forth, creating a huge breeze that blew out the candles. A great gust of blossoms flew across the garden as if in a blizzard.

Someone coughed at the garden gate and said, "Hello?"

Bay immediately stood, recognizing the voice. No, it couldn't be.

But there he was. Josh Matteson walked forward, looking around the garden in awe. He was wearing jeans and a sweatshirt and he was red with the cold, as if he had been standing outside for a while, working up enough nerve to come in. He looked beautiful here. Well, he looked beautiful everywhere, but he looked *right* here. There was no smoke curling off of him. Why had she never thought of this? Josh in the garden at first frost. It made perfect sense.

"It's even better than I imagined," Josh said, still coughing. "But I think I just swallowed a blossom."

Bay shot over to him like she'd been aimed and fired at him. She almost hugged him, but then stopped herself, partly for Josh's benefit, partly because the whole family was watching. She took his hands instead, drawing him closer to the table. "What are you doing here?" she asked happily.

"Your mother invited me."

"She did?" Henry asked from where the men were standing. As Bay and Josh got closer, Henry put out his arm and stopped him. "Whoa, son."

Josh stopped automatically. Bay gave her father an exasperated look.

"Men in this family, we learn quickly not to get too near the tree," Henry said with a smile. "You think the blossoms are bad? Wait until it has apples."

"Hear, hear," Tyler said, holding up his beer.

"Stay on this side," Henry told Josh. "It's the best side to be on."

Josh smiled and looked at Bay. "I think you're right."

Bay, in her T-shirt that read, MY LIFE IS BASED ON A TRUE STORY, looked up at the petals falling like snow and thought of her dream of Josh, how there were flurries around them in her dream, and it was just as she thought. She just had to wait.

"Definitely right."

16

Sydney let Josh take Bay home, and they were obviously taking the long way, because she and Henry made it back to the farmhouse before them. Henry had left the porch light on and they walked to the door in the cool darkness, their arms heavy with bags containing leftovers.

When they entered, they only made it as far as the couch before they collapsed, setting the bags on the floor beside them.

"We should put this food away," Sydney said.

"I'm so full I may never eat again," Henry groaned.

"You're going to have to. I can't eat all these leftovers alone." She grinned at him. "We could work off some of this tonight."

Neither of them moved. "You first," Henry said.

"Come here," she said, lifting a hand weakly.

"No, you come here."

"I'm too full. This may take a while. Who needs sleep?"

Henry laughed. "That reminds me of something my

granddad once told me. He said that when my father was a baby, he kept my granddad and grandmother up all night so many times that my granddad would fall asleep in the fields in the mornings. He said the cows would roll him into the barn and milk them-selves."

Sydney gave him a skeptical look. "The cows rolled him into the barn?"

"That's what he said. He'd wake up in the barn to find them milked and out in the fields again, as happy as, well, cows."

Sydney laughed, then snorted, which made Henry laugh, which made her laugh harder. She doubled over and slid off the couch to the floor. Henry went down with her.

They sprawled out side by side on their backs and their laughter subsided. Sydney was lying on something hard, so she reached under her and real-ized she still had the small night-light Fred had given her in her coat pocket.

She turned it on, and a circle of blue stars reflected on the ceiling.

"Where did you get that?" Henry asked, scooting his head closer to hers as they stared at the ceiling.

"Fred gave it to me."

"Why?" Henry asked.

"I have no idea," she said, the moment the doorbell rang. She sat up. "Did you lock the door? Bay must have forgotten her key."

"Maybe it's late trick-or-treaters," Henry said.

"I don't have any candy. Wait, maybe I have some gum."

"Gum will get the house egged for sure." Henry stood and held out his hand to help Sydney stand. "I'll take these to the kitchen," he said, picking up the bags as Sydney went to the door and opened it, smiling as she put the night-light back in her pocket.

But it wasn't Bay, or a trick-or-treater. At least, not the obvious kind.

Violet Turnbull was standing there in the glow of the porch light. Baby Charlie was asleep on her hip.

"Can I come in?" Violet asked. Despite the cold, she was wearing cut-off shorts with cowboy boots. The sweater she'd put on seemed like an afterthought. Charlie, at least, was wearing a flannel onesie.

Speechless, Sydney stepped back and let Violet enter.

"I'm sorry about breaking into the salon," Violet said. She looked around the living room, swaying back and forth jerkily, like nerves rather than trying to soothe Charlie. "Although, technically, it wasn't really breaking in, because I had a key."

"Are you here to return the money?" Sydney asked levelly, putting her hands in her coat pockets to hide how clenched they were.

"I already spent it. I told you, I needed the money to buy the Toyota."

"Then are you here to return the key?"

"I lost the key. You changed the lock, anyway," Violet said, not meeting her eyes.

That raised warning flags she'd always ignored before when it came to Violet. "And how do you know
that? Did you go back and try again?"

Violet disregarded the question, because they both
knew the answer. "I'm leaving tonight. I needed some
money to travel with."

Sydney sighed. "I'll give you what I have on me. It's
not much."

"I'm not here for money," Violet said as Sydney
turned to get her purse. "The heater doesn't work in
the Toyota, and Charlie and I were both cold."

Sydney hesitated. Was she really going to turn them
away? Of course not. "You can stay here for the night.
We'll figure something out."

"You're not listening to me!" Violet said, raising
her voice. Sydney's eyes went immediately to Charlie,
who frowned in his sleep. "It doesn't matter that the
heater doesn't work. I'm going south, where it's warm.
Charlie doesn't have a winter coat, but I figured he
didn't need one if we went somewhere warm. But he's
growing out of his clothes, and I realized I'd have to
buy more when we got there anyway. And I don't
have the money."

"But you just said you're not here for money."

Violet's face twisted in anger. No, not anger.
Anguish. Her eyes filled with tears.

"Just take him," she said, handing over the sleeping
baby.

"What?" Sydney's hands shot out of her coat pockets, dropping Fred's night-light to the floor as she took Charlie. Violet gave her no choice. It was either take him or let him fall.

Violet set the plastic tote bag she was carrying on the floor. "Some of his favorite toys are in there. The clothes that still fit him are there, too. And his birth certificate. I put some photos of me and him in there, so he doesn't forget what I look like. And I wrote a letter." Violet lifted the hem of her sweater and wiped her nose on it. "When I was nine, my mom left me with her friend Karen for almost a whole year when she went off with her boyfriend. I broke my arm, and Karen had a lot of trouble with DSS, because my mom, like, didn't leave any kind of instructions about custody and stuff. So that's in there. I want to be happy. And I want him to be happy, too. But we can't do it at the same time, you know? You probably think I'm the worst mother in the world."

Sydney shook her head. Motherhood, true motherhood, was what went on when no one else could see. How could she judge her when she didn't know the whole story?

"Leave a night-light on for him when he sleeps, okay? He doesn't like the dark."

Violet kissed his head, hiccuping with tears, then hurried out the door.

Sydney turned to find Henry standing in the doorway to the kitchen behind her, looking as stunned as she was.

* * *

There was frost on the ground Monday morning as Bay walked down the driveway to the bus stop. Phin was already there, his hands stuffed into his yellow hoodie, a black knit cap on his head.

He grinned when he saw her. "Welcome back to the bus stop, where the fun never ends. Not grounded anymore?"

"I'm not sure," Bay said as she approached. "There's a baby in the house now, so I think my mom forgot about taking me to school. I just kind of . . . slipped out."

Phin nodded with approval. "Bay Waverley, rule breaker."

She stopped beside him and stared at him, brows raised, as if waiting for him to say something.

"What?" he asked. "Why are you looking at me like that?"

"I finally watched the video everyone's been talking about, the one someone recorded on their phone of the fight at the Halloween dance," Bay said. "That blur of something that knocked the guy from Hamilton High off of Josh? In slow motion, it looked exactly like someone covered in a bedsheet."

Phin shifted his weight from foot to foot. "Huh. Is that so?"

"A bedsheet with a rosebud pattern. It was *you*," she said. "You sent him flying."

Phin didn't say anything.

She gave him a shove. He was still as bendy as a

straw. "Turns out, you really *are* the strongest man in town, Phineus Young."

He waited a few seconds before acknowledging, "No one was more surprised than me. You knew my dad, before he died. He was a hulk. But then I got to thinking, my grandfather Phin was skinnier than me. He was in his nineties, and people were still asking him to dig wells and break through ice on Lunsford's reservoir in the winter."

"Riva knows, I take it?" Bay asked with a smile. "Is that the reason she gave you that note on Friday?"

He took the note out of his jeans pocket. "I haven't read it yet. I'm savoring the possibilities."

Bay smiled at him. "Possibilities are good."

Phin tucked the note back in his pocket and they stood there, the world covered in a blanket of crystals, and waited for the bus to arrive.

Mary's Note: Sometimes the two most improbable things make the best combination.

Ingredients:

   2 cups whole grain spelt flour
   2½ cups unbleached all purpose flour
   1½ cup coarsely chopped figs
   2 tsp sea salt
   2 tbsp olive oil
   1 dry yeast packet
   1½ cups of warm water

Whisk four, salt, pepper, and yeast until blended, by hand or with whisk attachment of mixer.

Add olive oil and warm water. Knead for 10 minutes, or use dough hook attachment of mixer for 5 minutes, until dough is smooth and springy.

Oil a large bowl, place dough inside, and cover bowl with a damp hand towel. Let sit in a warm place for approximately 1 hour, or until dough has doubled in size.

Softly knead in the chopped figs and evenly distribute throughout the dough (lightly flouring your hands can make handling the dough easier), shape into an oval, then place on a baking sheet.

Snip three shallow lines into top of the dough with scissors, then lightly dust the dough with flour.

Let rise, uncovered, until dough swells a little more— 10–15 mins, or longer if the kitchen isn't warm.

Place tray in 350° oven for 40–45 mins until crust is slightly brown and the loaf sounds hollow when tapped on the underside.

Cool on a wire rack.

Acknowledgements

The year everything changed. I think we all have years like that, when our lives splinter in to very clear *befores* and *afters*. One of those years for me was when I wrote *Garden Spells*, the first Waverley Sisters book. It began as a simple story about two sisters reconnecting after many years. Then the apple tree started throwing apples and the story took on a life of its own, and my life hasn't been the same since.

For the befores and afters that made *First Frost* possible, many thanks to my mom, Louise; my dad, Zack; Sydney Allen; Hanna Allen; Michelle Pittman; Heidi Caramack; Billy Swilling; the Loopy Duetters, for their support during the bone-dry writing years; Andrea Cirillo, Kelly Harms and everyone at the Jane Rotrosen Agency, for taking a chance on a strange little garden book; Shauna Summers, Nita Taublib, Irwin Applebaum and everyone at Bantam, for feeding and watering it and making it grow; the amazing Jen Enderlin, for giving new life to a cranky old apple tree, and the whole team at St. Martin's Press, for your good humor and creativity. Most of all, to my readers, for your unfaltering support and enthusiasm for *Garden Spells*, without which I never would have stopped and asked, *What happened after?*

Lastly, I can't think of a year everything changed more than in 2011, when I was diagnosed with cancer. My life before and my life after are so vastly different that sometimes I think they were lived by two separate people. Many of you have been with me on this journey from the beginning, many joined me in the middle, and many have come in after. To all of you, I want to say a special thanks for being a part of my life—before, after, and everywhere in between.

I just celebrated my third year in remission.